THE HOUSE BY THE MEDLAR TREE

Giovanni Verga

Dover Publications, Inc.
Mineola, New York

Bibliographical Note

The House by the Medlar Tree, first published by Dover Publications, Inc., in 2015, is an unabridged republication of the edition published by Grove Press, New York, in 1953. The book was originally published in Italian in 1881 under the title *I Malavoglia.*

Library of Congress Cataloging-in-Publication Data

Verga, Giovanni, 1840-1922.
    [Malavoglia. English]
    The house by the medlar tree / Giovanni Verga.
        pages cm
    ISBN-13: 978-0-486-79404-4
    ISBN-10: 0-486-79404-0
    I. Title.
    PQ4734.V5M313 2015
    853'.8—dc23

2014041208

Manufactured in the United States by Courier Corporation
79404001   2015
www.doverpublications.com

TRANSLATOR'S NOTE   *The House by the Medlar Tree* is a translation of *I Malavoglia*, first published in 1881.

Some explanation of a few points seems preferable to interlarding the text with footnotes. The action begins in 1863, i.e., three years after the destruction by Garibaldi's expedition of the decrepit Kingdom of the Two Sicilies (the régime of "King Bomba's son," p. 3) which led to its incorporation in the new Kingdom of Italy. Petty insurrections throughout Sicily accompanied Garibaldi's expedition, and one of these constituted "the diabolical revolution that had happened when the tricolour handkerchief had been hoisted on the church tower" (p. 3). It was, of course, the Italian Government which introduced taxation, not Garibaldi, to whom that unpleasant innovation is attributed on p. 34.

The name Malavoglia means "Ill-will." The title "Don" implies in the language of the Malavoglia that its owner "does nothing," i.e., no manual work. A *mastro* is an artisan or skilled labourer, e.g., a bricklayer. A "master" (as I have translated *padron*), e.g., Master 'Ntoni, is self-employed. The Fariglioni, more commonly Faraglioni, are tall, often pointed rocks, characteristic of Sicily and Capri; according to tradition they were thrown by the blinded Polyphemus at the fleeing Odysseus. The lupins which led to so many troubles for the Malavoglia were not cultivated for their flowers. They were *Lupinus albus*, which has been cultivated in the Mediterranean area since ancient times for forage, for ploughing in to enrich the land and for its round, flat seeds which form an article of food. The "Three Kings" are part of the constellation of Orion. Mena's rejection of Alfio Mosca, and his ready acceptance of her final explanation (p. 262) may be surprising to those unaware of the Sicilian code according to which a woman's dishonour, or appearance of dishonour (in this case that of her sister, Lia), disgraced not only the woman herself but also her female relatives. Finally some weights, measures, etc. An *onza* in Sicilian currency was equivalent to 12.75 lire; a *tarì* to about 0.85 lire; a *carlino* to half a *tarì*; and a *grano* to one-tenth of a *carlino*. A *salma* was 275.1 litres and a *rotolo* about 800 grammes.

Eric Mosbacher

ONE The Malavoglia had once been as numerous as the stones on the old Trezza road. There had been Malavoglia at Ognina and Aci Castello; all good, honest, sea-going folk, just the opposite of what their name implied. In the parish register they were actually called Toscano, but that didn't mean a thing, because for generations, in fact ever since the world began, they had been known at Ognina, Trezza and Aci Castello as Malavoglia, and they had always had boats at sea and their own roof over their heads. But now all that was left of them was old Master 'Ntoni's family, who lived in the house by the medlar tree at Trezza and owned the Provvidenza, which was drawn up on the river bed below the public wash-place, near Uncle Cola's Concetta and Master Fortunato Cipolla's Carmela, which was a bigger boat.

The storms which had scattered the other Malavoglia to the four winds had done no very great harm to the house by the medlar tree or to the boat drawn up below the public wash-place; and Master 'Ntoni, to explain the miracle, would show his clenched fist, which looked as though it were made of walnut, and say: "To manage an oar the five fingers of the hand have to help one another."

He used also to say: "Men are like the fingers of the hand; the thumb must play the thumb's part, and the little finger must play the little finger's part."

Master 'Ntoni's family really was arranged like the fingers of the hand. First came the thumb, himself, who arranged all the feasts and festivals; next his son Bastiano, called Bastianazzo, because he was as huge and burly as the St. Christopher painted under the arch of the fish-market at Catania; big and burly though he was, it never entered his head to question anything his father said; he wouldn't even blow his nose without his father's permission; and when he had been told to take La Longa as his wife, he had taken her without a moment's hesitation. Next came La Longa, a little woman who stuck to weaving, salting anchovies and bearing children, like the good housewife that she was. Then came the grandchildren. The eldest was 'Ntoni, a great lout of twenty, who was always getting cuffed by his grandfather, and sometimes kicked as well, to restore his balance in case the cuff had been too hard. Next came Luca, who, his grandfather used to say, had more sense than his big brother, and then Mena, short for Filomena, who was nicknamed St. Agatha, because she was always at her loom. As the saying is, woman at the loom, hen in the coop, and mullet in January! After Mena came Alessio, or Alessi for short, who was the very image of his grandfather, though he hadn't learned yet how to blow his own nose; and last of all Lia, short for Rosalia, who was neither fish nor flesh nor good red herring yet. When they filed into church on Sunday it looked like a procession.

Old Master 'Ntoni remembered many sayings and proverbs that he had learnt from his elders, because, as he said, what the old folks said was always true. One of his sayings was: "You can't sail a boat without a helmsman." Another was: "You must learn to be sexton before you can be Pope." Another was: "Do the job you know; if you don't make money, at least you'll make a living." And another: "Be satisfied to do what your father did, or you'll come to no good." And he had many other sensible sayings as well.

That was why the house by the medlar tree prospered, and Master 'Ntoni passed at Trezza for a prudent and long-sighted man, and he would have been made a councillor of the commune if Don Silvestro, the communal secretary, who was a wily one, had not gone about telling everybody that he was a rotten reactionary, of the kind that favoured the Bourbons, and was plotting for the return of King Bomba's son, in order to be able to boss the village just as he ruled the roost at home.

As a matter of fact Master 'Ntoni didn't even know King Bomba's son by sight, but always looked after his own affairs. "The head of a household can't go to sleep when he likes," he used to say. "The man in charge has to give an account of his stewardship."

In December, 1863, 'Ntoni, the eldest of the grandchildren, was called up for service in the navy. Master 'Ntoni went to see all the village bigwigs about it, all the people able to pull strings. But Don Giammaria, the parish priest, told him he must put up with it, because it was the consequence of the diabolical revolution that had happened when the tricolour handkerchief had been hoisted on the church tower. Master 'Ntoni next went to see Don Franco, the chemist, who started chuckling in his big beard and rubbing his hands, and swore that if they ever succeeded in setting up a republic all taxation and conscription officials would be done away with immediately, because there would be no more army or navy any more, and if necessary the whole people would go out to fight for their country. At this Master 'Ntoni begged and implored Don Franco for the love of heaven to start his republic quickly, before his grandson 'Ntoni was sent for, as though Don Franco kept a republic up his sleeve; and the conversation ended with the chemist's losing his temper. Don Silvestro, the communal secretary, roared with laughter at all this, and ended by saying that by greasing the palm of certain people whom he knew they might be able to find something wrong with his grandson and get him exempted. Unfortunately he was a fine, big, strapping lad, of the kind they still turn out at Aci Trezza, and when he went for his medical the doctor told him that all that was wrong with him was that he was planted as solid as a pillar on two great feet that looked like the leaves of a prickly-pear tree. But in some weathers feet like that are better than a smart pair of town boots for standing on the deck of a cruiser, so they took 'Ntoni without so much as a by-your-leave. When the conscripts went to report to the barracks at Catania, La Longa trotted breathlessly beside her long-striding son, and kept telling him always to wear the scapulary of the Virgin Mary round his neck, and if he ever met an acquaintance who was coming back to the village he must send back a letter by him, and they would forward him the money to pay for the notepaper.

His grandfather, being a man, kept silent, but he had a lump in his throat too, and he avoided looking at his daughter-in-law, as though he had quarrelled with her. They walked back to Trezza in silence, with heads bent. Bastianazzo, who had been out fishing, hurriedly tidied up the boat and went to meet them at the top of the road; but when he saw them like that, carrying their boots, he had no spirit to open his mouth either, but walked back home with them in silence. La Longa promptly vanished into the kitchen, as though she were in an enormous hurry to be alone again with her old pots and pans, and Master 'Ntoni said to his son: "Go and say something to the poor thing; she's very upset."

Next day they all went to the station at Aci Castello to see the train with the conscripts going through to Messina. They had to wait for more than an hour, squeezed in the crowd outside the railings; but at last the train came in, with the poor boys hanging their heads out of the windows, just like cattle being taken to market, and waving. What with the singing and the laughter and the din, it was just like the fair at Trecastagni. In the noise and excitement of all those people you nearly forgot the pang you felt in your heart. "Good-bye, 'Ntoni!" "Good-bye, mother!" "Good-bye, don't forget! Don't forget!" A few feet away from them, by the edge of the road, was Mother Tudda's Sara, mowing hay for their calf, but Venera Zuppidda whispered to everybody that the girl had really come to wave good-bye to Master 'Ntoni's 'Ntoni, who had often spoken to Sara over the garden wall; Venera Zuppidda had seen them with her own eyes, as true as she was born. At all events 'Ntoni waved to Sara, and Sara stood with her hook in her hand and watched the train until it left. La Longa felt as if 'Ntoni's wave of the hand to Mother Tudda's Sara had been stolen from her; and for a long time afterwards she always turned her back on Sara when she met her in the village square or at the wash-place.

Then the whistle blew and the train moved out, and

the noise drowned the singing and the good-byes. The crowd of onlookers scattered, leaving only a few old cronies and idlers clinging to the railings without quite knowing why. Then they started drifting away too, and Master 'Ntoni, guessing that his daughter-in-law must have an unpleasant taste in her mouth, bought her two centesimi worth of lemon water.

To comfort La Longa, Venera Zuppidda kept saying to her: "Now set your heart at rest, because for five years you must act as though your son were dead, and you mustn't think about him."

But in the house by the medlar tree they went on thinking about him. La Longa was reminded of him every time she laid the table and found one plate extra under her hand. There was a particular kind of running bowline for securing the sheet that 'Ntoni could tie better than anyone else; and they missed him when they had to pull on a rope as taut as a violin-string, or haul the Provvidenza to her moorings—a job for which you really needed a winch. "This is where we need 'Ntoni!" his grandfather would exclaim, panting with exertion. "Do you think I've got the wrist that that lad has?" And the rhythm of her loom reminded 'Ntoni's mother of the rhythm of the engine that had drawn him away from her, and of the dismay with which it had filled her—dismay that still pounded rhythmically in her heart.

His grandfather had a number of strange arguments to comfort himself and the family with. "Do you want to know what I really think?" he'd say. "A little discipline will do the lad good; he used to prefer going out and enjoying himself on Sundays to using his hands to earn a living"; or: "After he has discovered the bitter taste of bread away from home, he won't complain any more about the meals he gets when he comes back!"

Eventually 'Ntoni's first letter arrived from Naples and set the whole village in a commotion. He said that in Naples the women wore long, silk skirts which swept the pavement, and that there was a Pulcinella show on the jetty and that *pizze*, the kind that gentlefolk ate, were on sale at two centesimi each, and that it wasn't at all like Trezza, where there was no way of spending a farthing unless you went to Santuzza's tavern; at Naples, he said, you couldn't possibly manage without money. "Are we to send the young glutton money to spend on *pizze?*" his grandfather grumbled. "But it's not his fault, it's the way he's made; he's just like a mullet, which would even swallow a rusty nail. If I hadn't held him in my arms at his christening, I should have sworn that Don Giammaria had put sugar in his mouth instead of salt!"

At the wash-place, when Mother Tudda's Sara was there, the Mangiacarrubbe girl said: "The ladies dressed in silk were just waiting for Master 'Ntoni's 'Ntoni, of course! They had never seen a pumpkin in that part of the world before!"

The others all held their sides with laughter; after that all the girls who were sour and on the shelf used to refer to 'Ntoni as the Pumpkin.

'Ntoni also sent his photograph home, and all the girls at the wash-place saw it, because Mother Tudda's Sara passed it round—the girls all passed it to each other under their aprons—and the Mangiacarrubbe girl was livid with jealousy. He looked like the Archangel Michael in flesh and blood. With his feet standing on a carpet and a curtain behind his head, like the one in the picture of the Madonna at Ognina, he looked so handsome and clean and sleek that even the mother who

bore him wouldn't have recognised him. Poor La Longa
never tired of gazing at the carpet and the curtain and
the pillar against which her son was standing as stiff as
a poker, with his hand resting on the back of a beautiful armchair; and she thanked God and the saints for
placing him in the midst of such elegance. She kept
the picture on the chest of drawers, under the glass
dome with the statue of the Good Shepherd to whom
she told her beads, and she thought she had a treasure
there on the chest of drawers, or so Venera Zuppidda
said, and Sister Mariangela la Santuzza had another
one just like it, in case anybody wanted to see it—it
had been sent her by Mariano Cinghialenta, and it was
kept nailed up on the counter at the tavern, behind
the bottles.

But after some time 'Ntoni found himself a friend
who could write, and then he started complaining
about the horrors of life on board ship, and the discipline, and his superiors, and the over-cooked soup
and the tight boots. Master 'Ntoni complained that a
letter like that wasn't worth the twenty centesimi for
the stamp, and La Longa grumbled at the writing,
which reminded her of fish-hooks, and complained that
'Ntoni couldn't say anything good about anything.
Bastianazzo shook his head and said no, it wasn't right,
and if it had been himself, he'd always have put cheerful things in his letters, to make people laugh and be
cheerful. As he said this he pointed a finger as huge as
the pin of a rowlock at the letter—if only out of sym-
pathy for poor La Longa, who couldn't reconcile herself to her boy's being away, and behaved just like a
cat that has lost its kittens. Master 'Ntoni went off
secretly and had the letter read to him by the chemist,
and then as a check he had it read to him all over
again by Don Giammaria, whose way of thinking was

diametrically opposite, and, when he felt convinced that he really knew what the letter said, he went over it again with his son and daughter-in-law.

"Didn't I say that the lad should have been born rich, like Master Cipolla's son, so that he could spend his whole time scratching his belly without doing anything?" he said.

Meanwhile it was a bad year, and now that Christians had learned to eat meat on Fridays, just as though they were Turks, the only thing left to do with fish was to give it away as alms for the souls of the dead; and on top of it there were not enough hands left to manage the boat now, and sometimes they had to hire Menico della Locca or someone else to help them out. What the King did was this. As soon as a lad grew fit to earn a living he took him away and made him a conscript; but while he was still young and a burden to his family, the family had all the trouble of bringing him up. And what for? Just to have him turned into a soldier or a sailor; and there was also the fact that Mena had just turned seventeen, and was starting to make the boys turn and look at her when she went to mass. Man is fire and woman straw; and the devil comes and blows on them. To keep the boat and the house by the medlar tree going was no light task.

To help out, Master 'Ntoni had arranged a deal with Uncle Crocifisso, who was known as Dumbbell. Master 'Ntoni arranged to buy some lupins on credit from Uncle Crocifisso and to sell them at Riposto, where Cinghialenta said there was a ship from Trieste looking for cargo. Actually the lupins were somewhat the worse for wear; but there were no others at Trezza, and sly old Dumbbell knew that the Provvidenza was moored idly below the wash-place, uselessly eating up sun and water, so he held out for his price. "All right," he said, "if you don't like it, don't take it, but in all conscience I can't take a centesimo less, as sure as I have a soul for which I shall have to answer to God," and he shook his head, which really looked like a bell without a clapper. This conversation took place outside the church door at Ognina on the first Sunday in September, which was the feast of the Virgin Mary, to which a big crowd had come from all the neighbouring villages. Piedipapera was there too, and he succeeded by his jokes and witticisms in getting them to agree on a price of two *onze* and ten a *salma*, to be paid off on the "never-never" system at so much a month. That's the way it always ended with Uncle Crocifisso—you had to bully and cajole him to get him to agree, because he had the terrible failing of not being able to say no. "You see! You can't say no even when you ought to!" Piedipapera said with a grin.

La Longa heard about the deal while they were all sitting with their arms on the table, talking after dinner, and it took her breath away; an enormous sum like forty *onze* was too much for her. But women have no courage for business, and Master 'Ntoni had to explain that if all went well the deal would mean bread for the whole winter, as well as earrings for Mena; Bastiano would go to Riposto with Menico della Locca, and they would be back in a week. Bastiano snuffed the candle without saying a word. That was how the lupin deal and the Provvidenza's voyage was decided on. The Provvidenza was the oldest of the village boats, but she had the reputation of being lucky. Maruzza still felt sick at heart, but she said nothing, because it was not her business, and she quietly set about tidying the boat and getting everything ready for the voyage—she put the fur-lined coat under the stretcher, and bread, a jar full of oil, and onions in the locker.

When the men went to fetch the lupins they had a terrible argument, which lasted all day long, with that usurer Uncle Crocifisso, who had sold them a pig in a poke, because the lupins turned out to be rotten. Old Dumbbell swore that he hadn't known it, as true as God's word. He said you couldn't back out of a fair bargain, and he had no intention of incurring damnation for his immortal soul by doing so. Piedipapera made a great noise, swearing black and blue that he had never known anything like it in the whole of his life, and he cursed and swore trying to get them to agree. He thrust his hand into the heap of lupins and displayed them before God and the Holy Mother of God, calling on Them to witness. Finally, red in the face, breathless and beside himself, he made a last desperate proposal, which he flung in the face of Uncle Crocifisso, who was stubbornly facing the Malavoglia, who were standing there with the sacks ready in their hands. "Well then, instead of paying so much a month, pay at Christmas and you'll save a *tarì* a *salma*! Are you satisfied now, God help you?" And he started filling the sacks.

The Provvidenza left on Saturday evening. The evening bell should have been rung, but wasn't, because Mastro Cirino, the sexton, was taking a pair of new boots to Don Silvestro, the communal secretary. The girls had all gathered round the fountain like a flock of sparrows, and the evening star was shining bright —it looked like a lantern hung on the Provvidenza's yard. Maruzza, with Lia beside her, stood on the shore, not saying anything, while her husband unfurled the sail and the Provvidenza rocked like a duckling on the waves, which were broken by the Fariglioni rocks. "When it's clear to the south and dark to the north, safely to sea you may put forth," Master 'Ntoni quoted, standing on the shore and looking towards Etna, which was covered with clouds.

Menico della Locca, who was in the Provvidenza with Bastianazzo, shouted something which the sea swallowed up. "He says that you can give the money to his mother, La Locca, because his brother's out of work," Bastianazzo said, and that was the last time his voice was heard.

TWO The lupin deal was the talk of the village, and all the women came to their doors to watch La Longa and Lia pass on their way home.

"You'll make a pile of money. It's the chance of a lifetime," Piedipapera called out, hobbling along on his lame leg behind Master 'Ntoni, who went and sat with Master Fortunato Cipolla and Menico della Locca's brother, who were taking the air on the church steps. "Master Cipolla's waiting for rain for his vines, and you're waiting for a west wind for the Provvidenza. You know the saying: a choppy sea means a fresh wind. The stars are bright tonight, and at midnight the wind will change. Can't you feel it now?"

Some carts were heard, slowly passing along the road.

"There are always people going about the world, night and day," Master Cipolla remarked.

Now that neither sea nor country were visible any longer it seemed as though there were nothing in the world but Trezza, and everyone wondered where the carts might be going at that time of night.

"Before midnight the Provvidenza will have turned the Capo dei Mulini," Master 'Ntoni said, "and she won't be troubled by the fresh wind any longer."

Master 'Ntoni could think of nothing but the Provvi-

denza, and when not talking about his own affairs
didn't talk at all; in fact he took no more part in the
conversation than a broomstick.

This caused Piedipapera to say to him: "You ought
to join in the argument about the King and the Pope
at the chemist's. You'd cut a fine figure there with them!
Can't you hear them shouting?"

"That's Don Giammaria arguing with the chemist,"
said La Locca's son.

La Longa had gone home, lit the lamp and sat down
with her winder on the balcony to fill the bobbins she
was using for the warp of the week.

"Mena is heard but not seen," her neighbours said.
"She's busy at her loom night and day!"

"That's how girls ought to be occupied, instead of
standing by the window," Maruzza replied. "If out of
the window she idly stares, she's not a girl for whom
anyone cares, as the saying is."

"All the same, with so many men passing by, some
girls do find themselves husbands by standing at the
window," Cousin Anna remarked from the doorway opposite.

Cousin Anna had good reason for talking as she did,
because that good-for-nothing son of hers, Rocco, had
let himself be caught up in the Mangiacarrubbe girl's
apron strings, and she was one of the girls who spent
their time gazing out of the window as bold as brass.

Grazia Piedipapera, hearing the conversation in the
street, appeared at her doorway, with her apron full
of the beans she was shelling, and started grumbling
at the mice, which had made so many holes in her sack
that it was just like a colander. To listen to her, you'd
have thought that mice had the intelligence of Christians and did it on purpose to annoy her. After this
the conversation became general, because the accursed

little beasts had done just as much damage in Maruzza's house. Cousin Anna's house had been full of
mice ever since her cat died; that cat had been worth
its weight in gold, and it had died as a result of being
kicked by Piedipapera. "Grey cats are best for catching
mice; they would hunt down a mouse in the eye of a
needle," one woman said, and another said that no one
should ever open the door at night to let the cat in,
because that's how an old lady at Aci Sant' Antonio
had been murdered. "Three days before some thieves
had stolen the old lady's cat," she said, "and they
brought it back half-dead with hunger, and they let it
miaow outside her door. Naturally she didn't have the
heart to leave it out in the street at that time of night,
so she opened the door, and that's how the thieves got
in!"

Nowadays there were so many rogues and vagabonds
about that you never knew what was going to happen
next. At Trezza faces that had never been seen before
were to be seen upon the rocks; strangers came and
pretended they were going fishing, but sometimes they
stole the washing that was laid out to dry. That was
how Nunziata had lost a new sheet. Poor girl! to be
robbed like that when she was working herself to the
bone looking after her young brothers, whom her father
had left on her hands when he went away to seek his
fortune in Alexandria in Egypt! Nunziata had been
left just like Cousin Anna had been when her husband
died, with Rocco, the eldest of her children, still only
knee-high; and now poor Cousin Anna had had all the
trouble of bringing up that good-for-nothing Rocco,
only to see herself robbed of him by the Mangiacarrubbe hussy!

In the midst of all this Venera Zuppidda, the wife of
Mastro Turi, the caulker, who lived at the end of the

street, suddenly appeared on the scene—she always turned up suddenly to say her piece, just like the devil in the litany; she seemed to spring from nowhere, because no one ever saw where she came from. "Your son Rocco has never helped you in any case," she said to Cousin Anna. "As soon as he has any money in his pockets he goes and spends it all at the tavern!"

Venera Zuppidda always knew everything that was going on in the village, and they used to say that she went from house to house on her bare feet, snooping and eavesdropping, carrying her spindle high in the air to prevent it from catching on the stones. But her spindle was only an excuse. What she was really doing was snooping. Her vice was that she was always as truthful as Holy Scripture, and, as people did not like hearing the truth about themselves, they said she had an evil tongue, of the kind that dripped gall. A bitter tongue drips gall, and Venera Zuppidda really was bitter, because of her daughter Barbara, for whom she had not been able to find a husband, the girl being so proud and spiteful; but in spite of this her mother would be satisfied with nobody less than Victor Emmanuel's son for her.

"And where is Nunziata all this time?" La Longa asked a swarm of ragged little children who were whimpering on the doorstep of the cottage opposite. As soon as they heard their sister's name mentioned they all started howling at the top of their voice.

"I saw her going up to the lava field to collect some bundles of broom. Your son Alessi was with her," Cousin Anna replied.

The children stopped howling to listen, and then started whimpering again. After a moment the eldest, who was standing on a big stone, said:

"I don't know where she is!"

The neighbours had all come out of their houses like snails in a shower, and there was a continuous buzz of conversation from door to door all the way down the little street. Even Alfio Mosca's window was open—Alfio Mosca of the donkey cart—and a strong smell of broom came out through it. Mena had left her loom, and came out on the balcony too.

"Ah! St. Agatha!" the neighbours exclaimed with pleasure, and they all started making a fuss of her.

"Why don't you start thinking about getting your Mena married?" Venera Zuppidda asked Maruzza in a whisper. "She'll be eighteen this Easter. I know, because she was born the year after the earthquake, like my Barbara. But he who wants my daughter Barbara must first please me!"

At that moment a rustling of branches was heard coming down the street, and Alessi and Nunziata arrived. They were almost invisible under their enormous bundles of broom.

"Ah! Nunziata!" the neighbours called out. "Weren't you frightened up on the lava at this time of night?"

"I was with her," Alessi replied.

"I was late with Cousin Anna at the wash-place, and then I had no wood for the fire."

The girl lit the lamp and started briskly getting everything ready for dinner, while her little brothers followed her about the room, like a brood of chickens following a hen. Alessi put down his bundle and stood in the doorway, with his hands in his pockets, watching her gravely.

"Nunziata!" Mena called out from the balcony. "Come over here for a little when you've put the pot on to boil!"

Nunziata left Alessi to look after the fire and went

over to the balcony, where she sat hand in hand with St. Agatha, to enjoy a few minutes' rest too.

"Alfio Mosca's cooking beans," Nunziata remarked after a while.

"He's like you, poor chap, with no one at home to get his dinner ready for him in the evening when he comes home tired."

"That's quite true, he cooks and does his own washing and mends his own shirts." There was nothing about her neighbour Alfio that Nunziata didn't know; she knew his house like the back of her hand. "Now he's going to fetch firewood," she said. "Now he's looking after his donkey." You could see his lantern moving about in the yard or in the shed. St. Agatha laughed, and Nunziata said that Alfio only needed a skirt to be just like a woman.

"When he gets married," Mena said, "I expect his wife will go round with the donkey cart and he'll stay at home and mind the babies!"

A group of women in the street were talking about Alfio Mosca too. They were saying that Venera Zuppidda had said that even La Vespa didn't want him for a husband, because she owned a fine plot of land, she said, and she didn't propose throwing herself away on a man with nothing to his name but a donkey cart. A cart is nothing but a hearse, as the saying is. The designing creature was said to have set her eyes on her uncle, old Dumbbell.

The girls overheard this, and took Mosca's part against the horrid Vespa woman; and Nunziata felt her heart full, because of the contempt with which they spoke of poor Alfio, just because he was poor and had no one in the world, and suddenly she said to Mena:

"If I were grown-up, I'd take him if they gave him to me!"

Mena was just going to say something, but instead she abruptly changed the subject.

"Will you be going to Catania for the Feast of the Dead?" she asked.

"No, I shan't be able to, because I can't leave the house alone."

"We're going if the lupin deal turns out all right. Grandfather said so."

Then she thought for a moment, and added:

"Alfio Mosca generally goes there too, to sell his nuts."

Then they both fell silent, thinking about the Feast of the Dead, to which Alfio Mosca generally went to sell his nuts.

Meanwhile Tino Piedipapera, presiding over the gathering on the church steps rather like the president of a court of justice, was delivering one judgment after another.

"I tell you that before the revolution things were different," he said. "The fish have grown vicious now!"

"The revolution has nothing whatever to do with it," said Master 'Ntoni. "The anchovies feel a nor'wester twenty-four hours in advance. It has always been like that! The anchovy is a much cleverer fish than the tunny. Beyond the Capo dei Mulini now they sweep up tunny-fish from the sea with close-meshed nets."

"I'll tell you what the trouble is," said Master Fortunato. "It's those damned steamers going backwards and forwards, beating the sea with their paddle-wheels! The fish are frightened and disappear. What do you expect?"

La Locca's son had been listening to the conversation, gaping and scratching his head. "If that were the case," he said suddenly, "there'd be no more fish at Syracuse or Messina either, because that's where the

steamers go. But they take fish away from Messina
and Syracuse on the railway by the ton!"

At this Master Cipolla lost his temper. "Settle it for
yourselves!" he said. "I wash my hands of the whole
thing! It doesn't matter a straw to me anyway, because
I've got my vines and my land to provide me with a
living."

Piedipapera gave La Locca's son a smack on the
head to teach him manners. "Blockhead!" he said.
"Keep quiet when your elders and betters are talking!"

The lad went off, shouting and punching himself on
the head, as if to show that everyone took him for a
dunce just because he was La Locca's son. Master
'Ntoni sniffed the breeze and said: "If the nor'wester
doesn't drop before midnight, the Provvidenza will
have time to turn the cape."

Some slow, sonorous strokes fell from the church
tower. "One hour after sunset," said Master Cipolla.

Master 'Ntoni made the sign of the cross, and said:
"Peace to the living and rest to the dead."

Piedipapera sniffed in the direction of the priest's
house and said: "Don Giammaria is having fried vermicelli for dinner tonight!"

At that very moment Don Giammaria passed on his
way home, and he said good evening to them all, even
to Piedipapera, because in these times it was necessary
to be friendly even with rogues; and Piedipapera, who
still had the appetising smell of fried vermicelli in his
nostrils, called out: "Eh! Don Giammaria! Fried vermicelli this evening!"

"Would you believe it?" Don Giammaria muttered.
"Would you believe it? They even know what I eat!
They spy even on the servants of God, and count every
mouthful they eat! All out of hatred for the Church!"

At that moment he bumped into Don Michele, the ser-

geant of the customs guards, who used to walk about
with a pistol on his paunch and with his trousers tucked
into his boots, looking for smugglers. "They don't count
the mouthfuls that those people eat!" he said.

When Maruzza heard the clock strike she hurried
back into the house to lay the table. The gossips in the
street had dispersed and, as the village gradually went
to sleep, you began to hear the sea snoring away, not
many yards away at the end of the little street. Every
now and then the snore rose to a snort, rather as
though somebody kept rolling over in bed. The only
noise in the village now came from the tavern. The
little red light was still visible outside it, and you could
hear the loud voice of Rocco Spatu, for whom every
day was a holiday to be celebrated.

"Rocco Spatu's a happy man," Alfio Mosca said from
his window after an interval, though it seemed as
though nobody was there any more.

"Oh! Are you still there, Alfio?" answered Mena, who
had stayed on the balcony to wait for her grandfather.

"Yes, I'm here, Mena. I'm eating my supper here,
because when I see you all gathered round the lamp
on the table I don't feel so lonely. Sometimes I feel so
lonely that it takes away my appetite!"

"Aren't you a happy man, Alfio?"

"Oh! A man wants so many things to make him
happy."

Mena did not answer. After another silence Alfio
said:

"I'm going to Catania tomorrow for a load of salt."

"Will you be going there for the Feast of the Dead?"

"God knows! This year the few nuts I've got are all
rotten."

"Alfio will be going to town to find himself a wife,"
said Nunziata from the doorway opposite.

"Is that true?" asked Mena.

"Well, Mena, if that was all that was necessary to find a wife, there are plenty of girls in my own village, without my having to look any farther."

"Look at all the stars twinkling up there," said Mena, after another interval. "They say they're souls from purgatory on the way to paradise!"

"Listen," said Alfio, after he too had looked up at the stars. "You, who are St. Agatha, if you dream of a lucky number, tell me, and I'll put my shirt on it, and then I'll be able to think about getting married."

"Good night," Mena answered.

The stars twinkled more and more brightly, as though they had caught alight, and the Three Kings were shining over the Fariglioni, with their arms crossed, like St. Andrew. The sea murmured quietly at the end of the street, and at long intervals you heard the noise of a cart passing in the dark, bouncing over the stones, and going about the world, which is so big that if you walked and walked and walked and kept on walking for ever, day and night, you would never come to the end of it. There were actually people going about the world at this moment who knew nothing whatever about Alfio Mosca, or about the Provvidenza, which was at sea, or about the Feast of the Dead at Catania. So thought Mena to herself as she waited for her grandfather on the balcony.

Before her grandfather at last shut the door he went out on the balcony several times to look at the stars, which were brighter than they should have been, and he muttered, "It's an ugly sea!"

Rocco Spatu was shouting himself hoarse near the lantern outside the tavern door. "He whose heart is happy always sings," said Master 'Ntoni.

THREE After midnight the wind rose as though the devil were behind it. It shook the windows, and howled as though all the cats in the village were on the roof. The sea roared round the Fariglioni as if all the oxen from the fair at Sant' Alfio were bellowing, and day dawned blacker than the soul of Judas. It was an ugly Sunday in September, treacherous September, which can let loose a storm at you as suddenly and unexpectedly as a shot from among the prickly-pear trees. The village boats were drawn up on the beach and securely moored to the big stones below the washplace. The children shouted and whistled with delight every time they caught sight of a distant sail, scudding through the mist as though the devil were after it, but the women made the sign of the cross, as though they could see the poor devils on board with their own eyes.

Maruzza La Longa, as was only right, said nothing, but she couldn't keep still for a moment, and was constantly on the move in the house and yard; in fact, she behaved just like a hen about to lay an egg. The men were at the tavern, or at Pizzuto's barber's shop, or at the butcher's shed, staring out at the rain. Nobody was on the shore, except Master 'Ntoni, who was there because of the cargo of lupins he had at sea in the Provvidenza, with his son Bastianazzo on board into the bargain; and La Locca's son, who had nothing to lose on board the Provvidenza, except his brother Menico. While Master Fortunato Cipolla was having his shave in Pizzuto's shop, he said he wouldn't give two farthings at that moment for Bastianazzo and Menico della Locca and the Provvidenza with her cargo of lupins.

"Everyone tries to be a trader and get rich nowadays," he said, with a shrug of the shoulders; "and then, when they've lost the mule, they go round looking for the halter!"

Sister Mariangela la Santuzza's tavern was crowded. That drunkard Rocco Spatu was there, shouting and spitting enough for ten; and Tino Piedipapera, Mastro Turi Zuppiddo, Mangiacarrubbe, Don Michele, the sergeant of the customs guards, with his trousers tucked into his boots and his pistol on his paunch, as though this were weather for chasing smugglers, and Mariano Cinghialenta. That great elephant, Mastro Turi Zuppiddo, went about playfully distributing to his friends punches that would have been sufficient to fell an ox, as though he still had his caulking mallet in his hand; and Cinghialenta started shouting and swearing, to show that he was a carter and a man of courage, too.

Uncle Santoro, squatting in what little shelter there was outside the door, was waiting with outstretched hand for someone to pass, so that he could beg for alms.

"Between the two of them, father and daughter must do very nicely, thank you, on a day like this, with so many people coming to the tavern."

"Bastianazzo Malavoglia's worse off than Uncle Santoro at this moment," Piedipapera answered. "Mastro Cirino may well ring for mass for them; they've roused the wrath of God Almighty with that cargo of lupins they have at sea!"

The wind made the dried leaves and the women's skirts fly, so that every now and then Vanni Pizzuto, with his curly hair, which was as glossy as silk, kept turning to look at the passers-by, holding the customer he was shaving by the nose with one hand and resting the other on his hip; and the chemist, with that huge hat of his, which made him look as though he were wearing an umbrella on his head, was standing at the entrance to his shop, pretending to have important business to discuss with Don Silvestro, the communal secretary, in the hope that his wife would not make him go to church; he was chuckling in his beard at the subterfuge and winking at the girls going by, tripping over the puddles.

"Master 'Ntoni wants to be a Protestant today, like Don Franco, the chemist," Piedipapera remarked.

"If you turn round again to look at that shameless Don Silvestro, I'll smack your face on the spot!" Venera Zuppidda said to her daughter as they crossed the square. "I don't like that man!"

At the last stroke of the bell Santuzza handed over the tavern to the care of her father and went off to church, taking her customers with her. Poor Uncle Santoro was blind, and so it was no sin if he didn't go to mass; and Santuzza lost no business, because she could tell every one of her customers by his step, so she could keep her eye on the bar from the church door without seeing it.

"Devils are in the air today," Santuzza said, crossing herself with holy water. "It's a day to drive one to sin!"

Near her Venera Zuppidda was squatting on her heels, rattling off her beads and thrusting hostile glances in every direction, as though she were angry with the whole village. To those willing to listen she said: "La Longa isn't coming to church, although her husband's at sea in this gale! No wonder the Lord chastises us!" Even Menico's mother was in church, although she was too distracted to do anything but watch the flies buzzing about.

"We must pray even for sinners," Santuzza replied. "That's what good souls are for!"

La Vespa then chimed in. "Do you know what I think?" she said. "It's all the fault of Uncle Crocifisso, who let them have the lupins on credit. Credit should never be given without security; for experience shows that the matter will end in the loss of your goods, your wits and your friend!"

Uncle Crocifisso was on his knees before the altar of Our Lady of the Sorrows with his beads in his hand, and he was reciting the verses of the rosary in a nasal voice which would have touched the heart of the devil himself. Between one Ave Maria and the next everybody talked about the lupin deal and the Provvidenza out at sea, and La Longa, who was going to be left with five children on her hands.

"Nowadays," said Master Cipolla, shrugging his shoulders, "everybody is discontented with his lot and wants to take heaven by storm."

"The fact is that today will be a bad day for the Malavoglia," Mastro Zuppiddo announced.

"I shouldn't like to be in Bastianazzo's shoes," said Piedipapera.

Evening came down sad and cold. From time to time a squall came from the north, followed by fine, gentle rain. It was one of those evenings when, if your boat is safely drawn up with its hull nice and dry on the sand, you enjoy sitting with the youngster on your knees, watching the steam rising from the pot and listening to your wife's slippers padding about the house behind you. That Sunday—which promised to last all Monday as well—all the idlers preferred spending the evening at the tavern, and even the doorposts seemed to enjoy reflecting the warmth of the fire, and Uncle Santoro, who had been put outside to rest his chin on his knees and hold out his hand to beg, had moved close in, to warm his back a bit, too.

"He's better off at this moment than Bastianazzo," said Rocco Spatu, lighting his pipe in the doorway.

He put his hand in his pocket and, without further thought, actually gave Uncle Santoro two centesimi.

"You're wasting your money, giving alms as a thanksgiving to God for being in safety," Piedipapera said to him. "There's no danger of your ever coming to poor Bastianazzo's end!"

Everyone laughed at this sally, and then stood at the doorway, gazing silently at the sea, which was as black as the lava field.

Master 'Ntoni had been pacing up and down all day long, as restlessly as if he had been bitten by a tarantula. The chemist asked him whether he wanted a tonic; or was he going out for a walk in this weather? "A fine Providence, eh? Master 'Ntoni?" he actually said. But everyone knew that the chemist was a Protestant and a Jew.

La Locca's son, who was standing outside the tavern with his hands in his pockets, because there was no money in them, said:

"Uncle Crocifisso has gone with Piedipapera to look for Master 'Ntoni, to make him admit in the presence of witnesses that he gave him the lupins on credit."

"That means that he must think that the Provvidenza's in danger too."

"My brother Menico's on board the Provvidenza, with Bastianazzo."

"We were just saying that if your brother Menico doesn't come back you'll be the head of the household."

"He went because Uncle Crocifisso was willing to give him half-a-day's pay for a day's fishing, but the Malavoglia offered him full pay," La Locca's son answered, not understanding. The others burst out laughing and left him standing there, gaping.

At dusk Maruzza took her children to the lava field, from where a big expanse of sea was visible, to wait. When she heard the way the sea was howling she was terrified, but she scratched her head and remained silent. The little girl started crying, and the little group, all alone in the lava field at that time of day, looked like souls in torment. The child's crying hurt the poor woman, and she felt it was a bad sign. She didn't know what to do to quieten the child, so she started singing to her, but she too had tears in her voice.

Women, on the way back from the tavern with a jar of oil or a bottle of wine, went over and chatted to La Longa for a moment, as though it were a perfectly normal thing to do, and one or two friends of her husband Bastianazzo—Master Cipolla or Master Mangiacarrubbe, for instance—walking over to the lava field to see what the sea was like, and in what sort of mood the old snarler was settling down for the night, talked to her and enquired after her husband, and stayed for a few minutes to keep her company, smoking their pipes in silence or talking in whispers among themselves. The poor woman, alarmed at these unusual attentions, looked at them in terror, and hugged her baby to her breast as though they wanted to rob her of it. In the end the hardest, or most compassionate, of them took her by the arm and led her home. She let herself be led, muttering: "Holy Mother of God! Holy Mother of God!" Her children followed her, clinging to her skirts, as though they too were afraid that thieves were about. When they passed the tavern all the customers crowded to the smoky doorway and watched her pass in silence, as though she were already an object of curiosity.

"*Requiem aeternam*, may he rest in peace," Uncle Santoro muttered under his breath. "Poor Bastianazzo always gave me alms when Master 'Ntoni left him any money in his pockets!"

"Holy Mother of God! Holy Mother of God!" poor Maruzza, who did not yet know that she was a widow, kept muttering.

Outside the balcony of her house a group of neighbours were waiting for her, talking in whispers. When they saw her in the distance, Grazia Piedipapera and Cousin Anna came forward to meet her, with their hands on their bellies, without saying anything. Then she clutched her hair with her hands, and with a shriek of despair dashed into the house.

"What a misfortune!" they said in the street. "And the boat was loaded! More than forty *onze* worth of lupins!"

FOUR   The worst of it was that the lupins had been bought on credit, and Uncle Crocifisso was not to be put off with soft words and rotten apples as the saying is. That's why he was called Dumbbell, because if anyone tried putting him off with promises instead of hard cash he would be deaf in that ear. "We'll have to think about credit," he would say. He was the soul of generosity, and made his living by lending money to friends; that was all the work he did. He used to stand in the square all day long, with his hands in his pockets, or spend his time leaning against the church wall, wearing a tattered old coat for which nobody would have given him a farthing; but he was rolling in money, and if anyone asked for a small loan he would lend the money at once, but on security, because without security experience shows, as the saying is, that the matter will end in the loss of your goods, your wits and your friend.

If he lent you twelve *tarì*, the condition would be that it must be repaid punctually on the following Sunday, with one *carlino* extra, as was only right, because friendship plays no part in business. He would also buy up a whole catch of fish at a cut price if the poor devil who owned it was in urgent need of cash; but the fish had to be weighed in his scales, which some people— the type that is never satisfied—said were as false as Judas, having one arm longer than the other, like St. Francis Xavier; and, if it was wanted, he would advance the money to pay a crew's wages, and he only wanted the principal back and didn't demand any interest, only a *rotolo* of bread and a portion of wine per head. That was all he wanted, because he was a Christian and would have to answer to God for all his actions in this world. In short, he was the good angel of all who were in distress. He had discovered a hundred ways of being of service to his fellow-men, and, though he never went to sea, he owned boats and gear and everything else, which he lent out to those who did not have them, contenting himself with taking one third of the haul for himself, plus a share for the boat, which counted as one member of the crew, and a share for the gear, if gear were hired too. The outcome was that the cost of the boat ate up all the profit, so that it came to be known as the devil's boat. When he was asked why he didn't go to sea and risk his life like the others, instead of skimming the cream of the fishing without exposing himself to danger, he would reply: "Well, and supposing an accident happened, which heaven forbid, and I left my bones out there, who would there be to look after my business?" He looked after his business all right, and he would have lent his shirt if he could have raised money on it; and it was useless trying to argue with him because, as soon as you started, he grew hard of hearing and of understanding too, and all he could say was: "There's no fraud about a fair bargain"; or: "You can tell an honest man on the day his debt falls due!"

Now, because of the lupins that the devil had eaten, his enemies were laughing in his face; and at the funeral service he had to recite the De Profundis for Bastianazzo's soul, wearing a hood, like the other members of the Confraternity of the Good Death.

The church windows were sparkling, and the sea was smooth and shining, so that it did not at all seem the same sea that had robbed La Longa of her husband and, now that the weather had turned fine again, the members of the Confraternity were in a hurry to get through with the service and go back to their business.

This time the Malavoglia were in church, squatting on their heels, wetting the floor with their tears, as though the dead man, with his cargo of lupins, really lay between the four boards which Uncle Crocifisso had let them have on credit, because he had always known Master 'Ntoni as an honest man. But if Master 'Ntoni proposed cheating him out of his money, on the pretext that Bastianazzo was drowned, he was mistaken, because as sure as God was in his heaven, cheating him would be cheating Christ, for the bargain he had made with him was as sacred as the Sacred Host, for he had laid those five hundred lire at the feet of the crucified Christ. If Master 'Ntoni tried any nonsense, by heaven, he would go to prison. After all, the law was the law, even at Trezza.

Meanwhile Don Giammaria hurriedly swung the holy water sprinkler four times over the bier, and Mastro Cirino started walking round the church, putting out the candles with his extinguisher. The members of the Confraternity, with their arms in the air, struggling out of their hoods, started stepping over the benches on their way out, and Uncle Crocifisso went over to offer Master 'Ntoni a pinch of snuff to cheer him up, for after all an honest man leaves a good name behind him and goes to paradise. That was what he said to those who asked him about the lupins. "I'm not worried about the Malavoglia," he said, "because they're honest folk, and would never consent to leaving poor Bastianazzo's soul at the devil's mercy." Master 'Ntoni could see with his own eyes, he said, that no expense had been spared in honour of the dead man. The mass had cost so much, the candles so much, the funeral procession so much. He counted it out on his fingers, which were covered with the cotton gloves worn by members of the Confraternity. The children gaped at all the expensive things which were there because of their father—the bier, the candles and the paper flowers. The baby girl, seeing the shining candles and hearing the organ music, started crowing with delight.

The house by the medlar tree was full of people. The proverb says that sad is the house in which a husband is mourned. Everyone who passed, seeing the little Malavoglia with their dirty faces and their hands in their pockets, shook his head and said: "Poor Maruzza! Now sorrows are beginning in her house!"

All her friends brought something, as is the custom—macaroni, grapes, wine, and all God's good gifts; to eat it all you would have needed a heart at peace. Even Alfio Mosca turned up, carrying a hen in either hand. "Take these, Mena," he said. "I wish I'd been in your father's shoes, I swear! At least my death wouldn't have hurt anyone, and no one would have wept for me!"

Mena, leaning against the kitchen door, with her

face hidden in her apron, felt her heart beating as though it were going to leap from her breast, like those poor animals that she was holding. St. Agatha's dowry had gone down with the Provvidenza, and the visitors to the house by the medlar tree were thinking that Uncle Crocifisso would be getting his claws into it, too.

Some of the visitors, after remaining screwed to the high-backed chairs, went away without saying a word, like the real codfish that they were. But those sufficiently bright to say a few words tried to keep up a smattering of conversation, to chase away melancholy and distract the poor Malavoglia a little, because they had been weeping like fountains for two days. Master Cipolla said there had been an increase of two *tarì* a barrel in the price of anchovies; that might interest Master 'Ntoni, if he still had any for sale. He, Master Cipolla, had fortunately kept back about a hundred barrels, which he had laid in at a good price. They even talked about Bastianazzo, God rest his soul; nobody would have expected such a thing to happen to him, a man in the prime of life, simply bursting with health, poor chap!

The mayor, Mastro Croce Callà, who was known as the Silkworm and also as Giufà, was there too, with the communal secretary, Don Silvestro. Giufà stood there with his nose in the air; people said he was like a weather-cock, waiting for the breeze to tell him which way to turn next; he stared now at one speaker and now at the next, as though he really were looking at the leaves in the wind, and wanted to eat the words that everybody spoke; and when the communal secretary laughed he laughed too.

For the sake of a laugh Don Silvestro brought the conversation round to the subject of the death duty payable because of Bastianazzo, and so managed to get in a joke which he had picked up from his lawyer. He had taken such a fancy to this joke, after it had been properly explained to him, that he never failed to work it into the conversation when he paid a visit of condolence.

"At least you have the pleasure of being related to Victor Emmanuel, since you will have to pay him his share!" he said.

Everybody held his sides and rocked with laughter, because the saying is that there must be no wedding without tears and no visit of condolence without a laugh.

The chemist's wife made a grimace at these sallies, and sat holding her gloves on her belly and with a long face, as people do in towns in these circumstances; the mere sight of her was enough to reduce you to silence, as though she were the corpse. That was the reason why she was known as "the Lady."

Don Silvestro behaved like a complete lady's man and, on the pretext of offering the newcomers chairs, was continually on the move, making his polished shoes squeak. "All tax collectors ought to be burned alive!" said Venera Zuppidda, who was as sour as a lemon, glowering at Don Silvestro as though he were a tax collector. She knew very well what certain pen-pushers, who had no socks to wear under their polished shoes, were after; they wanted to worm their way into people's houses and lay their hands on their daughters and their dowries. "My beauty, I don't want you, I want your money," they said. That was why she had left her daughter Barbara at home. "I don't like those faces," she had said.

Donna Rosolina, the priest's sister, who looked as red as a turkey-cock and was fanning herself with her handkerchief, started grumbling at Garibaldi, whose fault it was that taxation had been introduced. It was perfectly disgusting, she declared. Nowadays life was impossible, and nobody got married any more. "Why should Donna Rosolina care?" Piedipapera whispered. Meanwhile Donna Rosolina, to impress on Don Silvestro what an excellent housekeeper she was, had started telling him about all the things she was busy with. She had twenty yards of warp on the loom, and there were the vegetables to dry for the winter, and the tomato purée to make—she knew a special way of making it that kept it fresh right through the winter. In her opinion, you needed a woman to run a house properly; but a woman with sense in her fingers; not one of those chits who were long in the hair but short in the brains, as the saying was, and thought of nothing but dolling themselves up all day long; because then the husband was sunk, like poor Bastianazzo, poor soul, may he rest in peace.

"God bless him!" whispered Santuzza. "He died on a fated day, the eve of the day of Our Lady of the Sorrows, and now he is among the angels and the saints in paradise, praying for us poor sinners. The Lord will provide for those who love Him, as the saying is." Bastianazzo was a good man, she said, the kind that didn't go about prying into their neighbours' affairs and speaking ill of them and sinning against them, as so many did.

At this Maruzza, who was sitting at the foot of the bed, looking like Our Lady of the Sorrows herself— she was as pale and as washed out as a rag—started sobbing more loudly than ever, and Master 'Ntoni, who was all bent up and looked a hundred years older, gazed at her and gazed at her and shook his head, and did not know what to say, because of Bastianazzo, who was like a thorn in his side, as though a dog-fish were gnawing at his heart.

"Santuzza has honey in her mouth," Grazia Piedipapera remarked.

"Acting the hostess," Venera Zuppidda replied. "It's her trade! If you don't know your trade you should shut up shop, as the saying is. If you can't swim, you drown!"

"Now they're going to put a tax on salt," said Mangiacarrubbe. "The chemist said he saw it printed in the paper. Then there'll be no more salting of anchovies, and we may as well break up our boats for firewood!"

"Good heavens above!" exclaimed Mastro Turi, the caulker. He was just about to raise his fist and say something when he caught his wife's eye, so he swallowed what he was going to say and kept it to himself.

"With the bad year that we're in for," said Master Cipolla—it hadn't rained since St. Claire's Day—"if it hadn't been for the storm in which the Provvidenza was lost, which came like a real blessing from heaven, the hunger this winter would have been thick enough to cut with a knife!"

Everyone started talking about his own troubles, partly to comfort the Malavoglia by showing them that they were not the only ones to have them. Troubles, whether great or small, alas! alas! afflict us all, as the saying is, and those standing outside in the yard were looking up at the sky, because a little more rain would have been as welcome as a feast. Master Cipolla knew the reason why it no longer rained as in the past.

"The reason why it doesn't rain any more," he said, "is that they have put up those accursed telegraph wires, which draw all the rain and carry it away!"

Mangiacarrubbe and Tino Piedipapera were aghast at this piece of information, because there were telegraph poles all along the Trezza road; but Don Silvestro started laughing—he cackled just like a hen—and Master Cipolla rose indignantly from the low wall on which he was sitting and started denouncing all ignoramuses and donkeys. Did they not know that the telegraph carried news from one place to another? That happened because there was a kind of juice inside the wire, just like the sap in a vine-branch, by which the rain was drawn down from the clouds and taken away to where there was more need of it. They could go and ask the chemist, who had said so himself! That was why they had made the law which said that anyone who broke a telegraph wire must go to prison. After this Don Silvestro was left with nothing to say, so he put his tongue in his pocket and held his peace.

"By all the saints in paradise, we ought to cut down all the telegraph poles and burn them!" Mastro Turi Zuppiddo declared, but nobody felt inclined to agree with him. To change the subject everybody started looking at the garden.

"A fine bit of land!" said Mangiacarrubbe. "When it's well cultivated it provides food for all the year round."

The Malavoglia house had always been one of the best in Trezza; but now, with Bastianazzo dead and 'Ntoni a conscript and Mena, for whom a husband must be found, and all those idle mouths to feed, it was a house leaking at every joint.

What could the house be worth? They all craned their necks over the garden wall and stared at it, trying to work it out. Don Silvestro knew better than anyone what it might be worth, because he had all the papers in his office at Aci Castello.

"Do you want to bet twelve *tarì* that all is not gold that glitters?" he asked, showing everybody a new five-lire piece.

He knew that the house was assessed at five *tarì* a year. At this they all started working out on their fingers what the house, complete with garden and everything, might be worth if it were sold up.

"Neither the house nor the boat can be sold, because they're both assigned to Maruzza!" someone said. They had grown so heated that their voices could be heard from the room where the mourners were weeping the dead. In the end Don Silvestro dropped a bombshell. "Of course they were assigned to Maruzza, as part of the marriage settlement!" he admitted.

Master Cipolla, who had talked to Master 'Ntoni about the possibility of marrying Mena to his son Brasi, shook his head and said no more.

"In that case," said Mastro Turi Zuppiddo, "the real sufferer is Uncle Crocifisso, who loses the money he advanced for the lupins."

Everyone turned towards Dumbbell, who had joined the group to see what was going on and was sitting quietly in a corner, listening to what they were saying. He sat with his mouth open and his nose in the air—even his mouth and nose seemed to be calculating how many tiles and joists there were in the roof and working out the value of the house. A few inquisitive visitors popped their heads out of the door and pointed him out to each other with a wink. "He looks just like a bailiff with a writ of execution," they said with a sneer.

The gossips who knew about Master 'Ntoni's conversations with Master Cipolla said that now Maruzza must get over her mourning and arrange the match for Mena quickly. But poor Maruzza's head was full of other things.

Master Cipolla turned away coldly and left without saying anything; and when everybody had gone the Malavoglia were left alone in the yard. "Now we are ruined," said Master 'Ntoni, "and Bastianazzo is better off than we are, because he doesn't know!"

At this, first Maruzza and then all the others started crying again, and the children, seeing their elders crying, cried too, although their father had been dead for three days. The old man walked up and down without knowing what he was doing, but Maruzza stayed motionless at the foot of the bed, as if there were nothing in the world now left for her to do. When she spoke all she said was: "Now there is nothing in the world left for me to do." Her eyes were staring, and she seemed to have no other thought in her head.

"No!" replied Master 'Ntoni. "There is the debt to Uncle Crocifisso to be paid off. It must never be said of us that when we lost our money we grew dishonest!"

The thought of the lupins served to drive the thorn of Bastianazzo deeper into his heart. Faded leaves were falling from the medlar tree, and the wind blew them about the yard.

"He went because I sent him," Master 'Ntoni said, "just as those leaves are blown about by the wind. If I had told him to throw himself from the Fariglioni with a stone round his neck, he would have done so without complaining. At least he died with the house and the medlar tree still his, down to the last leaf! And I, an old man, am still left. The days are long for a poor man!"

Maruzza said nothing, but there was a question hammering in her brain and gnawing at her heart; the question of what had happened that night. She had the Provvidenza constantly before her eyes. If she closed them she could still see the Provvidenza, out towards the Capo dei Mulini, where the sea was smooth and blue and boats were scattered about like so many gulls sunning themselves on the surface. You could count them one by one—there was Uncle Crocifisso's boat and there was Barabba's; there was Uncle Cola's Concetta, and there was Master Fortunato's Carmela; it broke your heart to look at them; and you could hear Mastro Turi Zuppiddo, who had lungs like an ox, singing away as he hammered; and a smell of tar rose from the river-bed, and at the wash-place Cousin Anna was beating her washing on the stones; and Mena was quietly weeping in the kitchen.

"Poor girl!" her grandfather muttered. "The house has collapsed about her too; and Master Fortunato went away coldly, without saying anything."

He started touching one by one the tools that were piled in a corner, with trembling hands, as the old do; and seeing Luca, who was wearing his father's coat, which came down to his heels, he said to him: "That will keep you warm when you go out to work; because now you will have to help us all to pay off the debt."

Maruzza put her hands over her ears to avoid hear-ing La Locca, who had been on the balcony outside the door since early morning, and wouldn't listen to reason, but kept shrieking to them in that stupid, crazy voice of hers to give her back her son.

"She acts like that because she's hungry," Cousin Anna said in the end. "Uncle Crocifisso is fed up with them all now, because of that lupin deal, and won't give her anything any more. Now I'll take her some-thing, and then she'll go away."

Poor Cousin Anna had left her washing and her little girls to come and lend a hand, because Maruzza was behaving just as though she were ill. If they had left her alone she wouldn't even have thought of lighting the fire and putting the pot on to boil, and they would all have died of hunger. The proverb says that neigh-bours must act like the tiles on the roof, which supply one another with water. Meanwhile the children's lips were white with hunger. Nunziata came and helped too, and Alessi, whose face was tear-stained from having cried so much because his mother was crying, helped by looking after Nunziata's little ones, to prevent them from getting in the way like a brood of chickens, because Nunziata liked having her hands free when she worked.

"You know your job," Cousin Anna said to her. "Your dowry when you grow up will be your own two hands!"

FIVE   Mena knew nothing about the plan to marry her to Master Cipolla's Brasi, to help her mother to get over her grief. The first person to tell her about it some time afterwards was Alfio Mosca, when he met her outside the garden gate on his way back from Aci Castello with his donkey cart. "It's not true! It's not true!" Mena exclaimed; but then she grew confused, and when he went on to explain how and when he had heard about it from La Vespa, at Uncle Crocifisso's house, she suddenly grew as red as a beetroot.

A wild look came into Alfio Mosca's eyes. Seeing the way the girl, wearing that black handkerchief round her neck, fidgeted with the buttons on her doublet and stood now on one leg and now on the other, he would willingly have paid something to be able to get away. "Listen, it's not my fault!" he said. "I heard them talking in Dumbbell's yard while I was chopping up the carob tree which was blown down in the storm on St. Claire's Day, you remember? Uncle Crocifisso gives me the odd jobs about the house now, because he won't have anything to do with La Locca's son since the turn his brother served him in connection with that cargo of lupins." Mena was standing with the latch of the garden gate in her hand, but she couldn't make up her mind to open it. "Well, if it isn't true, why are you blushing?" Alfio Mosca continued. In all conscience Mena didn't know why she was blushing. She only knew Brasi Cipolla by sight, and apart from that she knew nothing whatever, but she went on standing there, fidgeting with the latch of the garden gate. Alfio started talking about how enormously rich Brasi Cipolla was; after Naso, the butcher, he had the reputation of being the best match in the whole village, and all the girls had their eyes on him. Mena stared openeyed at Alfio as he spoke, and then abruptly said goodnight and left him. Alfio indignantly went to see La Vespa and complained at her having told him lies, which resulted in his quarrelling with people.

"I don't tell lies!" La Vespa replied. "I only told you what Uncle Crocifisso said!"

"Lies?" exclaimed Uncle Crocifisso. "Lies? I don't imperil my immortal soul by telling lies! What I told you I heard with my own ears. I also heard that there's a mortgage on the Provvidenza as part of the marriage settlement, and that the house is assessed at five *tarì* a year."

"We shall see!" La Vespa said, rocking herself to and fro with her hands behind her back against the doorpost. "We shall see whether you're speaking the truth or not! We shall see! You men are all alike. Not one of you is to be trusted!"

Sometimes Uncle Crocifisso didn't seem to hear what was said to him, and that's what happened now. Instead of rising to the bait, he went off like a bird leaping from bough to bough, talking about the Malavoglia, whose hearts were set on match-making, without a thought for that little matter of forty *onze*.

Eventually La Vespa lost patience and exclaimed:

"If they listened to you, nobody would ever get married!"

"All I want is what belongs to me! That's all I'm interested in. It's no concern of mine whether people get married or not!"

"If it's no concern of yours, whose concern is it, I should like to know? Thank goodness everybody doesn't think the way you do, putting things off again and again!"

"What hurry are you in?"

"I am in a hurry! You have time, but if you think others are willing to wait an eternity, you're very much mistaken!"

"This is a bad year," said Dumbbell. "It's no time to be thinking of such things."

At this La Vespa placed her hands on her hips and let him have a piece of her mind.

"Now listen," she began. "This is something that I've been wanting to tell you for a long time! After all, thanks be to heaven, I've got my own little bit of property, and I don't have to go down on my knees and beg for a husband. Do you suppose that if it hadn't been for your leading me up the garden path all this time I shouldn't have found a hundred husbands—Vanni Pizzuto, or Alfio Mosca or Cousin Cola, who was glued to my skirts before he went away to do his military service and wouldn't let me so much as tie up my own shoe-lace? All of them were frantic with impatience, and wouldn't have kept me dangling on a string all this time, from Easter to Christmas, like you have!"

This time Uncle Crocifisso put his hand behind his ear to hear what she was saying, and when she'd finished he tried some soothing syrup.

"Yes, I know you're a sensible girl, that's why I care for you," he said. "I'm not one of those who run after you just for the sake of your plot of land! I'm not one of those who would start squandering all your money at Santuzza's tavern as soon as they had laid their hands on it!"

"It isn't true that you care for me!" she answered, pushing him away with her elbows. "It isn't true! If you really cared for me, you know what you'd do, and you'd see that I've nothing else in my mind!"

She turned her back on him angrily, but, without realising it, kept on prodding him with her shoulder. "You don't care for me a bit!" she said. Her uncle was offended at this insulting suggestion. "You're talking like this to lead me into sin," he started grumbling. Did it mean nothing at all to her that they were kith and kin? Wasn't the plot of land part and parcel of the family too? Hadn't it always belonged to the family, and wouldn't it have remained so if his brother, God rest his soul, hadn't decided to marry, with the result that La Vespa had come into the world? That was why she had always been the apple of his eye, and why he had never thought of anything but her welfare.

"Listen," he said. "Supposing I assigned you the Malavoglia debt, which is forty *onze*, and with interest and expenses might amount to as much as fifty, in exchange for your plot of land? The house by the medlar tree would be of far more use to you than the plot of land!"

"You keep the house by the medlar tree and I'll keep my plot of land!" La Vespa answered sharply. "I know what to do with my plot of land!"

At this Uncle Crocifisso lost his temper too. Yes, he said, he knew what she wanted to do with her plot of land; she wanted to throw it away on that penniless Alfio Mosca, who was making eyes at her, all because he was in love with her land! He never wanted to see

Alfio Mosca about the house or yard again. After all he, Uncle Crocifisso, had red blood in his veins too.

"Now you're pretending to be jealous!" La Vespa exclaimed.

"Of course I'm jealous!" replied Uncle Crocifisso. "Madly jealous!" He'd be quite willing to pay five lire to have Alfio Mosca's bones broken. The reason why he didn't do so, however, was that he was a God-fearing Christian. But nowadays being an honest man didn't pay. All it did was to lead you up the street where they sold you a rope to hang yourself with. The proof was that time after time he had walked up and down outside the Malavoglia house, all for nothing, and now people were starting to laugh at him, saying he was just like those who went to pray regularly to Our Lady of Ognina, making his pilgrimage to the house by the medlar tree! All the Malavoglia did when they saw him was to raise their hats. That was as near to paying as they got. As soon as the Malavoglia children saw him appear at the end of the street they vanished, as if he were the bogeyman; but so far not a word had been said about paying for the lupins, and the Feast of the Dead was approaching, and all Master 'Ntoni was thinking about was marrying off his granddaughter.

To relieve his feelings he went to see Piedipapera, who, he told everybody, had been responsible for getting him into this mess. People said, however, that the real reason why he went to Piedipapera's was to have a peep at the house by the medlar tree, and at La Locca, who was perpetually hanging round it, because she had been told that her Menico had gone out in the Malavoglia boat, so she believed that if she waited long enough outside the house he would eventually turn up. As soon as she saw her brother Crocifisso she started shrieking like a bird of ill omen. This upset him more than ever. "That woman will drive me to sin!" he muttered.

Piedipapera told him to be patient. "The Feast of the Dead hasn't come yet. Do you want to suck Master 'Ntoni's blood? In any case, you haven't lost anything, because you know perfectly well that the lupins were rotten!" he said.

Uncle Crocifisso knew nothing of the sort. All he knew was that he was in God's hands, and that the Malavoglia children didn't dare play on the balcony when they saw him at Piedipapera's doorstep.

And if he met Alfio Mosca with his donkey cart, Alfio would raise his hat to him too, as bold as brass. This was another thing that made his blood boil, he was so jealous of his niece's plot of land. "Making love to my niece to cheat me of that plot!" he grumbled to Piedipapera. "A good-for-nothing who's only fit for leading his donkey cart around and hasn't got a penny to his name! A rascally pauper, who pretends to be in love with my ugly witch of a niece's pig's snout just for the sake of her property!"

When he had nothing else to do Uncle Crocifisso would go and squat next to Uncle Santoro outside Santuzza's tavern—they looked like a couple of beggars sitting side by side. Uncle Crocifisso didn't go to the tavern to buy a pennyworth of wine, but started whining just like Uncle Santoro, as though he were begging too. "Listen, Uncle Santoro," he said, "if you see my niece La Vespa around when Alfio Mosca comes to deliver his load of wine, just keep an eye on what they're up to, will you?" And Uncle Santoro, with his beads in his hand and his unseeing eyes, said yes, yes, of course he would, Uncle Crocifisso could depend on him, that was just what he was there for; not a fly passed without his knowing it. He was so eloquent in his assurances to

Uncle Crocifisso that his daughter Mariangela had enough of it, and asked why on earth he should meddle in Dumbbell's affairs, which had nothing whatever to do with him, especially as Dumbbell never spent a ha'penny in the tavern but stayed outside where it didn't cost anything.

Alfio Mosca had no thoughts for La Vespa, however. If anyone was on his mind, it was Master 'Ntoni's Mena, whom he saw every day in the yard or on the balcony, or when she went to feed the chickens in the fowl-house. When he heard the clucking of the two hens that he had given her he had a strange feeling—he felt as though he himself were in the yard of the house by the medlar tree; and if he had not been a penniless carter he would have asked for St. Agatha's hand and have carried her off in his donkey cart. When he thought of all this, any number of things to say to her would crowd into his mind, but when he saw her he was tongue-tied, and could only talk about the weather and the load of wine he was on his way to deliver at Santuzza's, and about his donkey, which could carry four hundredweight better than a mule, poor beast.

Mena stroked the poor beast, and Alfio smiled as though she were stroking him. "Ah! Mena, if only my donkey were yours!" he said. Mena shook her head, and her heart grew full at the thought that it would have been better if the Malavoglia had been carters, because then her father wouldn't have been drowned.

"The sea is salt, and the seaman dies at sea," she said.

Alfio was in a hurry to deliver Santuzza's wine, but he couldn't tear himself away, and he stayed talking to Mena about what a fine thing it was to be a tavern-keeper; for a tavern-keeper could always make a profit, whatever happened; if the price of wine went up he only had to put more water in the barrel. "That's how

Uncle Santoro made his money," said Alfio. "Now he begs just to fill in the time!"

"Do you make a good living, carting wine?" Mena asked.

"Yes, in the summer, when I can go on working in the evening, I don't do so badly. This poor beast earns its keep. When I've laid a little money aside, I'll buy a mule and set up as a real carter, like Cinghialenta."

The girl was all intent on what Alfio was saying. Meanwhile the grey olive tree was rustling as though it were raining, and scattering dried, crumpled leaves about the street. "Now that winter's coming, all that will have to wait until next summer," Alfio went on. Mena followed with her eyes the shadows of the clouds, which were chasing each other across the fields and scattering like the leaves of the grey olive tree. The thoughts in her head were chasing each other too, and she said: "You know, Alfio, there's nothing in that story about Master Fortunato Cipolla's son, because first we've got to pay off the lupin debt."

"I'm very glad to hear it," Mosca answered, "because then you won't be leaving the neighbourhood."

"Now that 'Ntoni's coming back from the navy, grandfather and all of us are going to help each other to pay off the debt. Mother has taken in some cloth to weave for the Lady."

"The chemist's trade's a fine trade too," Mosca remarked, but at this moment Venera Zuppidda appeared at the end of the street with her spindle in her hand.

"Good heavens, people are coming!" Mena exclaimed, and vanished into the house.

Alfio whipped up his donkey and made as if to go away too.

"Why are you in such a hurry, Alfio?" Venera Zuppidda called out. "I wanted to ask you if the wine you're taking to Santuzza's is from the same barrel as last week's!"

"I don't know. They give me the wine in casks."

"It's vinegar, only fit for salads!" Venera Zuppidda declared. "It's nothing but poison! That's how Santuzza has made all her money! That's the trade to be in nowadays if you want to go ahead! Otherwise you only go backwards, like a lobster, as the Malavoglia have been doing. Have you heard that they've fished up the Provvidenza?"

. "No. I haven't been here, but Mena knew nothing about it."

"We've only just heard! Master 'Ntoni dashed over to Il Rotolo to watch her being towed back. The old man went so fast, he seemed to have a new pair of legs. With the Provvidenza the Malavoglia will be able to set themselves on their feet, and Mena will be a good match again!"

Alfio did not reply, because Venera Zuppidda was staring straight at him with those beady, yellow eyes of hers. He said he was in a hurry to deliver the wine to Santuzza's. "He won't tell me a thing!" Venera Zuppidda muttered. "As if I hadn't seen them with my own eyes! It's like trying to hide the sun with a net!"

The Provvidenza was towed back all smashed up, just as they had found her beyond the Capo dei Mulini, with her nose among the rocks and her keel in the air. In a moment the whole village, men and women alike, had hurried down to the shore, with Master 'Ntoni in the midst of the inquisitive throng. One or two men actually kicked the Provvidenza's side to show how cracked up and useless she was, as though she no longer belonged to anybody, and poor Master 'Ntoni felt as if he'd been kicked himself. "A fine Providence you have!" said Don Franco, who had come down to have a look, in his shirt-sleeves and with his big hat on and smoking his pipe.

"She's good for nothing but firewood," said Master Fortunato Cipolla. Mangiacarrubbe, who knew what he was talking about, said that the boat must have gone down suddenly, without even giving the crew time to call on Christ's help, because the sea had swept away sails, yard, oars and everything, and had not left a peg in its place.

"This was daddy's place, where the new rowlock is," said Luca, who had climbed on to the side, "and the lupins were underneath here."

But no trace of the lupins was left, because the sea had swept everything clean. That was why Maruzza had stayed indoors, for she never wanted to see the Provvidenza again.

"The hull's sound, and something might still be made of her," Mastro Zuppiddo, the caulker, finally decided. He too kicked the Provvidenza's side a few times with his great feet. "With four ribs I'll make her shipshape again. But she won't be able to stand up to heavy seas any more. A big wave broadside-on would sink her like an old tub. But you could still use her for fishing off the rocks and in fine weather." Master Cipolla, Mangiacarrubbe and Cola stood by and listened without saying anything.

"Yes," Master Fortunato concluded gravely. "Rather than break her up for firewood . . ."

"I'm delighted to hear it," said Uncle Crocifisso, who was standing there too, with his hands behind his back. "We're Christians, and we must rejoice at the good fortune of others. As the proverb says: Wish your neighbour good fortune, because it will benefit you."

All the children had climbed into the Provvidenza,

the young Malavoglia among them. "When we've re-
paired the Provvidenza properly," Alessi said, "she'll
be like Uncle Cola's Concetta." The boys made a great
business of helping to shove and heave the boat up outside Mastro Zuppiddo's door, where there were big
stones for holding boats up and a pitch-boiler and a
whole stack of ribs and planks leaning against the wall.

Alessi was always squabbling with the boys who
wanted to climb into the boat and help to blow on the
fire under the pitch boiler, and when they wouldn't go
away he threatened them, with tears in his eyes, that
soon they would have to look out, because his brother
'Ntoni was coming home.

'Ntoni had sent in his papers and got his discharge,
though Don Silvestro, the communal secretary, had
found out that if he stayed in the navy for only another
six months his brother Luca would be exempt from
service altogether. But, now that his father was dead,
'Ntoni wouldn't stay in the navy even a week longer
than necessary. He, 'Ntoni, had had to do his service,
and Luca, who had been at home when the disaster
had happened, could do the same. After the news of
his father's death came, but for those pigs, his superior
officers, he wouldn't have done a stroke!

Luca said he would be perfectly willing to do his
service in exchange for 'Ntoni. "When he comes back
you'll be able to put the Provvidenza to sea, and there
won't be any need for me," he said.

"There's a real Malavoglia for you!" Master 'Ntoni
said in delight. "He's the living image of his father Bastianazzo, who had a heart as great as the sea and as
kind as the mercy of God."

One evening, after the boats had come in, Master
'Ntoni came home breathless with excitement, and
said: "The letter's come! Mastro Cirino just gave it

to me, while I was on the way to the Pappafavas with
the lobster pot!" La Longa went as white as a sheet
with delight, and everyone hurried into the kitchen to
look at the letter.

'Ntoni arrived with his cap pulled over one ear and
wearing his naval shirt, which his mother kept feeling
as she walked behind him in the midst of all the friends
and relations who went to meet him at the station. In
a moment the house and the yard filled with people,
just as they had after Bastianazzo's death, though this
had happened some time ago now, and nobody thought
about it any more. There are some things that only the
old go on thinking about, as if they had happened only
yesterday. La Locca, for instance, still sat against the
wall outside the Malavoglia house, waiting for her
Menico, and looking up and down the street every time
she heard a footstep.

SIX The day on which 'Ntoni came home was a
Sunday, and he went from door to door to greet his
friends and acquaintances, and everybody turned and
looked when he passed by. A troop of friends followed
him everywhere, and all the girls looked out of the
window. The only one who wasn't to be seen was
Mother Tudda's Sara.

"She's gone to Ognina with her husband," Santuzza
told him. "She married Menico Trinca—he was a wid-
ower with six children, but he's as rich as a pig!"

Venera Zuppidda, who had seen Master 'Ntoni's
'Ntoni and Sara talking by the vineyard wall, and had
gone to the station when 'Ntoni left specially to see
whether Sara was there to say good-bye to him, was
very anxious to see what sort of a face 'Ntoni would
pull at this piece of news. But time had passed for him

too—out of sight, out of mind, as the saying is—and 'Ntoni now wore his cap jauntily over one ear.

"I don't like these chits who flirt with two or three men at the same time," the Mangiacarrubbe girl said, drawing the corners of her handkerchief under her chin and trying to look like a little Madonna. "You see, if I were fond of anybody, I wouldn't change him even for Victor Emmanuel or Garibaldi!"

"I know whom you're fond of!" said 'Ntoni, placing his hand on his hip.

"You don't know anything of the sort, 'Ntoni, they've been telling you a pack of lies. One day, if you're passing my way, I'll tell you the truth!"

"Now that the Mangiacarrubbe girl has set her eyes on Master 'Ntoni's 'Ntoni, it'll be a godsend for Cousin Anna," Venera Zuppidda remarked.

'Ntoni went swaggering off, with his troop of friends behind him, and he would have been delighted if every day had been Sunday, so that he could have paraded his naval shirt about the village. In the afternoon he entertained his friends by having a fight with Vanni Pizzuto, who had no fear of God or man, though he had never been in the navy, but Vanni ended up on the ground outside the tavern with a bloody nose. Rocco Spatu, however, turned out to be stronger than 'Ntoni and managed to floor him.

"Rocco Spatu's as strong as Mastro Turi Zuppiddo," the onlookers said. "He'd earn a fine living if he were only willing to work!"

"I know how to use this," said Pizzuto, showing his razor, in order not to admit being beaten.

'Ntoni, in fact, enjoyed himself all day long. In the evening the whole family sat round the table talking, and his mother kept asking him questions, and the boys kept gazing at him in admiration, though they

were half-asleep, and Mena kept touching his cap and
his shirt with the stars on it, and examined them to see
how they were made, and his grandfather told him
that he had found work for them in the Carmela, the
big boat owned by Master Cipolla.

"I took them on out of charity," Master Fortunato,
sitting outside the barber's shop, explained to anybody
who cared to listen. "When Master 'Ntoni came to me
under the elm tree and asked me whether I needed
men for my boat, I agreed, because I didn't like to say
no. I've never been in need of men for the Carmela!
But a friend in need is a friend indeed, as the saying is.
Master 'Ntoni's so old that if you do anything for him
you can't expect anything in return!"

Master 'Ntoni said that when Mastro Bastiano had
mended the Provvidenza they would have their own
boat to go out in, and there would be no need to go
out working for others.

It was two hours before dawn when he woke his
grandson next morning, and 'Ntoni would have liked
to stay in bed a little longer. When he emerged yawning into the yard Orion was still high over Ognina, and
in the opposite direction the Pleiads were shining,
and there were so many stars twinkling in the sky that
they looked like sparks against the bottom of a black
frying pan. "It's like when reveille was sounded 'tween
decks; it's as bad as being in the navy!" 'Ntoni grumbled. "What was the use of coming home?"

"Be quiet!" Alessi answered. "There's grandfather
getting the gear ready, and he got up an hour before
we did!"

Alessi was the pattern of his father Bastianazzo, God
rest his soul. Master 'Ntoni kept busily moving about
the yard with a lantern in his hand. Outside you could
hear the footsteps of men going down to the sea and

knocking at doors to call their companions. But when the Malavoglia reached the shore, and saw the stars mirrored in the dark sea, and heard the sleepy murmur of the sea on the pebbles, even 'Ntoni was moved.

"Ah!" he exclaimed, stretching his arms. "It's a fine thing to come home. This bit of shore knows me!" Master 'Ntoni always used to say that if you were born a fish you ended by going back to the sea. A fish can't stay out of water, as the saying is.

When they were out at sea and had furled the sail and the Carmela started slowly moving round in a circle, leaving a trail of nets behind her like the tail of a snake, the other men started making fun of 'Ntoni and the way he had been jilted by Sara.

"Pork and fighting men don't last, as the saying is," one of them remarked. "That's why Sara jilted you."

"You'll find a faithful woman when the Turks are converted to Christianity," Uncle Cola said.

"In Naples I had all the girls I wanted," 'Ntoni answered. "They used to follow me about, just like stray dogs!"

"In Naples you had a cloth uniform and a cap with the name of your ship on it, and you wore boots," Barabba pointed out.

"Are the girls in Naples as pretty as they are here?"

"The girls here are not fit to clean their boots! There was one girl I had who had a silk dress and red ribbons in her hair and an embroidered bodice and golden epaulets, just like the captain's; and a fine girl she was —all she had to do was to take her master's and mistress's children out for walks!"

"It must be fine living in those parts!" said Barabba.

"Steady on the port side!" Master 'Ntoni called out.

"In the name of Judas, you're driving us on the nets," Uncle Cola, who was at the tiller, started shouting.

"Stop your talking there! Are we here to scratch our bellies or to do the job?"

"It's an eddy that's drawing us back," said 'Ntoni.

"Keep quiet, you son of a bitch!" Barabba shouted. "With all those fine ladies you've got in your head, you'll end by losing us our day's work!"

"Say that again and you'll get this on your head!" answered 'Ntoni, raising his oar.

"What's the meaning of this?" said Uncle Cola from the stern. "Is this what you learned in the navy? Can't one speak a word to you any more?"

"I'll clear out!" 'Ntoni answered.

"Clear out, then, because Master Fortunato can easily find somebody else, with all his money!"

"The servant should be patient, the master prudent," observed Master 'Ntoni.

'Ntoni, not being able to clear out, went on rowing, muttering to himself, and to restore peace Mangia-carrubbe said it was time for breakfast.

At that moment the sun broke through, and in the cool of the morning a draught of wine was very welcome indeed. The crew of the Carmela settled down to their breakfast with a will, sitting with their bottles between their legs, while the boat slowly drifted in the middle of the big circle of nets.

"The first to talk will get a kick in the pants," Uncle Cola announced.

To avoid being kicked in the pants they all started chewing away like oxen, looking at the waves, which were rolling in from the open sea without breaking. Waves of that kind look just like great swollen, green bladders, and even on sunny days remind you of overcast skies and leaden seas.

"Master Cipolla won't be pleased with us tonight,"

said Uncle Cola. "But it's not our fault! You can't catch fish when the water's cold."

Uncle Cola had broken his own rule, so Mangia-carrubbe first kicked him soundly in the pants and then replied:

"In the meantime, as we are here, let's wait till we've pulled the nets in."

"The swell's coming straight in from the open sea and ought to help us," remarked Master 'Ntoni, while Uncle Cola nursed his sore behind.

"Have you got a cigar stub for me?" Barabba asked 'Ntoni Malavoglia, now that the silence was broken.

"I haven't got a stub," said 'Ntoni, forgetting all about the quarrel of a little while before. "But here, take half mine!"

The crew of the Carmela, sitting in the bottom of the boat with their backs against the stretchers and their hands behind their heads, started quietly singing, to avoid going to sleep, for the bright sunlight made them half close their eyes. Barabba snapped his fingers each time a mullet leapt out of the water.

"They've got nothing else to do," said 'Ntoni, "so they amuse themselves by jumping out of the water!"

"This is a good cigar," said Barabba. "Are these what you smoked in Naples?"

"Yes, I smoked any amount of them."

"The corks are beginning to sink," Mangiacarrubbe pointed out.

"Do you see where the Provvidenza was lost, with your father?" Barabba said. "Over there on the cape, near where those white houses are picked out in the sunlight, and the sea's all golden."

"The sea is salt and the seaman dies at sea," 'Ntoni replied.

Barabba passed him his bottle, and then they started

grumbling in whispers about Uncle Cola, who bullied the crew of the Carmela as unmercifully as though Master Cipolla were there in person to see what they were doing.

"It's all to make people think that the big boat couldn't be worked without him," Barabba added. "The bloody policeman!"

"Now he'll say that it was all due to him that we've got such a fine haul, in spite of the cold sea. Just look how the nets are sinking; you can hardly see the corks now!"

"Let's pull in the nets, boys," Uncle Cola called out. "Because if a swell comes it'll tear them out of our hands."

"Ohi! oohi!" the men started rhythmically shouting as they hauled on the rope.

"Holy St. Francis!" Uncle Cola exclaimed, "it hardly seems possible that we should have a haul like this in spite of the swell, thanks be to God!"

The fish gleamed and glittered in the sun as the nets came to the surface, and soon the whole of the bottom of the boat was full of living silver. "Now Master Fortunato will be pleased," muttered Barabba, flushed and sweating with the exertion, "and he won't grudge us our three *carlini* for the day's work."

"Isn't it just our luck to have to break our backs for other people?" 'Ntoni remarked. "And then, when we've scraped a little money together, the devil comes and takes it away again."

"What are you grumbling at?" said his grandfather. "Doesn't Master Fortunato give you your day's pay?"

The Malavoglia worked night and day to try and save some money. La Longa took in weaving and washing. Master 'Ntoni and his grandsons hired them- selves out by the day, and did what they could. Sometimes, when he was doubled up with sciatica, Master 'Ntoni stayed in the yard, mending nets or lobster pots, or repairing gear, for he was master of every branch of the fisherman's calling. Luca went to work on the railway bridge for fifty centesimi a day, although his brother 'Ntoni said it wasn't worth it, because of the shirts he wore out carrying stones in a basket on his back, but Luca didn't care if he wore out his shoulders as well as his shirt. Alessi caught lobsters among the rocks, or worms for bait, which could be sold for one lira a *rotolo*; sometimes he went as far as Ognina or the Capo dei Mulini, and came back with his feet bleeding. But a lot of money was eaten up by having to pay Mastro Zuppiddo every Saturday for repairing the Provvidenza; to scrape together forty *onze* you had to mend a lot of lobster pots, and carry a lot of stones on the railway, and sell a lot of bait at one lira a *rotolo*, and do a lot of washing, with the water up to your knees and the sun beating down on your head. The Feast of the Dead had come and gone, and Uncle Crocifisso did nothing but walk up and down the little street, with his hands behind his back, looking like a basilisk.

"This little matter will end up in court!" he kept telling Don Silvestro and Don Giammaria, the priest.

When Master 'Ntoni heard what Dumbbell was saying, he assured him that there would be no need to go to court. "The Malavoglia have always been honest, and there has never been any need to take them to court," he said.

"That's no concern of mine," replied Uncle Crocifisso, leaning against the wall of the shed in the yard in which his vine branches were being stacked. "All I know is that I want my money!"

As a result of the priest's intervention, Dumbbell

agreed to wait for his money till Christmas, accepting as interest in the meantime the seventy-five lire that Maruzza had put away, ten centesimi at a time, in the stocking under the mattress.

"You see how it is," grumbled Master 'Ntoni. "We're slaving night and day for Uncle Crocifisso. As soon as we manage to scrape a lira together Uncle Crocifisso comes along and grabs it!"

His grandfather and Maruzza consoled themselves by building castles in the air for the following summer, when there would be anchovies to salt and prickly pears to sell at ten for a *grano*, and they made big plans for the tunny-fishing and for catching swordfish, at which good money could be earned; and in the meantime Mastro Turi would have the Provvidenza ready again. They would talk about all this on the balcony, or sitting round the table after dinner, and the children would listen attentively, with their chins in their hands. But 'Ntoni, who had been out in the world, found this sort of talk boring, and preferred going out and hanging about the tavern, where there were always a lot of people engaged in doing nothing, and even Uncle Santoro, who was about as badly off as it was possible to be, made an easy living, just by holding out his hand to passers-by and muttering Ave Marias; or he would go to Mastro Zuppiddo's, on the pretext of seeing how the Provvidenza was getting on, but really to talk to Barbara, who had just added a few branches to the fire under the pitch boiler when 'Ntoni appeared.

"You're always busy, Barbara," 'Ntoni said to her. "You're the mainstay of the family. That's why your father won't let you get married!"

"He won't let me get married to anyone who isn't good enough for me," Barbara answered. "Like should stay with like; everyone should stay with his own people."

"I should be only too willing to stay with your people, if you were willing, Barbara!"

"What things you say, 'Ntoni! Mother's in the yard, and she can hear every word you say!"

"Those branches are green and won't burn. Let me help!"

"Is it true that you come this way to see the Mangia-carrubbe girl looking out of the window?"

"I come this way for quite different reasons, Barbara. I come here to see how the Provvidenza's getting on."

"She's getting on fine. Father said you'll be able to launch her on Christmas Eve!"

With the approach of the Christmas novena the Malavoglia were continually coming and going in Mastro Turi Zuppiddo's yard. Meanwhile the whole village was getting ready for Christmas. In every house pictures of the saints were decorated with branches and oranges, and the children followed the bagpipes about when they played in front of the illuminated shrines beside the doors. The statue of the Good Shepherd in the Malavoglia house was the only one to be left in darkness, while Master 'Ntoni's 'Ntoni spent his time strutting about the village like a turkey-cock.

"Will you at least remember that it was I who melted the pitch for you, when you're out in the Provvidenza again?" Barbara Zuppidda said to him.

Piedipapera kept saying that all the girls in the village were wild about 'Ntoni.

"I'm the one who's wild!" Uncle Crocifisso complained. "If 'Ntoni gets married and they give Mena a dowry, what with that assessment there is on the house, and all those mortgage complications that came out at the last moment, I should like to know where the money for the lupins is coming from! Here's Christmas coming already, and I haven't heard a word from the Malavoglia yet!"

Master 'Ntoni went to see him again in the village square, or in the shed. "What can I do if I haven't got the money?" he said. "You can't draw blood from a stone! Give me until June, or take the Provvidenza or the house by the medlar tree. They're all I've got."

"I want my money," replied Uncle Crocifisso, leaning against the wall. "You said the Malavoglia were honest people, and it's no good talking to me about the Provvidenza and the house by the medlar tree!"

Uncle Crocifisso fretted so much about his money that he lost his sleep and his appetite, and he couldn't even console himself by saying that he would take the matter to court, because whenever he did so Master 'Ntoni promptly sent Don Giammaria or the communal secretary round to see him and appeal to him to have pity on the Malavoglia, and he couldn't go about his business in the square any longer because everybody kept telling him that it was tainted money he was after. He couldn't even relieve his feelings by talking to Piedipapera, because Piedipapera only replied that the lupins were rotten anyway, and that his, Piedipapera's, part in the matter had merely been that of an intermediary, and that in any case it no longer had anything to do with him. But one night Uncle Crocifisso had an idea. He was so excited by it that for the rest of the night he couldn't sleep a wink. As soon as it was daylight he went to see Piedipapera, and found him stretching his arms and yawning at the front door. "You must pretend to have bought the debt from me," Uncle Crocifisso said to him, "and then we shall be able to issue a court order against the Malavoglia, and nobody will be able to say that you're a usurer, just because you're trying to get your money back, or that the money's tainted!"

"Is that the wonderful idea you had during the night?" exclaimed Piedipapera scornfully. "Did you wake me at dawn to tell me that?"

"I came to talk to you about the vine branches. If you want them, you can come and take them away!"

"Then you can apply for the court order," Piedipapera replied, "but you must pay the costs!"

That good woman Grazia Piedipapera appeared in her nightgown and said to her husband: "What did Uncle Crocifisso come to see you about? Why can't you leave the Malavoglia alone with all their troubles, poor souls?"

"You mind your own business!" Piedipapera replied. "Women are long in the hair and short in the brains." And he hobbled off to drink a glass of herb beer at Vanni Pizzuto's.

"They're preparing an unhappy Christmas for those poor Malavoglia," said Grazia Piedipapera with her hands across her belly.

Outside every house was a shrine decorated with leaves and oranges, and when they came to play the bagpipes in the evening the candles in the shrines were lit, and the litany was sung, so that each house had its own festival. Children played games with nuts in the street, and when Alessi stopped and stood and watched them with his legs apart, they said to him:

"You go away if you haven't any nuts to play with! Now they're going to take your house away!"

Sure enough, on Christmas Eve the bailiff came in a carriage and set the whole village in a commotion. He went to the Malavoglia house and left a sheet of paper with a stamp on it on the chest of drawers, next to the statue of the Good Shepherd.

"Did you see the bailiff calling at the Malavoglia's?" Venera Zuppidda exclaimed. "Now they're done for!"

Her husband, who was completely taken aback at having turned out to be right after all, started shouting and making a terrible row.

"By all the saints in Paradise!" he shouted. "Didn't I say that I didn't like that 'Ntoni hanging about the house?"

"Don't you meddle in affairs you don't understand!" his wife answered. "'Ntoni's visits are our affair! That's the way that girls get married—unless, of course you want the girl to be left on our hands!"

"What? Marry him now that the bailiff has called?" Venera Zuppidda laid her hands on his face.

"So you knew the bailiff was coming, did you? When something's going to happen you never lift a finger in good time! You just make a fuss afterwards! In any case the bailiff doesn't eat people!"

It's true that the bailiff doesn't eat people, but the Malavoglia behaved as though they had been struck by a thunderbolt. They just sat in a circle in the yard, staring at each other, dumbfounded. There was no sitting down to table in the Malavoglia house on the day that the bailiff called.

"There you are!" said 'Ntoni. "We're caught like rats in a trap, and now they send the bailiff to wring our necks!"

"What are we to do?" said La Longa.

Master 'Ntoni didn't know what they were to do, but in the end he took the piece of paper with the stamp on it and went with his two eldest grandsons to see Uncle Crocifisso and asked him to take the Providenza, because Mastro Bastiano had just finished repairing it. The old man's voice quivered, just as it had done after the death of his son Bastianazzo.

"It's no use talking to me," Dumbbell answered. "It's no concern of mine any longer. I've sold my interest to Piedipapera. You must settle it with him!"

As soon as he saw the procession approaching Piedipapera started scratching his head. "What do you expect me to do?" he asked them. "I'm only a poor man, and I need the money. The Provvidenza is useless to me, because it's not my trade. But, if Uncle Crocifisso is willing, I'll help you to sell her. Wait here, I'll be back in a minute!"

The three unhappy Malavoglia sat on the wall and waited miserably. They didn't have the heart even to look at each other, but cast long glances down the road, waiting for Piedipapera to come back. In the end he came back, walking very, very slowly, though he could walk quickly enough when he chose, in spite of his lame leg.

"Uncle Crocifisso says the Provvidenza's as useless as an old boot, and he can't do anything with her," Piedipapera called out, while he was still quite a long way away. "I'm sorry, but I couldn't do anything with him!"

So the Malavoglia went home again, still with that piece of stamped paper.

Something had to be done, however, because they had heard it said that that piece of stamped paper, lying there on the chest of drawers, would end by eating up, not only the chest of drawers and the house, but the whole family.

Maruzza suggested that they should ask the advice of Don Silvestro, the communal secretary. "Take him those two hens, and he'll be able to tell you something," she said.

Don Silvestro said there was no time to lose, and sent them to a fine lawyer, Dr. Scipioni, who lived in the Via degli Ammalati in Catania, opposite Uncle Crispino's stables. He was a young man, but, so far as talking was concerned, none of the old lawyers could hold a candle to him, though they charged five *onze* to open their mouths, while he was satisfied with only twenty-five lire.

When the Malavoglia appeared, Dr. Scipioni was busy rolling cigarettes, and he made them go away and come back again two or three times before he would let them in. The best of it was that they all walked in procession, one behind the other, and at first La Longa, carrying her small daughter, went with them to help them state their case, and so they lost a whole day's work. When the lawyer had read the papers, and had begun to grasp what it was all about from the confused answers which were all that he was able to get from Master 'Ntoni, while the others sat around glued to their chairs, scarcely daring to breathe, he suddenly burst out laughing, and the others joined in, without knowing why, because it relieved the tension and enabled them to breathe freely again. "You must do nothing at all!" the lawyer said. "You must do absolutely nothing at all!" When Master 'Ntoni repeated that the bailiff had called, the lawyer said: "Let him call every day if he likes. The more often he calls, the sooner the creditor will tire of the expense. There's nothing he can get from you, because the house is mortgaged, and we'll put in a claim against the boat in the name of Mastro Turi Zuppiddo. Your daughter-in-law has nothing whatever to do with the purchase of the lupins!"

The lawyer went on talking for a long time, without so much as spitting or scratching his head; in fact they felt he was giving them far more than twenty-five lire worth. Master 'Ntoni and his grandsons felt their mouths watering as they listened; he put such a fine defence into their mouths that they felt like rattling it off too; and they went away overwhelmed and dazed by all the lawyer's arguments, and kept repeating his words and gesticulations all the way home. This time Maruzza had not gone with them, and when she saw them coming home with red cheeks and shining eyes she felt a great weight had been lifted from her shoulders, and her whole expression grew serene as she waited for them to explain what the lawyer had said. Instead, they looked at each other without saying a word. In the end poor Maruzza nearly died of impatience.

"Well?" she asked.

"There's nothing to worry about!" Master 'Ntoni calmly replied.

"What did the lawyer say?"

"He said there's nothing to worry about!"

"But what did he say?"

"Oh, he knows how to talk! He has a moustache. God bless those twenty-five lire!"

"But what did he say?"

Master 'Ntoni looked at his grandson, and his grandson looked at him.

"Nothing!" Master 'Ntoni eventually replied. "He told us to do nothing at all!"

"We shan't pay anything," young 'Ntoni announced, more boldly. "We shan't pay anything at all, because he can't take either the house or the Provvidenza. We don't owe him anything at all!"

"But what about the lupins?"

"That's true! What about the lupins?" Master 'Ntoni repeated.

"The lupins?" 'Ntoni said. "We didn't eat the wretched lupins! Uncle Crocifisso won't find them in our pockets! He can't get anything from us! The lawyer said he should repay us our expenses."

A moment of silence followed. Maruzza didn't seem to be convinced.

"Did he say we shouldn't pay, then?"

'Ntoni scratched his head, and his grandfather added:

"It's true that he let us have the lupins, and we must pay for them."

There was no answer to that. Now that the lawyer was no longer present, the lupins must be paid for. Master 'Ntoni shook his head and muttered:

"The Malavoglia have always paid what they owe. Uncle Crocifisso can take the house and the Provvidenza and everything else, but the Malavoglia have always paid what they owe!"

The old man was confused, and his sister-in-law wept silently into her apron.

"We must go and see Don Silvestro," Master 'Ntoni said eventually.

With one accord grandfather, daughter-in-law, grandsons and granddaughters, not forgetting even the little one, went once more in procession to the communal secretary to ask what they should do to pay off the debt without Uncle Crocifisso's having to send them any more stamped paper, which would end by eating up the house, the boat and all of them. Don Silvestro, who was well versed in the law, was passing the time making a trap-cage to give to the Lady's children. His behaviour was quite different from the lawyer's, and he let them talk and talk while he went on with his cage-making. In the end he told them what to do. "Well, if Signora Maruzza puts her hand to it, it can easily be arranged," he said. The poor woman could not imagine what she would have to put her hand to.

"You must sign a document agreeing to the sale," Don Silvestro explained, "and abandon your mortgage, although you didn't buy the lupins."

"We all of us bought the lupins," La Longa murmured, "and the Lord punished us by taking my husband!"

The poor, ignorant Malavoglia, sitting motionless on their high-backed chairs, looked at one another, and Don Silvestro laughed privately to himself. Then he sent for Uncle Crocifisso, who arrived chewing a dried chestnut, having only just finished his lunch. His little eyes were shining brighter than usual. At first he wouldn't listen. He said he wasn't interested, because the whole thing had nothing whatever to do with him any longer. "I'm just a low wall," he said, "which everybody sits on when he feels inclined, and all because I can't talk like a lawyer and state my case. They make out that all I own is stolen property, but what they do to me they do to the crucified Christ . . ." And he went on grumbling and muttering to himself, standing with his back against the wall and his hands in his pockets, and you couldn't understand a word he was saying, because of the chestnut in his mouth. Don Silvestro had to sweat blood to convince him that Malavoglia were not trying to cheat him, since they wanted nothing better than to pay off the debt, and Bastianazzo's widow was sacrificing her mortgage for the purpose. "The Malavoglia are willing to make any sacrifice to avoid a lawsuit," Don Silvestro said, "but, if you force them to it, they'll start sending out stamped papers too, and you'll never hear the end of it. You must have a little charity, after all. Would you like to bet that if you stick your heels in the ground like a mule you won't get anything out of them at all?"

"If you approach me from that side, of course, I've

got nothing to say," Uncle Crocifisso replied, and he promised to talk things over with Piedipapera. "I'd make any sacrifice for the sake of friendship," he said. Master 'Ntoni knew what he was willing to do for a friend, he said, and he offered him his open snuff-box, stroked the little girl's hair, and gave her a chestnut. "Don Silvestro knows my weak side," he said. "I can't say no. I'll talk to Piedipapera this evening, and ask him to wait till Easter; provided, of course, that Maruzza puts her hand to it." Maruzza did not know what she was expected to put her hand to, but she said she would do it immediately. "You can send for those beans that you asked me for that you wanted to sow," Uncle Crocifisso said to Don Silvestro before going away.

"All right, all right," Don Silvestro replied. "I know that for your friends your heart is as big as the ocean!"

In public Piedipapera protested vigorously at the postponement that he said Uncle Crocifisso had imposed on him. He shouted and tore his hair and said he was being ruined. By persuading him to take over the Malavoglia debt for five hundred lire Uncle Crocifisso had condemned him and his wife Grazia to starvation for the whole winter. When he mentioned the sum of five hundred lire, it took poor Grazia's breath away, because she couldn't imagine where such a large sum of money had come from. She tried to put in a good word for the Malavoglia, who were good people —everybody in the neighbourhood had always known them as honest and decent folk. Uncle Crocifisso started taking their part too.

"They've said they will pay, and if they can't pay, you get the house," he said to Piedipapera. "La Longa has said that she'll put her hand to it herself. Nowadays everyone has to manage as best he can!"

At this Piedipapera lost his temper, put on his jacket and went away, cursing. So far as he was concerned, he said, Uncle Crocifisso and his wife could do what they liked, as he didn't count any more and was no longer master in his own house.

SEVEN   It was a sad Christmas for the Malavoglia. To add to their troubles, Luca's number—a low, poor man's number—came up in the conscription lottery. But the family had grown hardened by now, and there were fewer complaints than when 'Ntoni went off. 'Ntoni walked with his brother to the station, with his cap pulled over one ear—it might have been he who had been called up—and reminded him that he had done his service himself, and that it wasn't so bad, after all. It was raining that day, and the road was one long puddle.

Luca told his mother it was a long way to the station, and said he didn't want her to come with him. He stood with his bundle under his arm, watching the rain on the medlar tree. Then he kissed his grandfather's and his mother's hand and kissed Mena and the rest of them.

So La Longa watched him walking away under the umbrella, accompanied by his brothers and sisters, picking his way from stone to stone because the street was nothing but one big puddle. The boy, who was as sensible as his grandfather, rolled up the bottoms of his trousers on the balcony, although he was going to be put into uniform and wouldn't be wearing them again.

He won't write for money while he's away, the old man said to himself. If God grants him long life, he'll set the house by the medlar tree on its feet again! But, just because he was made of that stuff, God did not grant him long life; and later, after the news came that he was dead, the thought that she had allowed him to walk away in the rain, without going with him to the station, plagued La Longa like a thorn in her flesh.

"Mother!" said Luca, turning back because it made his heart bleed to leave her grieving on the balcony, like Our Lady of Sorrows, "when I come back, I'll let you know in good time, so you can come and meet me at the station!" Maruzza never forgot those words of Luca's; to her dying day she sorrowed because he was not there to see the Provvidenza launched again; this was a second thorn in her flesh. The launching of the Provvidenza was just like a festival, and the whole village turned out to see. Barbara Zuppidda appeared with her broom to sweep up the chips and shavings. "I'm doing it for your sake," she said to Master 'Ntoni's 'Ntoni, "because the Provvidenza belongs to you!"

"With that broom in your hand, you look like a queen!" 'Ntoni replied. "There's not another house-keeper like you in the whole of Trezza!"

" 'Ntoni, now that you're taking the Provvidenza away, you know quite well that we shan't be seeing you round here any more!"

"Of course you will. It's the quickest way to the lava field, anyway!"

"You'll be coming this way to see the Mangia-carrubbe girl. She puts her head out of the window every time you pass."

"I'm leaving the Mangiacarrubbe girl to Rocco Spatu, because I've got other ideas in my head."

"What with all those pretty girls you met while you were away, who knows what ideas you've got in your head?"

"There are pretty girls here too, Barbara, you can take it from me!"

"Really?"

"Really!"

"And are you interested in them?"

"Of course I'm interested in them, but they're not interested in me, because of the smart young men they see passing the window in polished shoes."

"By Our Lady of Ognina, I don't even look at their polished shoes! Mother says polished shoes are meant to steal our dowries and everything else too. One fine day, she says, she's going out into the street with her distaff to have things out with that Don Silvestro, if he doesn't leave me alone!"

"Are you being serious, Barbara?"

"Yes, really!"

"I'm very pleased to hear it!"

"Listen, what about coming with me to the lava field on Monday, when my mother goes to the fair?"

"On Monday my grandfather won't leave me free for a moment, now that the Provvidenza's being launched!"

As soon as Mastro Turi said that the boat was ready, Master 'Ntoni came to fetch her with his grandsons and all his friends, and on the way down to the sea through the crowd of onlookers the Provvidenza rocked and floundered over the stones as though she were seasick.

"Heave! Heave this way!" Mastro Zuppiddo shouted louder than the rest as they sweated and shouted, pushing and pulling the boat down the slipway. "Leave her to me!" he called out when she ran into an obstruction, "or I'll pick her up like a baby and put her in the sea by myself!"

Some said that with those great arms of his Mastro Turi was perfectly capable of it. Others remarked that now things would be looking up again for the Malavoglia. They said that Mastro Turi had magic in his fingers. The Provvidenza had looked as useless as an old boot, but now just look at what he'd done with her!

The Provvidenza, shining with new pitch and with a fine streak of red paint along her side and a statue of St. Francis, with a beard that looked like cotton wool, at the stern, really did look quite different now, so much so that even La Longa was reconciled to her for the first time since the day when she had come back without her husband. Ever since the bailiff had called, La Longa had been afraid, and that was why she made her peace with the Provvidenza.

"Long live St. Francis!" everyone shouted when they saw the Provvidenza pass, and La Locca's son shouted louder than the rest, hoping that Master 'Ntoni would now be able to give him work. Mena came out on the balcony and wept again, but this time with happiness, and even La Locca rose and went with the crowd that followed the Malavoglia.

"Oh, Mena, this must be a fine day for you all," said Alfio Mosca from his window opposite. "It must be like the day when I shall buy my mule!"

"Will you sell the donkey?"

"What do you expect me to do? I'm not rich, like Vanni Pizzuto. If I were, I certainly shouldn't sell it."

"Poor beast!"

"If I could afford to feed another mouth, I should marry and not live a dog's life all by myself," said Alfio, with a laugh.

Mena did not know what to say to this, and Alfio went on:

"Now that you've got the Provvidenza at sea again, they'll be marrying you to Brasi Cipolla."

"Grandfather hasn't said anything about it!"

"He'll tell you later! There's plenty of time yet. Who knows what may happen between now and your wedding day, or what roads I'll be travelling with my cart! They tell me there's work for everybody on the railway on the plain beyond Catania. Now that Santuzza has made an arrangement with Massaro Filippo for the new wine, there'll be no more work for me here!"

Although things were beginning to look up again for the Malavoglia, Master Cipolla shook his head and said that they weren't so very much better off after all—he knew where the blemishes were under the new pitch.

"A patched-up Providence!" sneered the chemist. "She's nothing but a sham, like our constitutional monarchy! You'll see that Master 'Ntoni will lose his house and his boat!"

"They'll end by making us pay even for the water we drink. Now they say there's going to be a tax on pitch. That's why Master 'Ntoni was in such a hurry to have his boat finished. And he still owes Mastro Turi fifty lire!"

"The sensible one was Uncle Crocifisso, who sold the Malavoglia debt to Piedipapera."

"If things don't go well for the Malavoglia now, Piedipapera will get the house by the medlar tree and the Provvidenza will go to Mastro Turi."

Meanwhile the Provvidenza had taken to the water like a duck. She seemed to revel in the cool, green water lapping against her sides and the sun playing on her new paint. Master 'Ntoni felt happy too, as he stood with his legs apart and his hands behind his back, frowning slightly, as sailors do when trying to pick something out against the sunlight; for a fine, winter sun was shining, and the fields were green and the sea was glittering and the blue sky looked endless. Thus eyes which had wept and seen all things the colour of pitch looked again upon sunshine and fine winter weather, and renewal came to all things, even to the Provvidenza, for a little pitch and new paint had sufficed to make her as good as new again; only eyes that wept no more and were closed in death saw no renewal.

Maruzza, moving to and fro in front of her warp-frame arranging the weft, grieved that her husband Bastianazzo could not see all this rejoicing, for all those beams and shafts had been made for her by Bastianazzo with his own hands, on Sundays or rainy days, and fixed in the wall by him. Everything in the house still spoke of him. His oilskins hung in a corner, and a pair of nearly new boots were still under the bed. Mena, as she softened the warp, was sad at heart too, thinking about Alfio, who was going to La Bicocca and was thinking of selling that poor, wretched donkey of his. The young, alas! have short memories, and have eyes only for the rising sun; only the old, who have seen the sun go down so many times, look in the direction of sunset.

"Now that the Provvidenza has been launched," said Maruzza, seeing her daughter silent and absorbed, "your grandfather has started talking to Master Cipolla again. I saw them from the balcony this morning, outside Peppi Naso's shed."

"Master Fortunato is rich and has nothing else to do. That's why he hangs about the village square all day long," Mena replied.

"Yes, and his son Brasi is well provided for too. Now that we've got our boat back, and our menfolk won't have to go out working for others, we'll drag ourselves out of the mire again; and if the souls in purgatory intercede for us, and help us to pay off the debt to Uncle Crocifisso, we shall start being able to think of other things. Your grandfather keeps his eyes open, don't you worry, and, as for the future, there's no need to feel that you've lost your father, because your grandfather's like a second father to you!"

Soon afterwards Master 'Ntoni arrived, carrying an enormous load of nets—they completely hid his face. "I went to fetch them from the Carmela," he said. "They must be looked at carefully, because tomorrow we're going out in the Provvidenza."

"Why didn't you let 'Ntoni help you?" Maruzza answered, holding on at one end while the old man spread out the nets, which uncoiled endlessly, like the tail of a snake.

"I left him at Mastro Pizzuto's," he said. "The poor lad has to work the whole week. A load like this keeps you warm even in January!"

Alessi laughed, seeing his grandfather all red and bent with the exertion.

"Poor La Locca's just outside," his grandfather said to him. "Her son's hanging about the square out of work, and they've got nothing to eat."

Maruzza sent Alessi out to La Locca with some beans, and the old man, wiping the sweat from his brow with his shirt-sleeve, said: "Now that we've got our boat back, if we get through to the summer, with God's help we shall be able to pay off the debt." The debt was all that he could think about, and he sat under the medlar tree and gazed at his nets as though they were already full.

"Now we must lay in a stock of salt before they put a tax on it, if they're going to," he went on. "We must pay Mastro Zuppiddo with the first money we earn; he promised me that then he'd let me have a supply of casks on credit."

"Five *onze* from Mena's weaving are in the chest of drawers," Maruzza remarked.

"Bravo! I don't want to borrow from Uncle Crocifisso any more, because I've had misgivings about him ever since the lupin deal; but he'd advance us thirty lire for the first time we went out with the Provvidenza."

"Leave Uncle Crocifisso alone!" exclaimed La Longa. "Uncle Crocifisso's money brings misfortune. I heard the black hen clucking last night!"

"Poor thing!" the old man exclaimed, smiling at the sight of the black hen, which was strutting about the yard with her tail up and her comb hanging over her ear, as though it were no affair of hers. "All the same, she lays eggs every day!"

At this Mena appeared in the doorway and spoke. "There's a whole basketful of eggs," she said. "On Monday, if Alfio Mosca goes to Catania, he can take them and sell them in the market."

"Yes, it all helps to pay off the debt," said Master 'Ntoni. "But you should eat eggs occasionally, when you feel like it."

"We don't feel like it!" said Maruzza, and Mena added: "If we eat them, how can Alfio Mosca take them to market? Now we're going to put duck's eggs under the broody hen—we can get eighty centesimi each for the ducklings."

Her grandfather looked at her and said: "You're a real Malavoglia, my girl!"

Meanwhile the chickens were scratching in the sunlight in the yard, and the broody hen, with her feathers dangling, was stupidly shaking her beak in a corner. Under the green branches along the wall in the kitchen garden, warp was hanging to bleach in the sun, with stones at the bottom to keep it stretched. "All this means money," Master 'Ntoni repeated, "and with

God's help they won't turn us out of the house. House of mine, mother of mine, as the saying is."

Meanwhile Piedipapera was saying: "Now the Malavoglia must pray to God and St. Francis for a good fishing season."

"With the seasons we've been having lately, they certainly must!" Master Cipolla answered. "The fish in the sea must be afflicted with the cholera too!"

Mangiacarrubbe nodded his head in agreement, and Uncle Cola started talking about the tax they were proposing to put on salt; if they taxed salt, the anchovies in the sea need have no anxiety in the future, and need not worry any more about the paddle-wheels of passing steamers, because it wouldn't be worth anyone's while to go out fishing.

"They've thought up something else as well," said Mastro Turi Zuppiddo, the caulker. "They're thinking of putting a tax on pitch!" Those who had no interest in pitch made no comment, but Mastro Zuppiddo declared that he would put his shutters up, and that in future those who wanted their boats caulked could use their wives' chemises. At that moment the whistle of an engine was heard, and a train emerged from the tunnel in the side of the hill, with as much smoke and clatter as though the devil were inside it.

"There you are!" Master Fortunato announced. "What with the railway on one side and steamers on the other, Trezza is becoming impossible to live in!"

The proposal to put a tax on pitch caused an uproar in the village. Venera Zuppidda went out on her balcony, fuming with rage, and announced to the world that this was another piece of wickedness on the part of Don Silvestro, who was trying to ruin the village because he had been rejected as a suitor for her daughter's hand. She wouldn't even be seen walking next to him in a procession, let alone marry him, and her daughter wouldn't either! Whenever Venera Zuppidda talked about her daughter's future husband, she spoke as though she herself were to be the bride. She declared that Mastro Turi would put up his shutters, and then she would like to know how the village would manage to keep its boats at sea; they would all have to eat one another to keep themselves alive. All the other women started appearing at their doorways with their distaffs in their hands and started shouting that all tax collectors ought to be killed and their papers consigned to the flames; and the offices in which the papers were kept ought to be burned down too. When the men came back from the fishing, they left their gear to dry and stood at their windows, watching their wives hatching riot and revolution.

"It's all because Master 'Ntoni's 'Ntoni came back!" Venera declared. "He's always hanging about after my Barbara!"

The excitement spread from door to door, rising like the waves of the sea in a storm. Don Franco, wearing his enormous hat, rubbed his hands with glee, and declared that the people was at last raising its head. When he saw Don Michele pass, with his pistol on his belly, he laughed in his face. The excitement gradually spread from the women to the men, who went about looking for each other for mutual support before letting their tempers rise; or they wasted their time standing with folded arms, gaping and listening to the chemist preaching revolution in the village square, but preaching in whispers, so that his wife upstairs shouldn't hear. He told them not to waste their time worrying about trifles like the salt tax and the pitch tax; that would be foolish. What was needed, he said, was a clean sweep; the people must be king. Some, however, turned their

backs on him with a sneer, saying: "The chemist wants
to be king himself! He's a revolutionary because he
wants the people to hunger," and instead of listening
to any more of it, went off to Santuzza's tavern, where
there was good wine that quickly went to your head,
as well as Cinghialenta and Rocco Spatu, who were as
good at getting angry as ten ordinary men. Now that
all the excitement about taxation had flared up again,
they would soon be talking about the tax on "hair,"
as they called the tax on beasts of burden, and of in-
creasing the tax on wine. By the Holy Mother of God,
if that happened things would come to a pretty pass!

The good wine made them shout, and shouting made
them thirsty, particularly as the tax on wine had not
gone up yet, and those who had been drinking rolled
up their sleeves and shook their fists at everything
and everybody, including the flies buzzing about the
bar.

"This is like a feast-day for Santuzza," they said. La
Locca's son, who had no money to buy drink, stood
outside the tavern door and shouted that now that
Uncle Crocifisso wouldn't give him any more work, even
at half pay, because of his brother Menico, who had
been drowned with the cargo of lupins, he was ready
to kill himself. Vanni Pizzuto shut his shop, because
obviously nobody else would be coming for a shave
that day. He put his razor in his pocket and spat and
shouted curses from a distance at those who were still
going about their business, with their oars over their
shoulders, and taking no interest in the hubbub.

"Those people don't care a fig for their country!"
Don Franco shouted, drawing at his pipe as though he
wanted to eat it. "They wouldn't lift a finger for their
country! They're scum!"

"Let him talk!" Master 'Ntoni said to his grandson,

who was ready to break his oar over the head of any man who called him scum. "All this talk won't put a crust of bread into our mouths or rid us of a penny of our debt!"

Uncle Crocifisso was another of those who kept to themselves instead of taking part in the excitement. Even when the tax collector drew blood from him, he used to swallow his anger, for fear that worse might follow. He was no longer to be seen in the village square, leaning against the wall of the church tower, but had slunk home and was hiding in the darkest corner of the house, rattling off Ave Marias to digest his anger at the shouting, excited mob, who would be ready to sack and burn the village and rob anybody who had a little money in the house. "He's the one who's right," they said in the village, "because he must have money by the shovelful. Now he's actually got the five hundred lire for the lupins from Piedipapera!"

But La Vespa, whose possessions were a plot of land, which she thought nobody could steal, went about shouting like a maniac on his behalf, with her face black with rage and her hair flying in the wind. Every six months they ate her uncle alive with the land tax, she declared, and if the tax collector ever dared set foot in her uncle's house again she would tear his eyes out with her own hands. She was continually going to Grazia Piedipapera's or Cousin Anna's or to the Mangiacarrubbes on one pretext or another, to find out how Alfio Mosca and St. Agatha were getting on, and she would have been only too pleased to have seen, not just St. Agatha, but the whole of the Malavoglia family wiped off the face of the earth. She told everybody it wasn't true that Piedipapera had bought the Malavoglia debt from her uncle, because Piedipapera had never owned five hundred lire in the whole of his life.

The Malavoglia were still completely at Uncle Crocifisso's mercy. In fact, her Uncle Crocifisso was so rich
that he could crush them like ants beneath his feet at
any moment he chose, and she had been wrong to turn
him down for the sake of a man who owned nothing
but a donkey cart, for she was the apple of her uncle's
eye, though, as it happened, he wouldn't open the door
to her just at the moment, for fear of having his house
looted and burned down.

Those who had something to lose, like Master Cipolla
and Massaro Filippo, the market gardener, did not
dare so much as show their noses out of doors, but
stayed at home with the door bolted; and his father
gave Brasi Cipolla an almighty cuff over the ear when
he found him at the front gate, gaping idly at the
throng in the village square. During the squall all the
big fish, even the stupid ones, stayed under water without showing themselves, leaving Silkworm, the mayor,
gazing skywards as though he were looking for a leaf
to nibble.

"Can't you see that they just use you as a puppet?"
his daughter Betta said to him, with her arms akimbo.
"Can't you see that they just make use of you for their
own purposes? Now you're in the soup, they turn their
backs on you and leave you to your own devices! That's
what comes of letting yourself be led by the nose by a
mischief-maker like Don Silvestro!"

"I don't let myself be led by the nose by anybody,"
Silkworm replied with dignity.

Don Silvestro, however, maintained that the real
mayor was Silkworm's daughter, Betta, and that,
though Mastro Croce Callà wore the trousers, this was
a mistake.

After mass on the Sunday on which the communal
council was to meet, Don Silvestro went to the big

room in the municipal office, which used to be the headquarters of the National Guard, and calmly sat down at the deal table and started cutting quills to pass the time, while Venera Zuppidda and all her friends waited outside in the street, spinning in the sun, and shouting as if they wanted to tear the councillors' eyes out.

When Silkworm was sent for—he was busy on the wall of Massaro Filippo's vineyard—he put on his new jacket, washed his hands, brushed the dust from his trousers, but refused to move until Don Silvestro sent for him. In vain Betta shouted at him and pushed him out of the doorway by the shoulders, telling him that as he made his bed so must he lie on it, and that, if those who were opposed to Don Silvestro would let him remain mayor, he should let them have their way. But Mastro Callà had seen the crowd of women outside the council office with their distaffs in their hands, and this time he dug in his heels and was as stubborn as a mule. "I won't go unless Don Silvestro comes for me," he repeated, with his eyes nearly popping out of his head. "Don Silvestro will find a way out!"

"I'll find a way out for you!" Betta told him. "If they don't want a tax on pitch, well, don't have one!"

"Bravo! And where is the money to come from?"

"Where is the money to come from? Get it from those who have it—Uncle Crocifisso, for instance, or Master Cipolla and Peppi Naso!"

"Bravo! But they're the councillors!"

"Then turn them out and get some new ones! They won't be able to keep you on as mayor if everyone else wants to get rid of you! You must satisfy the majority!"

"Hark at the way women talk! As if it were the majority on whom I depended for support! The mayor is appointed by the councillors, and not by anybody else. Whom would you have as councillors? Would you take the beggars off the streets?"

"Then keep the councillors and get rid of that crafty Don Silvestro!"

"Bravo! And then who'd act as secretary? You or I or Master Cipolla? Who is there, apart from Don Silvestro, who could possibly be secretary? Your advice is worse than a philosopher's!"

This left Betta with nothing to say, so she relieved her feelings by abusing Don Silvestro, who had made himself master of the village and had them all in his pocket.

"Bravo!" repeated Silkworm. "You see, when he's not there I don't know what to say. I should like to see you in my shoes!"

At last Don Silvestro arrived, with a face that looked harder than a brick wall and his hands behind his back, whistling a tune. "Well, don't lose heart, Mastro Croce," he said, "the heavens are not falling this time!" Mastro Croce permitted himself to be led away by Don Silvestro, and to be placed at the deal council table in front of the big inkpot. The only councillors present were Peppi Naso, the butcher, looking sleek and red-faced, who was afraid of nothing in the world, and Tino Piedipapera.

"Piedipapera's got nothing to lose!" Venera Zuppidda shouted from the doorway. "He comes here to suck the blood of the poor! He's like a leech, battening on his neighbours and aiding and abetting others in their crooked deals! Thieves and assassins, the lot of you!"

Piedipapera at first pretended to be indifferent, because of the dignity of his office, but in the end he lost patience, rose on his lame leg and ordered Mastro Cirino, the communal beadle, who was responsible for the maintenance of public order, and therefore wore a

red cap when he was not acting as sexton, to make the
woman hold her tongue.

"You'd like to silence everybody, wouldn't you, Piedipapera?"

"As if everybody didn't know the rôle you play, closing your eyes when Master 'Ntoni's 'Ntoni comes to talk
to your daughter Barbara!" Piedipapera answered.

"It's you who keep your eyes closed while your wife
makes herself useful to La Vespa, who comes to your
door every day looking for Alfio Mosca, while you just
hold the candlestick for them! That's a fine occupation!
But Alfio Mosca doesn't want to have anything to do
with her, I tell you! He's got Master 'Ntoni's Mena in
his head, and you're wasting lamp oil if you've promised him to La Vespa!"

"I'll break every bone in your body!" shouted Piedipapera, starting to hobble round the deal table.

"Now things are turning nasty," muttered Mastro
Croce Giufà.

"Now then, what sort of behaviour is this?" Don Silvestro shouted. "Do you think you're in the public
square? Will you take on a bet that I'll get rid of this
rabble for you? I'll settle this matter!"

But Venera Zuppidda wouldn't hear of the matter
being settled, and struggled violently with Don Silvestro, who pushed her and pulled her by the hair, and
finally managed to drag her away behind the farm gate.

"Now what is it that you're really after?" he asked
her when they were alone. "What does it matter to you
if they put a tax on pitch? Will you or your husband
have to pay it, by any chance? Won't the money have
to be found by those who want their boats mended?
Now just you listen to me! Your husband is a fool to be
angry with the council and to kick up all this fuss! Now
we've got to appoint new assessors to take the place

of Master Cipolla and Massaro Mariano, who are perfectly useless, and your husband might be one of
them!"

"I don't know anything about that," Venera Zuppidda replied, suddenly growing calm. "I don't inter-
fere in my husband's affairs! All I know is that he's
fuming with rage! If the thing's settled, all I can do is
to go and tell him!"

"Go and tell him, then! The thing's as certain as that
God's in His heaven, I tell you! Do I speak the truth
or not!"

Venera Zuppidda hurried off to tell her husband, who
was sitting in a corner looking as pale as death, carding
tow, but he refused to come out for all the money in the
world, and said they only wanted him to go and make
a fool of himself.

It was impossible to begin the council meeting because until Master Fortunato Cipolla and Massaro
Filippo, the market gardener, arrived there wouldn't
be a quorum, and they showed no sign of turning up,
so there was no way of knowing what the council was
going to decide. In the end it grew boring, and the
crowd of women started melting away along the low
wall of the farm.

Eventually the two missing councillors sent word
that they wouldn't be coming that day, because they
were too busy, but they said that if the other councillors
wanted to put on the tax they could do it without them.
"That's exactly what my daughter Betta said they
would do!" Mastro Croce Giufà muttered.

"Then get your daughter Betta to come and help you
out!" exclaimed Don Silvestro. After that Silkworm
didn't dare breathe another word, but went on muttering under his breath.

"Now you'll see that the Zuppiddi will come of their

own accord and offer me their daughter on bended knee," said Don Silvestro. "But I shan't take her unless they ask!"

The meeting adjourned without anything being decided. The secretary wanted a little more time to think things over. Meanwhile midday had struck, and most of the women had quietly slipped away. When the few who remained saw Mastro Cirino locking the door and putting the key in his pocket they went about their business too, talking about the insults that Piedipapera and Venera Zuppidda had flung at each other.

During the afternoon Master 'Ntoni's 'Ntoni heard about it all, and decided to show Piedipapera that it wasn't for nothing that he'd been in the navy. He met him near the Zuppiddi house, on his way back from the lava field, hobbling along on that lame leg of his, and started giving him a piece of his mind. He told him he was nothing but scum, and that he had better be careful not to talk ill of the Zuppiddi or their affairs, which were no concern of his. Piedipapera had a tongue in his head too.

"So you think you're somebody of importance, do you, now that you've come back from your travels?" he said.

"I'll break your bones if you say another word!" 'Ntoni answered.

People came to their doors as soon as they heard the two shouting, and by this time a crowd had gathered. This caused them to lose their tempers in earnest, and a scuffle started, and Piedipapera, who was cleverer than the devil himself, closed with 'Ntoni Malavoglia and went down with him in a heap to the ground, where 'Ntoni's two good legs gave him no advantage. They started rolling over each other in the mud, struggling and biting, just like Peppi Naso's dogs, and in the end Master 'Ntoni's 'Ntoni, with his shirt in shreds, had to seek refuge in the Zuppiddi's yard, while Piedipapera was led back home as bloody as Lazarus.

"Evidently I'm not mistress in my own house any more!" Venera Zuppidda was still shouting after she'd slammed the door in the neighbours' faces. "I'll give my daughter to whom I please!"

The girl, blushing deeply, had taken refuge inside the house, with her heart beating like a chicken's.

"This ear's half torn off," Mastro Turi Zuppiddo said, gently pouring water over 'Ntoni's head. "Tino Piedipapera bites worse than a Corsican dog!"

'Ntoni's eyes were still bloodshot, and he was determined to take the plunge.

"Listen, Venera Zuppidda," he said in front of everybody. "If I can't marry your daughter, I shan't marry at all!" The girl was listening from her room.

"That's not a matter to talk about now, 'Ntoni. But if your grandfather gives his consent, I wouldn't change you for Victor Emmanuel." Mastro Turi Zuppiddo stood there without saying anything and quietly gave him a towel to wipe himself with, and the result was that that evening 'Ntoni went home feeling very pleased with himself indeed.

As soon as the poor Malavoglia heard about his quarrel with Piedipapera, they started expecting the bailiff to arrive at any minute to turn them out of the house, because Easter was approaching, and in spite of all their efforts they had only managed to scrape together half the sum needed to pay off the debt.

"Now you see what comes of hanging about a house where there's a marriageable girl!" La Longa said to 'Ntoni. "Now everybody's talking about you. And I'm sorry for Barbara's sake."

"I'm going to marry her," said 'Ntoni.

"You're going to marry her?" exclaimed his grand-father. "What about your mother and me? Haven't we got any say in the matter? When your father wanted to marry your mother, he asked my permission first. Your grandmother was alive then, and she came and talked it over in the garden, under the fig tree. Now those ways have gone out of use, and old people don't count for anything any more. Once upon a time there was a saying: Listen to your elders, and you won't go wrong. Your sister Mena must get married first. Do you realise that?"

"Isn't it just my cursed luck!" 'Ntoni started shouting, tearing his hair and stamping his feet. "Work, work, work all day long, without ever going to the tavern or ever having a penny in my pocket! And now that I've found the girl I want I can't marry her! Why did I ever come back from the navy?"

"Listen!" his grandfather said, rising to his feet with difficulty, because of the pains in his back. "The best thing you can do is to go to bed. You should never talk like that in front of your mother!"

"My brother Luca in the navy is better off than I am!" 'Ntoni grumbled as he went off to bed.

EIGHT Luca, poor fellow, was neither better nor worse off. He did his duty as a sailor, as he had done it at home, and made the best of it. He didn't write often, it's true—stamps cost twenty centesimi each—and he didn't send his photograph home, because he had always been told as a boy that he had ears like a donkey's. But sometimes when he wrote he would slip into the envelope a five-lire note which he had man-aged to earn by doing odd jobs for the officers.

His grandfather had told 'Ntoni that his sister Mena

must be married first. Master 'Ntoni didn't talk about
Mena's marriage yet, but thought about it constantly
and, now that there was something in the chest of
drawers towards paying off the debt, he had worked
it out that after the salting of the anchovies he would be
able to pay Piedipapera in full, leaving the house free
for his granddaughter's dowry. So he had gone and had
several quiet conversations with Master Fortunato,
waiting on the shore for the Carmela to come in or
sitting in the sun outside the church when nobody was
about. Master Fortunato said that, if the girl had a
dowry, he didn't want to go back on his word, particularly as that young blockhead of a son of his was a continual source of anxiety to him, running after girls who
hadn't got a penny.

"A man is known by his word and an ox by its horns,"
he always said.

Mena's heart was often sad as she weaved, because
girls have a flair in these things. Now that her grandfather kept going out and having whispered conversations with Master Fortunato, and when he was at home
kept talking about the Cipolla family, she could not get
Alfio Mosca out of her mind; it was as though his picture were fastened to the beam of the loom, like those
of the saints. One evening she waited until late for
Alfio to come home with his donkey cart, standing with
her hands under her apron, because it was cold and
all the doors were shut and not a soul was to be seen
in the little street; and when he came she called out
"Good evening!" from the doorway.

"Are you going to La Bicocca on the first of the
month?" she said to him eventually.

"No, I'm not going yet," he answered. "I've got more
than a hundred loads to take to Santuzza's. What I do
after that's in God's hands."

Alfio got busy unharnessing the donkey and hanging up the harness and moving about in the yard with his lantern. Mena did not know what to say next.

"If you go to La Bicocca, who knows when we shall see each other again?" she said at last, her voice almost failing her.

"Oh? Why? Are you going away too?"

For a moment the girl made no reply, although it was dark and nobody could see. From time to time you could hear the voices of the neighbours from behind their closed doors, or the crying of a baby, or the clatter of plates from where a family was at dinner, and there was nobody to overhear them. "Now we've got together half the money we owe Piedipapera, and at the salting of the anchovies we'll have the rest."

Alfio left his donkey in the middle of the yard and came into the street.

"So you'll be getting married after Easter?"

Mena did not answer. "I told you so," Alfio went on. "I've seen Master 'Ntoni talking to Master Cipolla."

"It'll be as God wills," Mena said. "I wouldn't mind getting married if only I could stay here."

"What a fine thing to be rich like Master Cipolla's son, and to be able to choose a wife and live wherever one liked!"

Mena stayed for a moment, looking at the lantern hanging on the gate and the donkey eating nettles along the wall. "Good-night, Alfio," she said. Alfio Mosca said good-night too, and went back to put the donkey in its stall.

"That shameless St. Agatha!" exclaimed La Vespa, who was continually going to the Piedipapera's on the pretext of wanting to borrow an iron or making them a present of some beans she had picked. "That shameless hussy, St. Agatha, keeps pestering Alfio Mosca!

She doesn't leave him even a moment's peace to scratch
his head! Shame on her!" And off she went down the
street while Piedipapera closed the door, putting out
his tongue at her behind it.

"La Vespa's as vicious as a wasp in July," he sneered.

"Why should she worry so much about Mena?" his
wife asked.

"Because she has her knife into anyone who's getting
married, and now she has set her cap at Alfio Mosca."

"You ought to tell her I don't like it. As if it weren't
obvious that she comes here after Alfio Mosca! Venera
Zuppidda goes round telling everybody that we're en-
couraging them!"

"Venera Zuppidda would do better to mind her own
business, because she's got plenty to mind, what with
the way she encourages Master 'Ntoni's 'Ntoni to come
to the house, in spite of the fuss that the old man and
the rest of them make about it, because they won't
hear of his marrying Barbara, of course. Shut the window. Today I spent half-an-hour enjoying the scene
that 'Ntoni was playing with Barbara—my back's still
aching from bending up double, listening to them behind the wall. 'Ntoni had got away from the Provvidenza on the excuse of fetching a big gaff for mullet.
'What shall we do if grandfather won't consent?' he
said to her. 'We'll run away!' she said. 'Then it'll be
their business to see that we get married—they'll be
forced to consent!' I'd be willing to bet both my eyes
that her mother was there behind her, listening to the
whole thing. The old witch is playing a fine game!
When I told Don Silvestro, he said he'd be willing to
bet that Barbara would fall at his feet like a ripe plum.
Don't put the latch on the door, because I'm expecting
Rocco Spatu to come and talk to me."

Don Silvestro, to cause Barbara Zuppidda to fall at

his feet like a ripe plum, had thought out a plan which outdid anything that could have been devised even by the imp who decides which numbers shall come up in the lottery. His plan was to eliminate one by one all those who stood between him and Barbara. When there was no one left to marry her, he said, her parents would be forced to come and ask him of their own accord, and he would graciously accept the offer, like a salesman at the market when customers are scarce.

Among those who had been after Barbara were Vanni Pizzuto, at the time when he had gone to shave Mastro Turi when he had the sciatica, and Don Michele, who used to pass the time by making eyes at all the pretty girls he saw, because, except when he was at Santuzza's bar, he was bored with walking about with a pistol on his paunch and nothing whatever to do.

At first Barbara used to respond to his glances, but after her mother told her that customs men were nothing but idlers and scroungers, more like police spies than anything else, and that in any case all strangers ought to be driven out of the village, she slammed the window in his face, in spite of his moustaches and the gold braid on his hat, and Don Michele had to swallow his mortification. But out of sheer spite he went on walking up and down the street past her window, twirling his moustaches and wearing his hat pulled right down over his eyes. On Sundays he put on his feathered hat and went to look at the girl from Vanni Pizzuto's shop, on her way to mass with her mother. Don Silvestro took to going to the barber's for a shave too, and joined the group of men joking and warming themselves in front of the hot water brazier before they went to mass.

"Barbara Zuppidda doesn't seem to mind 'Ntoni Malavoglia's attentions," he remarked. "Would you like to bet twelve *tarì* that he marries her? Do you see him waiting for her with his hands in his pockets?"

Vanni Pizzuto left the soap on Don Michele's face and went over to the door.

"What a girl!" he exclaimed. "Just look at the way she walks, with her nose muffled up in her cape as though it were a spindle! And to think that that pumpkin 'Ntoni Malavoglia will get her!"

"If Piedipapera wants his money, 'Ntoni won't get her, you mark my words! If Piedipapera takes the house by the medlar tree, the Malavoglia will have other things to worry about!"

Vanni Pizzuto took Don Michele by the nose again to finish shaving him. "Well, and what have you got to say about it, Don Michele? You've had your eye on Barbara Zuppidda yourself. But that's a girl who makes everybody eat gall!"

Don Michele said nothing. He brushed himself, twirled his moustaches and put on his hat in front of the mirror. "You want more than a hat with a feather on it for a girl like that!" said Pizzuto with a grin.

Finally, on one occasion Don Michele said: "If it weren't for my feathered hat, I declare I'd take Barbara from under 'Ntoni Malavoglia's nose!"

Don Silvestro hastened to report this statement to 'Ntoni, and he added that Don Michele, the sergeant of the customs guards, was not a man to be trifled with, and that he ought to have things out with him.

"I laugh in the face of Don Michele, the sergeant of the customs guards," 'Ntoni answered. "I know what he's got against me. But this time he can go to blazes, and you can tell him from me that he could do better than wear out good shoe-leather walking up and down past Barbara Zuppidda's window, wearing his braided hat as proudly as a royal crown; because folk don't give a damn for him and his braided hat!"

'Ntoni glared at Don Michele whenever he met him, and winked at him significantly, to show he was a young man of spirit who had been in the navy and wasn't afraid of anything or anybody. Don Michele was too proud to give in to him, and went on walking up and down the street as before. But for the gold braid on his hat, he declared, he would beat 'Ntoni to a frazzle.

Vanni Pizzuto told everybody who came to his shop for a shave, or for cigars, or fishing tackle, or bone buttons at five for a *grano,* about the quarrel between Don Michele and 'Ntoni Malavoglia. "One day they'll break every bone in each other's body. Don Michele's hands are tied by that feathered hat of his. But he'd be willing to pay Piedipapera something to get rid of that pumpkin 'Ntoni for him." In the end even La Locca's son, who had nothing to do but dangle his arms in idleness all day long, started following them about to see how matters would end.

When Piedipapera went to the barber's for a shave and heard that Don Michele would be willing to pay him good money to get rid of 'Ntoni Malavoglia, the idea of being thought of such consequence in the village made him swell with pride like a turkey-cock.

"The sergeant would pay anything to have the hold over the Malavoglia that you have," Vanni Pizzuto went on. "Why did you let 'Ntoni get away with the yarn that he gave you a beating up?"

Piedipapera shrugged his shoulders and went on warming his hands in front of the brazier. Don Silvestro laughed and answered for him:

"Mastro Vanni would like Piedipapera to pick his chestnuts out of the fire for him," he said. "You know perfectly well that Venera Zuppidda won't have anything to do with strangers or anyone who wears a gold-braided hat. Mastro Vanni realises that if 'Ntoni Malavoglia were got out of the way he'd be cock of the walk and could go and court Barbara without any competition!"

Vanni Pizzuto said nothing, but the idea that Don Silvestro had put into his head kept him awake all night.

Not at all a bad plan, he said to himself. Not at all a bad plan. It all depends on getting hold of Piedipapera at the right moment, when he's in the right mood.

The right moment came sure enough, because one evening there was no sign of Rocco Spatu, and Piedipapera came two or three times to ask after him, looking white-faced and haggard-eyed, and the customs guards had been seen dashing about busily, with their noses down, like hounds on the trail, and Don Michele was with them, with his pistol on his belly and his trousers tucked into his boots. "You could do Don Michele a great service by getting rid of 'Ntoni Malavoglia for him," Pizzuto said, as Piedipapera concealed himself in the darkest corner of the shop to buy a cigar. "You'd be doing him a very great service indeed, and you'd make a friend of him for life!"

"Really!" Piedipapera muttered, for he was short of breath that night, and didn't say anything else.

During the night firing was heard from the direction of Il Rotolo and all along the beach—it sounded as though they were shooting quail. "Quail indeed!" the fishermen muttered, sitting up in bed to listen. "Those are quail with two legs, the kind that smuggle sugar and coffee and silk handkerchiefs. Last night Don Michele was walking about with his trousers tucked into his boots and his pistol on his belly!"

Piedipapera was at Pizzuto's shop for a glass of something even before daybreak, for the lamp was still
alight outside the door. The expression on his face was
like that of a dog that knows it has done something
wrong. Instead of making his usual jokes, he kept asking people what all the noise had been about during
the night, and whether anyone had seen Rocco Spatu
and Cinghialenta, and he took off his hat politely to
Don Michele, who had swollen eyes and dusty boots,
and insisted at all costs on buying him a drink. But
Don Michele had already been to the tavern, where
Santuzza had poured him out a stiff one, and said:

"What have you been risking your life for, in the
name of all the saints? Don't you realise that if you
get killed you'll cause the death of others too?"

"And what about my duty?" Don Michele replied.
"If I'd caught them red-handed last night, we'd have
made a fine thing out of it!"

"If they try to make you believe that it was Massaro
Filippo who was trying to smuggle his wine, don't you
believe a word of it, by this blessed scapulary of the
Virgin Mary that I unworthily wear on my bosom!
Those stories are all lies, spread by people without a
spark of conscience, who imperil their immortal souls
by speaking ill of their neighbours!"

"No, I know what the contraband was," said Don
Michele. "It was silk handkerchiefs, sugar and coffee.
They slipped through my fingers like eels. But I've
got my eyes on them, and they won't get away another
time!"

In Vanni Pizzuto's shop Piedipapera said to him:
"Have a glass, Don Michele, it'll do you good after the
sleep you've lost!"

But Don Michele was in a bad humour and simply
snorted.

"Take it, as he's offered it to you," Vanni Pizzuto said. "If Tino Piedipapera offers you a drink, it means he's in funds. He's got any amount of money, the cunning old rascal—so much money that he bought the Malavoglia debt; and now they pay him back by beating him up!"

Don Michele relaxed to the extent of laughing a little.

"By heavens!" Piedipapera exclaimed, banging his fist on the counter and pretending to get really angry. "I don't want to send that 'Ntoni lad to do penance in Rome!"

"Bravo!" Pizzuto said. "I certainly wouldn't take it lying down. Would you, Don Michele?"

Don Michele signified his agreement with a grunt. "I'll deal with 'Ntoni and his family as they deserve," Piedipapera went on. "I won't allow myself to be made the laughingstock of the whole village! You can set your mind at rest on that score, Don Michele."

And he went hobbling off, cursing aloud and saying to himself that it was necessary to keep in with these police spies. Still thinking of what could be done to keep in with them, he went to the tavern, where Uncle Santoro told him that there was no sign of Rocco Spatu or Cinghialenta yet, and from there he went to see Cousin Anna, who, poor thing, was pale and had not slept a wink either, and was standing at the door looking anxiously in every direction. Just outside the house he ran into La Vespa, who was coming to see whether by any chance Piedipapera's wife, Grazia, had a little yeast to spare.

"I've just met Alfio Mosca," he said to La Vespa, just for the sake of conversation. "He didn't have his cart with him, and I bet he was going to wander about in the lava field, behind St. Agatha's garden. You cannot

ask for more, than to love the girl next door; for court-
ing by the fence, saves both trouble and expense!"

"She's a fine saint to hang on the wall, that Mena!"
La Vespa exclaimed. "They're marrying her to Brasi
Cipolla, and she goes on flirting here, there and every-
where! Pooh! How disgusting!"

"Let her be! Let her be!" Piedipapera answered.
"They'll find out soon enough what sort of a girl she is!
People's eyes will soon be opened. But doesn't Alfio
Mosca know that they want to marry her to Brasi
Cipolla?"

"You know what men are like! If a chit of a girl so
much as looks at them, they all run after her to have a
good time. But when they're thinking of settling down
in earnest, they look for the kind of girl that I have in
mind!"

"Alfio Mosca ought to marry someone like you."

"I'm not thinking of getting married just now! But
he'd certainly find in me the kind of woman he ought to
have. I've got my little bit of land, and nobody's got
any hold over it, as they have on the house by the
medlar tree. If the north wind blows, the house by
the medlar tree will be carried right away. That'll be a
sight to see, if the north wind blows!"

"Let it be! Let it be! The weather isn't always fine,
and sometimes the north wind does blow. I'm going to
talk to your Uncle Crocifisso to-day about that little
matter that you know about!"

Piedipapera found Uncle Crocifisso only too ready
to talk about that little matter, which was dragging on
and on, with no end in sight. Long things turn into
snakes, as the saying is. Master 'Ntoni was still assuring
him that the Malavoglia were honest people and were
going to pay up, but he'd like to know where the money
was coming from. Everyone in the village knew what

everyone else owned down to the last penny, and for all their honesty the Malavoglia, even if they sold their souls to the devil, wouldn't be able to pay off even half the debt between now and Easter. Taking the house by the medlar tree would involve stamped paper and other expense besides, that he knew well enough, and Don Giammaria and the chemist were perfectly right when they talked about Government robbery. As sure as his name was Uncle Crocifisso, he hated not only the people who imposed the taxes but also the people who wished to do away with them—people who roused the village to a state of mind such that a man no longer felt safe with his property in his own house! When they had come and asked him whether he would like to be mayor, he had told them that that was a very bright idea, but if he became mayor and spent his time looking after their business, who the devil would there be to look after his? He, Uncle Crocifisso, preferred looking after his own business himself. Meanwhile Master 'Ntoni was thinking of marrying off his granddaughter, because he had been seen talking to Master Cipolla—Uncle Santoro had seen them; and Uncle Santoro had also seen Piedipapera acting as intermediary on behalf of La Vespa and making himself useful to that penniless Alfio Mosca, who was after her plot of land.

"And I assure you he'll get it," Piedipapera shouted in Uncle Crocifisso's ear to convince him of the fact. "It's no use your shouting and getting excited about it! Your niece is crazy about him, and spends her whole time running after him. Out of respect for you, I can't even shut the door in her face when she comes to talk to my wife, because, after all, she's your kith and kin, your niece!"

"Fine respect for me you show! Your respect for me will lose me that plot of land!"

"Of course you'll lose the plot of land! If the Malavoglia girl gets married to Brasi Cipolla, Alfio Mosca will be left high and dry, and he'll take La Vespa and her plot of land to console himself."

"To the devil with La Vespa!" Uncle Crocifisso finally exclaimed, thoroughly dazed by Piedipapera's eloquence. "I don't care a damn about her! What I'm worried about is the sins that the hussy drives me to. I want my money, which I earned with the sweat of my brow! Everybody makes it out to have been stolen, but everybody helps himself to it—Alfio Mosca, La Vespa and the Malavoglia. Now I'll go to law and take their house!"

"You're the boss. Say the word and I'll start proceedings at once!"

"No, not yet. We'd better wait till Easter. A man is known by his word and an ox by its horns. But I'll get my money down to the last penny, and I shan't agree to any more postponements for anybody's sake!"

Easter really was near. The hills were clothed in green and the prickly-pear trees were in flower again. The girls had sown basil in the window boxes, and white butterflies came and perched on them. Even the broom on the lava field was covered with poor, pale little flowers. In the morning steam rose from the green and yellow slates on the roofs, where sparrows chattered noisily until sunset.

Even the house by the medlar tree seemed to have a festive air. The yard had been swept, the gear was tidily arranged along the wall, the kitchen garden was green with cabbages and lettuces, the windows were wide open, the big room was flooded with sunlight and looked cheerful too, and everything spoke of the approach of Easter. Towards midday the old came out and sat in their doorways, and the girls sang at the wash-place. Once more carts were to be heard passing at night, and in the evening people were again to be heard gossiping outside in the street.

"Mena's getting married," they said. "Her mother's preparing the trousseau!"

Time had passed, and time takes away both good things and bad. Maruzza was perpetually busy with her scissors and needle, and Mena did not even ask for whom she was doing all this work, and one evening Brasi Cipolla was brought to the house by his father, Master Cipolla, together with the rest of the family.

"Here is Master Cipolla, who has come to pay us a visit," said Master 'Ntoni, showing them in, as though the whole thing were a surprise, though wine and toasted chickpeas were standing ready in the kitchen, and the women and children were all in their Sunday best. Mena, in a new dress and with a black handkerchief over her head, really looked like St. Agatha; Brasi simply couldn't take his eyes off her, but kept staring at her like a basilisk. He sat on the high-backed chair with his hands between his knees, secretly rubbing them with satisfaction every now and then. "Master Cipolla has brought his son Brasi, who is quite grown-up now," Master 'Ntoni continued.

"Yes, children grow up and elbow us into the grave," Master Fortunato replied.

"Now take a glass of wine—a glass of good wine," said La Longa, "and some of these chickpeas, which my daughter roasted. I'm sorry I wasn't expecting you, and so didn't prepare anything special."

"We were going for a walk quite near here," Master Cipolla continued, "and we said: 'Let us go and see Maruzza Malavoglia.'"

Brasi, still staring at Mena, started stuffing chickpeas into his pockets, and then the children got hold of the bag and started helping themselves, though Nunziata, talking in an awed whisper as though she were in church, vainly tried to stop them. Meanwhile the two old men had started talking under the medlar tree, with the women forming a circle round them, singing the girl's praises and saying what a fine housekeeper she was, and how she kept the house as clean as a new pin. "Cloth is judged by its texture and a girl by her bringing up," they said.

"Your granddaughter has grown up too," Master Fortunato remarked, "and it's time that she was married."

"That is what we desire, if the Lord should send us a good match," Master 'Ntoni replied.

"Marriages and bishops are made in heaven," La Longa added.

"A good horse never lacks a saddle," said Master Fortunato, "and a girl like yours can't fail to make a good match."

Mena was sitting by the young man's side, as is the custom, but she did not once lift her eyes from her apron, and on the way home Brasi complained to his father that she hadn't even offered him the plate of chickpeas.

"What do you expect?" Master Fortunato said when they were at a safe distance. "You talk like a mule in front of a sack of barley! As if the girl didn't have the rest of the company to think about! Just look, Giufà! You've spilled some wine on your trousers and ruined your new suit!"

Meanwhile Master 'Ntoni rubbed his hands with satisfaction. "It doesn't seem true that with God's help we've brought the ship safely into port," he said to his daughter-in-law. "Mena will have all she can possibly desire, and now we shall be able to settle our other little troubles, and you'll be able to say that poor old grandfather was right when he always said that laughter and tears come by turns!"

Next Saturday, towards evening, Nunziata came to fetch some beans for her children and said: "Alfio Mosca's going away tomorrow. He's packing all his things!"

Mena went white and stopped weaving.

In Alfio Mosca's house the lamp was alight and everything was in disorder. A little later he came and knocked at the door, and there was a certain expression on his face, and he kept tying and untying knots in the whip that he had in his hand.

"I came to say good-bye to you all, Maruzza, Master 'Ntoni, the children, and you too, Mena. I've finished carting the Aci Catena wine. Now that Santuzza has taken Massaro Filippo's wine, I'm going to La Bicocca, where there's work for me and my donkey."

Mena said nothing. Only her mother spoke and said: "Master 'Ntoni would like to see you. Won't you wait until he comes back?"

Alfio Mosca sat on the edge of the high-backed chair, with his whip still in his hand, and looked all round the room, except in the direction where Mena was sitting.

"When will you be coming back?" La Longa asked.

"Who knows?" Alfio answered. "I go where my donkey leads me! I shall stay at La Bicocca as long as the work there lasts. But I should like to come back soon, if I can make a living here."

"You must look after your health, Alfio. I've heard that at La Bicocca they're dying of malaria like flies!"

Alfio shrugged his shoulders, and said he couldn't help it. "I don't want to go away," he said, looking at the candle. "Aren't you going to say anything to me, Mena?"

Two or three times the girl's mouth opened, as though she were going to speak, but the words stuck in her throat.

"You'll be leaving the neighbourhood too, now that you're going to get married," Alfio went on. "The world's just like a stable. Some come and some go, and in the end everyone has changed places and nothing seems the same." He rubbed his hands and laughed as he spoke, but there was no laughter in his heart.

"Girls go where they're destined to go by God," said La Longa. "While they're young, they're always gay and carefree, but when they go out into the world they meet troubles and disappointments."

Master 'Ntoni and the boys came home, and Alfio Mosca said good-bye to them, but he couldn't make up his mind to leave. He lingered on the threshold, with his whip under his arm, shaking hands now with one and now with another, not forgetting Maruzza, and he kept saying "Forgive me for everything," as one does when saying good-bye to people whom one may never be going to see again. The only one whose hand he did not shake was St. Agatha, who stayed in the corner by her loom. But that, of course, is how girls ought to behave.

It was a fine spring evening, and the street and the yard were flooded with bright moonlight, and people were sitting out of doors, and girls were walking up and down arm-in-arm, singing. Indoors it was stifling, so Mena went out too, arm-in-arm with Nunziata.

"Now we shan't see the light in Alfio Mosca's house any more, and the house will be shut up," said Nunziata.

Alfio had loaded a good part of his things on to his

cart, and was putting the straw that was left over in the manger into a sack, while the beans for his supper were cooking over the fire.

"Will you be leaving before daylight, Alfio?" Nunziata asked him from the door of the yard.

"Yes, I've a long way to go, and that poor beast will need some rest during the day."

Mena said nothing, but leaned against the doorpost, looking for the last time at the loaded cart, the empty house, the half-stripped bed and the pot boiling over the fire.

"Are you there too, Mena?" Alfio exclaimed as soon as he saw her, dropping what he was doing.

Mena nodded her head in reply, while Nunziata, good housekeeper that she was, hurried over to skim the pot, which was just going to boil over.

"I'm so glad to be able to say good-bye to you," said Alfio.

"I came to say good-bye to you," she said, with tears in her voice. "Why are you going to La Bicocca if there's malaria there?"

Alfio started laughing, but it was forced laughter again, just as it had been when he had gone to say good-bye to her.

"What a question!" he replied. "And why are you marrying Brasi Cipolla, I should like to know? You have to do what you can, Mena. If I could have had my own way, you know what I should have done." She looked at him with shining eyes. "I should have stayed here, where even the walls know me, and I know my way about so well that I could even groom my donkey in the dark; and I should have married you, Mena, because I've had you in my heart for a long time, and I shall take you with me to La Bicocca, and wherever I go. But all this is idle talk, and you have to do what you can. Even my donkey goes where I make him!"

"Good-bye," said Mena. "I too have a thorn in my heart . . . and when I look at that closed window it will remind me that my heart has closed too, closed over that window as heavily as a mill-door. But it's the will of God. Now I must say good-bye and go away."

She started weeping quietly, with her hand over her eyes, and went away with Nunziata to weep under the medlar tree in the light of the moon.

NINE   Neither the Malavoglia nor anyone else in the village knew what Piedipapera and Uncle Crocifisso had up their sleeves. On Easter Day Master 'Ntoni put on his new coat, took the hundred lire from the chest of drawers and went to see Uncle Crocifisso.

"Have you brought all the money?" Uncle Crocifisso asked him.

"That's impossible, Uncle Crocifisso. You know how hard it is to scrape together a hundred lire. But something is better than nothing, and he who pays something on account is not a bad payer. Now that summer is coming, with God's help we shall pay off the rest."

"Why do you come and tell me this? You know that it's not my business now, but Piedipapera's."

"It's the same thing, because when I see you, it still seems to me that I owe the money to you. If you speak to Piedipapera, he won't refuse to wait till the feast of Our Lady of Ognina."

"This isn't enough even to pay the expenses," said Dumbbell, running the money through his fingers. "Go and talk to Piedipapera if you want him to wait, because it's no business of mine any longer!"

So Master 'Ntoni went to see Piedipapera, who started cursing and flinging his cap on the ground in his usual manner. He said he had no bread to eat, and he couldn't wait even till Ascension Day.

"Listen, Piedipapera," said Master 'Ntoni, with his hands joined as though he were praying to Almighty God, "now that my granddaughter's getting married, if you won't give me till St. John's Day, it would be better to kill me outright!"

"You're asking the impossible," Piedipapera shouted. "Cursed be the day and the minute when I got myself into this mess!" he went on, crumpling and tearing at his old cap.

When Master 'Ntoni reached home he was quite white in the face. "I got him to agree," he told his daughter-in-law, "but I had to beseech him as though he were Almighty God." The poor old man was still trembling, but he was glad that Master Cipolla knew nothing about the business and that his granddaughter's betrothal was not going to be shipwrecked.

On the eve of Ascension Day, while the children were playing round the bonfire, all the women gathered on the Malavoglia balcony, and Venera Zuppidda came to join them, to listen to what they were talking about and to say her own piece. Now that Uncle 'Ntoni was marrying off his granddaughter and the Provvidenza was at sea again, the Malavoglia were in good odour again with everyone, for nobody knew what Piedipapera had up his sleeve, not even his wife Grazia, who gossiped with Maruzza Malavoglia as though her husband had no evil in his heart. Every evening 'Ntoni went off to talk to Barbara, and he had confided to her that his grandfather had said that Mena must be married first. "After that it will be my turn," he added. So Barbara had sent St. Agatha a pot of basil, all decorated with pinks and with a beautiful red ribbon tied round it. This was the recognised invitation to friendship between women, and everyone made a fuss of St. Agatha, and even her mother had given up wearing her black handkerchief, because where there's an engaged couple it's unlucky to wear mourning; and they had written to Luca to tell him the news that Mena was getting married.

Poor Mena, however, was the only one who didn't seem happy; she seemed to be black at heart, and to see everything in dark colours, though the fields were strewn with flowers and the children were making garlands for Ascension Day, and though she herself climbed the ladder to help her mother put up the decorations over the doorway and the windows.

Every doorway was decorated with flowers, except Alfio Mosca's, which was dark and always shut, for there was no one to hang flowers on it for Ascension Day.

"That little minx St. Agatha!" La Vespa went about saying, fuming with rage. "What with all she said and all she did, she ended by driving Alfio Mosca out of the village!"

Meanwhile St. Agatha had been given her new dress, and they were waiting for the feast of St. John to take the sword-shaped silver hairpin from her hair and to part her hair in the middle before she went to church, and everyone who saw her pass said: "Bless the girl!"

Her poor mother felt full of rejoicing and gladness, because her daughter was marrying into a house where she would lack for nothing, and in the meantime she was constantly busy, cutting out and sewing. When Master 'Ntoni came back in the evening, he always insisted on seeing what she had done during the day, and when he went to town he always used to bring some little thing back. With the fine weather everything grew more cheerful again. All the children were earning money, some more and some less, and the Provvidenza was paying her way, and they worked out that with God's help they would be out of the wood by St. John's Day. Master Cipolla would spend the whole evening sitting on the church steps with Master 'Ntoni, talking about what the Provvidenza had done. Brasi, in his new suit, was continually hanging about the street in which the Malavoglia lived; and soon afterwards the news spread through the village that on the following Sunday the bride's hair was going to be parted and the silver sword-pin removed by Grazia Piedipapera, because Brasi Cipolla's mother was dead and the Malavoglia had asked her, to conciliate her husband; they had also invited Uncle Crocifisso and all their friends and relatives and the whole neighbourhood, without any exceptions whatever.

"I shan't go," said Uncle Crocifisso, standing with his back against the elm tree in the village square. "I've tasted too much bitterness, and I don't want to imperil my immortal soul. You go, because you're not involved, and no money of yours is at stake. We've still got time to send for the bailiff; the lawyer said so."

"You're the boss, and I'll do as you say. You don't care any more, because Alfio Mosca has gone away, but you'll see that as soon as Mena's married he'll come back for your niece!"

Venera Zuppidda, who, as a future connection of the Malavoglia, should have been invited to comb the bride's hair, created a terrible fuss because Grazia Piedipapera had been invited instead, particularly as her daughter had sent Mena a pot of basil. So little had she expected this affront that she had hurriedly finished a new dress for Barbara, specially for the occasion. 'Ntoni tried in vain to persuade her not to take such a trifling matter to heart, but to forget about it. Venera Zuppidda, with her hair tidily combed, but with her hands covered with flour, because she had started bread-making to demonstrate to all the world that she had lost interest in the Malavoglia invitation, replied:

"If you want Grazia Piedipapera you can have her! It's either she or I! You can't have both of us in the world!"

The Malavoglia were perfectly well aware that they had given the preference to Grazia Piedipapera because of the money they owed her husband. They had been as thick as thieves with Tino Piedipapera ever since Master Cipolla had made peace between him and Master 'Ntoni's 'Ntoni in Santuzza's bar.

"They lick his boots because of the money they owe him," Venera Zuppidda complained, "but they owe my husband money too. They owe him more than fifty lire for the Provvidenza! Tomorrow I'll see that I get the money!"

"Stop it, mother, let it be!" Barbara implored, but all the same she was put out at not being able to wear her new dress, and she almost regretted the money she had spent on the pot of basil she had sent to Mena; and 'Ntoni, who had come to fetch them, had to go home again with his tail between his legs, looking exceedingly uncomfortable in his new coat. After they had put the bread in the oven, mother and daughter went out into the yard to see what was going on in the Malavoglia house. The talking and the laughter could be heard all the way from their yard, and that made them angrier than ever. The house by the medlar tree was as full of people as it had been after Bastianazzo's death. Mena looked quite different without the silver sword-pin and with her hair parted in the middle, and all the women crowded round her, and there was so much talking and noise that if a cannon had been fired nobody would have noticed it. While the lawyer was getting all the papers ready, because Uncle Crocifisso had said that there was still plenty of time to send for the bailiff, Piedipapera was making the women laugh so much with his jokes that he might have been tickling them. Even Master Cipolla unbent to the extent of telling funny stories, at which only his son Brasi laughed. Everybody talked at once, while the children squabbled for beans and chestnuts between the grown-ups' feet. Even La Longa, poor woman, felt so happy that she forgot her sorrows; and Master 'Ntoni sat on the low wall alone, nodding his head and chuckling to himself.

"Your trousers aren't thirsty—be careful you don't give them another drink, like you did last time!" Master Cipolla said to his son. He said he felt in better form even than the bride, and he wanted to dance the *fasola* with her.

"Then there's nothing more for me to do here, and I may as well go home!" said Brasi, who was anxious to say something funny too, and felt annoyed at being left alone in the corner like a dunce, with nobody, not even Mena, taking any notice of him.

"This is Mena's party," said Nunziata, "but she's not enjoying it like everybody else."

At this Cousin Anna dropped a jug, in which there was still more than a pint of wine, as if by accident, and started shouting: "Hurrah! Hurrah! Broken crockery brings luck, and spilled wine's a good omen!"

"Now wine has been spilled on my trousers again!" grumbled Brasi, who had been very careful ever since the first accident to his new suit.

Piedipapera sat astride the low wall, with a glass between his legs, behaving as though he were the master of the house, because he had it in his power to send along the bailiff whenever he chose. "Not even Rocco Spatu's at the tavern today," he said. "Today all the merry-making's here. It's just like at Santuzza's!"

"It's much better here!" La Locca's son remarked. He had followed the crowd and had been brought in for a drink. "You can't get a drink at Santuzza's if you haven't got any money!"

Piedipapera, from his point of vantage on the wall, was looking at a little knot of people talking earnestly near the fountain, with faces as serious as though the end of the world were at hand. The chemist's shop was full of the usual idlers, making speeches to each other with the newspaper in their hands or gesticulating as though about to lay violent hands on each other. Don Giammaria was laughing, and took a pinch of snuff. You could see from there how much pleasure it gave him.

"Why haven't the priest and Don Silvestro come?" asked Piedipapera.

"I invited them," Master 'Ntoni answered. "They must be busy."

"They're over there at the chemist's. There's as much excitement as though the men were here selling lottery tickets. What the devil can have happened?"

An old woman crossed the village square, shrieking and tearing her hair as though she had heard that somebody was dead. A crowd had gathered outside Pizzuto's shop, just like when a donkey collapses under its load and everybody rushes to see what has happened; and women were standing and gaping from a distance, without daring to approach.

"I'm going to find out what's happened," said Piedipapera, slowly climbing down from the wall.

The centre of attraction in the middle of the crowd of people was not a fallen donkey but two sailors, with bandaged heads and kitbags on their shoulders. They were on their way home on leave, and they had stopped at the chemist's for a glass of herb beer. They were talking about a big naval battle which had taken place, in which, they said, ships as big as Aci Trezza, full of sailors, had been sunk. The things they described seemed as fantastic as the story of Roland or the exploits of the paladins of France as told on the esplanade at Catania; people gathered like flies to listen to them.

"Maruzza La Longa's son was on the Re d'Italia," remarked Don Silvestro, who had joined the crowd.

"I'll go and speak to my wife," said Mastro Turi Zuppiddo, "and persuade her to go to Maruzza's, because I don't like long faces between neighbours and friends."

Meanwhile poor La Longa knew nothing about what had happened, and was laughing and enjoying herself with her relatives and friends.

One of the sailors, gesticulating like a preacher, went on talking to all who were willing to listen. "Yes," he said, "there were Sicilians there too; there were men from all parts. Besides, you know, after they've sounded action stations between decks you don't distinguish between dialects any more—with carbines they all speak in the same way. Fine lads all of them, and what guts! I tell you that when you've seen what I've seen, when you've seen how those lads stuck it out and did their duty, you're entitled to wear your cap over one ear!"

The lad's eyes were shining, but he said it was nothing, it was because he had been drinking. "One ship was called the Re d'Italia," he said. "There was no other ship like her; she had armour-plate, which means that she had a bust just like you women, only the bust was made of iron, and you could fire a gun at it without doing it any harm. She sank in a flash, and we didn't see her again—there was as much smoke as though twenty brick furnaces were blazing."

"At Catania there was the devil's own excitement," the chemist chimed in. "There were such crowds round the people reading the newspapers that it might have been a public holiday!"

"Newspapers are nothing but printed lies," said Don Giammaria.

"They say it's a bad business. We've lost a big battle," said Don Silvestro.

Master Cipolla had come over to see what all the excitement was about.

"Do you believe it?" he said with a sneer. "It's all nonsense, put in to sell the newspaper!"

"But all the newspapers say that we've lost!"

"Lost what!" said Uncle Crocifisso, putting his hand to his ear.

"A battle."

"Who lost it?"

"I, you, everybody, the whole of Italy," said the chemist.

"I haven't lost anything!" replied Dumbbell, shrugging his shoulders. "It's Piedipapera's business now; let him worry about it!" And he looked at the house by the medlar tree, where the party was still going on.

"Do you know the truth of the matter?" Master Cipolla said. "It's just like when the commune of Aci Trezza went to law with the commune of Aci Castello about its boundaries! What has it got to do with you and me?"

"The truth of the matter," said the chemist, who had grown quite red in the face, "is that you're a lot of unpatriotic swine!"

"Just think of the mothers who've lost their sons,"

someone dared to remark. Uncle Crocifisso, who was not a mother, shrugged his shoulders.

Meanwhile the other sailor was talking. "I'll tell you what a battle's like," he said. "It's just like when there's a brawl in a smoky tavern, and men start shouting and plates and glasses start flying. Have you even seen that happen? That's just what it's like! At first, when you're behind the sandbags, fingering your carbine in the dead silence, you hear nothing but the noise of the engines, and you feel that they're pounding away inside your own belly, and that's all. Then, when the first shell's fired and the fun begins, you want to join in too, and chains couldn't hold you back; you can't help wanting to join in, any more than you can help it when the violin strikes up a dance at the tavern after you've eaten and drunk; and you point your carbine at any living being you can see in the smoke. On land it's quite different. A Bersagliere who came back with us to Messina was telling us that after the firing starts you feel your legs itching with the desire to charge forward with your head down. But Bersaglieri are not sailors, and they don't know what it's like to stand in the rigging with your hand steady on the trigger in spite of the rolling of the ship, with your comrades falling all round you like rotten pears!"

"By the Holy Mother of God," said Rocco Spatu, "I should have liked to have been there!"

Everyone stood and listened in stupefaction. Next the other lad described the blowing up of the Palestro. When they had passed near her she had been blazing like a stack of firewood, and the flames were as high as her foremast flag. But all the lads were still at their posts, by the guns or in the rigging. "Our captain asked them if they needed anything. The reply was 'No, thank you.' Then she passed to port, and we didn't see her again."

"I must say I don't like the idea of being burned alive," Rocco Spatu decided. "But I should like a bit of a scrap all the same!"

When Spatu went back to the tavern Santuzza said to him: "Ask those poor boys to come over here. They must be thirsty after the long way they've come, and they could do with a decent glass of wine! That Pizzuto poisons people with his herb beer, and he doesn't go to confession. Some people deliberately flout their consciences. So much the worse for them!"

Master Cipolla blew his nose quietly, and said that in his opinion everybody who took part in a battle must be mad. "Would you obey if the King told you to go and get yourself killed for his sake?"

"Poor chaps!" said Don Silvestro. "It's not their fault! They're forced to do it, because a corporal with a loaded rifle stands behind every soldier, watching in case he tries to run away; if he does try to run away, the corporal shoots him dead!"

"Oh, that's different. But it's a dirty business, all the same!"

Laughter and drinking went on the whole evening in the Malavoglia yard in the bright moonlight. It was late, and everybody was very tired, and slowly munching toasted beans, and some were quietly leaning against the wall and singing, when they came and told the story that the two sailors had brought to the village. Master Fortunato had left early, taking with him Brasi in his new suit.

"Those poor Malavoglia!" he said, meeting Dumbbell in the village square. "God is sending them trials in earnest. The evil eye must be on them!"

Uncle Crocifisso said nothing, but scratched his head.

He had nothing to do with the matter any more, he had washed his hands of it. It was Piedipapera's business now. But in all conscience he was very sorry.

Next day the news started going round that there had been a battle in the direction of Trieste between our ships and those of the enemy—nobody knew who the enemy was—and that many had been killed. Some said one thing and some another, and you had to make it out as best as you could from the bits and pieces you picked up. The neighbours came with their hands under their aprons to ask if Maruzza's Luca had been there, and stood and gazed at her round-eyed before leaving. As usual when some misfortune happened, the poor woman started spending her time waiting at the door, looking this way and that, as though she were expecting her father-in-law and the boys to come home from the sea earlier than usual. The neighbours asked her if Luca had written, and how long it was since she had heard from him. It had not struck her before that Luca had not written, and she lay awake all night, picturing the sea in the direction of Trieste, where the catastrophe had happened; and she saw her son, pale and motionless, looking at her with a strange, round-eyed, shining expression, and seeming constantly to say yes, as he had done when they had sent him away to be a sailor, and she felt a terrible thirst, an indescribable burning of the throat. Among all the stories which were going round the village, and which they had come and repeated to her, one story in particular stuck in her mind, a story of how one of the sailors had been rescued after twelve hours, just when the dogfish had been going to eat him and he was dying of thirst in the midst of all that water. La Longa, thinking about this man dying of thirst in the midst of all that water, had to help herself from the jug, as though she herself were the victim of that burning thirst; she opened her eyes in the dark, and the vision of the drowning man was constantly before her.

With the passing of the days, however, people stopped talking about what had happened. But, as no letter came from Luca, La Longa could neither work nor stay in the house; she spent her time going restlessly from door to door, as though in search of the answer to the question on her mind. "Have you ever seen a cat that has lost its kittens?" the neighbours said. The letter, however, did not come. Even Master 'Ntoni gave up going to sea and stayed tied like a lap-dog to his daughter-in-law's apron strings. Then somebody said to them: "Go to Catania, which is a big place, and they'll be able to tell you something."

In the big town the poor old man felt more lost than if he had been at sea at night without knowing which way to steer. In the end someone was kind enough to direct him to the harbour captain, who must surely have the news. There, after being sent from pillar to post, they were at last directed to an office where a clerk started turning over the pages of some big books and running his finger down the list of the dead. When they reached a certain name, La Longa, who had not been able to hear properly because of a whistling in her ears, and had been listening with a face as white as the paper in the big books, slowly collapsed to the ground, half-dead.

"It happened more than six weeks ago," the clerk said, closing the register. "It was at Lissa. Hadn't you heard yet?"

La Longa was taken home on a cart, and she was ill for several days. After this she was filled with a great devotion to Our Lady of the Sorrows, whose picture was on the altar of the little church. She felt that that long body, stretched on its Mother's knees, with blackened ribs and knees red with blood, was the portrait of her Luca, and she felt herself transfixed by all the silver swords which transfixed the heart of Our Lady of the Sorrows. Every evening, when the women went to benediction and Mastro Cirino rattled his keys before locking up, she was always to be found in the same place before the altar, and she came to be known as Our Lady of the Sorrows too.

"She's right," they said in the village. "Luca would have come home soon, and he would have earned his three lire a day. Every wind is contrary to a broken ship!"

"Have you seen Master 'Ntoni?" Piedipapera remarked. "Since the loss of his grandson he's turned into a complete owl! Now the house by the medlar tree is like an old boot, leaking at every joint, and every honest man must start thinking about his own interests."

Venera Zuppidda was still sulking, and remarked that now the whole family was dependent on 'Ntoni. A girl would have to think twice before accepting him as a husband.

"What have you got against the poor young man?" Mastro Turi asked.

"You be quiet, you don't understand a thing!" his wife shouted at him. "I don't like awkward complications! It's no business of yours anyway, so you go back to work!" And she turned the great, hulking man out of the house before you could say Jack Robinson.

Barbara was sitting on the terrace parapet, tearing off the dead petals of the pinks. There was a sulky expression about her mouth too, and she dropped into the conversation remarks such as: "Keep away from husbands and mules!" and "No girl gets on well with her mother-in-law!"

"When Mena's married, grandfather will give us the upstairs room," 'Ntoni said.

"I'm not used to living in a pigeon-loft!" Barbara answered, so sharply that on the way home her father, after looking round cautiously, said to 'Ntoni:

"Barbara will turn out just like her mother. Think twice before saddling yourself with her, otherwise the same will happen to you as happened to me!"

What Venera Zuppidda said was: "Before my daughter goes and sleeps in the pigeon-loft, I want to know what's going to happen to the house, and how that lupin deal is going to end!"

It ended with Piedipapera's insisting on getting his money. St. John's Day had come, and the Malavoglia, not being able to pay off the whole debt, had come and offered another payment on account; they hoped to scrape the remainder together by the olive harvest. The money had come out of his own mouth, Piedipapera declared, and left him with no bread to eat, as true as God's word. He couldn't live on air until the olive harvest.

"I'm sorry, Master 'Ntoni," he said, "but what do you expect? I've got to look after my own interests. St. Joseph shaved his own beard before shaving the others. Charity begins at home!"

When Uncle Crocifisso was alone with Piedipapera, he grumbled that a year would soon be up, and they hadn't seen a penny of interest yet. The two hundred lire that had been paid them barely covered expenses. "You'll see that when the olive harvest comes they'll ask you to wait till Christmas, and at Christmas they'll ask you to wait till Easter. That's the path that leads to ruin! But I earned my money with the sweat of my brow. Now one of them's in paradise and another's after the Zuppidda girl. They can't manage that broken-down old boat of theirs any longer, and they're trying to marry off the daughter. All that family thinks about is getting married! They're crazy about it, like my niece, La Vespa. You'll see that as soon as Mena's married Alfio Mosca will turn up again to lay his hands on La Vespa's plot of land!"

Next they started grumbling at the lawyer, who kept endlessly filling in documents before sending for the bailiff.

"It must be Master 'Ntoni who's getting him to go slow," Piedipapera remarked. "With a *rotolo* of fish you can buy ten lawyers!"

In the meantime he had broken in earnest with the Malavoglia, because Venera Zuppidda had removed his wife's things when they were laid out to dry at the wash-place and put her own in their place. Impudence of that kind was unpardonable. Venera Zuppidda had only had the nerve to do it because she had been egged on by that young braggart 'Ntoni. The Malavoglia really were beyond the pale, and he wouldn't have anything more to do with them.

The next thing that happened was that stamped papers started pouring in like rain, and Piedipapera said that this showed that Master 'Ntoni couldn't have bribed the lawyer heavily enough; it just proved what a stingy lot the Malavoglia were, and how much reliance could be placed on their promises to pay. Master 'Ntoni rushed off for help to the communal secretary and the lawyer, but this time Dr. Scipioni laughed at him and said that blockheads should stay at home, and that he should never have allowed his daughter-in-law to sign away the house, and that as he had made his bed, so must he lie on it.

"Listen to me," said Don Silvestro. "You had better give him the house; otherwise you'll lose the Provvidenza and everything else you've got in the world as well in expenses, and, what with going backwards and forwards to the lawyer's, you'll lose many days' work into the bargain."

"If you give us the house and the furniture," Piedipapera said to him, "we'll leave you the Provvidenza, so that you'll be able to earn your living, and you'll remain your own masters, and the bailiff won't come with any more stamped papers."

Tino Piedipapera bore Master 'Ntoni no ill will, and went and talked to him as though he were not in any way involved himself. He put his arm round Master 'Ntoni's shoulders and said to him: "I'm sorry, brother, it hurts me more than it hurts you to turn you out of your house, but what can I do? I'm a poor man! Those five hundred lire came out of my own mouth, and St. Joseph shaved his own beard first. If I were as rich as Uncle Crocifisso, I shouldn't do it, on my word of honour!"

The poor old man didn't have the courage to tell his daughter-in-law that they would have to leave the house by the medlar tree after living there for so many years. It was like leaving their country, going abroad, going away for ever, like those who had departed and not come back again, although they had intended to come back; for Luca's bed was still in its place, and so was the nail on which Bastianazzo used to hang his coat. But in the end they had to remove all their poor domestic chattels from their places, and every one of them left a mark behind in the place where it had been, and the house no longer seemed the same without them. They moved by night into the butcher's cottage which they had rented, as though the whole village did not know that the house by the medlar tree belonged to Piedipapera now, and that they would have to go. But at least no one saw them moving their goods.

Each time the old man loosened a nail on the wall, or moved from its place in the corner a small table that had been there for so long that it seemed at home nowhere else, he shook his head a little. Then they sat down to rest for a while on the straw that had accumulated in the middle of the room, and looked about, in case they had forgotten anything. But the old man soon got up and went out into the yard for some fresh air.

But straw was scattered everywhere there too, and bits of broken crockery and broken lobster pots; and in the corner there was the medlar tree, and the vine was in leaf over the doorway. "Let's go," he said. "Let's go, children. It's the same today or tomorrow." But he didn't move.

Maruzza looked at the door of the yard through which Luca and Bastianazzo had gone, and the little street down which her son had walked away with his trousers tucked up because it was raining, after which she hadn't seen him any more in his oilskins. Alfio Mosca's window was shut, and the vine was dangling from the wall, and everyone who passed tugged at it. Everyone had something to look at in the house, and when he went away the old man secretly placed his hand on the broken door, for which Uncle Crocifisso had said a couple of nails and a good piece of wood were needed.

Uncle Crocifisso came with Piedipapera to look the place over, and they talked loudly in the empty rooms, and their voices echoed as though they were in church. Piedipapera, having nothing to live on but air, had not been able to last out, and he had had to sell the debt back to Uncle Crocifisso in order to survive.

"What do you expect, Master 'Ntoni?" he said, putting his arm round the old man's shoulders. "You know I'm a poor man, and you know what five hundred lire means to me! If you had been rich, I should have sold the house to you!" But Master 'Ntoni couldn't bear walking about the house with Piedipapera's arm round his shoulders. Uncle Crocifisso arrived with a carpenter and a bricklayer, and all sorts of people started wandering about the house, as though it were the public square, saying that some bricks were wanted here and that that beam needed replacing, and that the doorpost needed mending, as though they owned it; they even said that the whole house ought to be whitewashed, which would change its appearance completely.

Uncle Crocifisso kicked the straw and the broken crockery about with his feet, and he picked up an old hat, which had belonged to Bastianazzo, and flung it into the kitchen garden, where it would serve for manure. Meanwhile the medlar tree was still quietly rustling in the wind, and garlands of daisies, faded now, still hung over the door and windows, where they had been put for Ascension Day.

La Vespa came to have a look too, with a stocking which she was knitting attached to her neck, and she examined everything, now that the place belonged to her uncle. "Blood is thicker than water," she said at the top of her voice, so that even the deaf should hear. "My uncle's property means as much to me as my little bit of land must mean to him!" Alfio Mosca's door just opposite being bolted and barred, Uncle Crocifisso let her talk without being able to hear. "Now that the chain's on Alfio Mosca's door," she said into Uncle Crocifisso's ear, "you can set your heart at rest and believe that I don't think about him any longer!"

"Don't worry," he said. "My heart is at rest."

After this the Malavoglia no longer dared show

themselves in the street or at church. They went all
the way to Aci Castello for mass, and no one greeted
them any longer, not even Master Cipolla, who went
about saying: "Master 'Ntoni should never have forced
such a shocking match on me. After letting his daughter
sign the house away, it was as good as cheating his
neighbour!"

"It's just as my wife said it would be," Mastro Zuppiddo said. "She says even the dogs avoid the Malavoglia now!"

That stupid young fool Brasi still hankered after
Mena, however. After all, she had been promised him.
He stamped his feet with rage, and behaved just like a
child in front of a toy-stall at a fair when its parents
refuse to buy it something.

"Do you think I stole your property, you young
booby, to be willing to throw it away on a girl who
hasn't got a penny?" his father told him.

They even took away Brasi's new suit, and to console
himself he went and hunted lizards in the lava field, or
sat astride the low wall by the wash-place, and he
swore that, as they refused to give him a wife, and had
even taken back his new wedding suit, he would do
absolutely nothing at all, and go on doing it, even if
they killed him. Luckily Mena didn't see him as he was
now, because the Malavoglia, poor things, always
stayed indoors in the butcher's cottage they had rented
in the Strada del Nero, near the Zuppiddi house. If he
chanced to see them in the distance, he hurriedly hid
behind the wall or among the prickly-pear trees.

Cousin Anna, who saw everything from the stream-
bed where she laid out her washing to dry, said to
Grazia Piedipapera: "Now poor St. Agatha's worse off
than an old saucepan on the shelf—just like my girls,
who haven't got a dowry."

"Poor girl!" Grazia Piedipapera answered, "and she had even had her hair parted!"

Mena took it calmly, however, and had put the silver sword-pin back in her hair, without saying anything to anybody. She had plenty to do in the new house, where everything had to be put in place, and from which the medlar tree and Cousin Anna's and Nunziata's doors were not to be seen. Her mother gazed long and searchingly at her as she worked, and spoke to her caressingly when she asked her to pass the scissors or to hold the skein of wool for her, for she felt deeply for her daughter, now that everyone's back was turned on her. But the girl sang like a starling, for she was eighteen years old, and at that age, when the sky is blue, there is laughter in your eyes and the birds sing in your heart. Besides, she confided in her mother's ear while they laid the warp, she had never had much liking for that young man. Her mother was the only one who read her heart, and said a kind word for her in her trouble. "At least if Alfio Mosca were here, he wouldn't have turned his back on us," she said. "But when the new wine is ready he'll come back!"

The womenfolk did not turn their backs on the Malavoglia. But Cousin Anna, with all the work she had to do because of her unmarriageable daughters, was always busy, and Grazia Piedipapera was ashamed to show herself, after the way her husband had treated the poor Malavoglia. Grazia Piedipapera had a good heart, and did not say, like her husband: "Leave them alone. They've got nothing left in the world. What do they matter to you?" The only one who came to see them every now and then was Nunziata, carrying the smallest of her children, with the others following in a troop behind her. But even she had her own affairs to worry about.

That's how the world is made. As Venera Zuppidda said to Master 'Ntoni's 'Ntoni: "Everyone must look after his own interests. Everyone must look after his own interests before thinking about other people's. Your grandfather doesn't give you any money, so what obligation are you under to him? If you get married, you must set up your own household, and what you earn, you earn for yourself!"

"That's a fine way to talk," 'Ntoni replied. "Now that my family are in the street, you want me to abandon them. How could my grandfather run the Provvidenza and feed the whole family if I left him in the lurch?"

"Then you must settle it for yourselves," Venera Zuppidda exclaimed, turning her back on him and starting to rummage in one of her boxes or to look for something in the kitchen, setting up an appearance of great activity to give herself something to do and avoid looking him in the face. "My daughter's not stolen property, and has nothing to be ashamed of. One might close one's eyes to the fact that you haven't got a penny, because you're young and you've got the strength to work, and you're a fisherman and one of us, particularly as husbands are scarce nowadays, what with this fiendish conscription which takes all the young men away from the village. But if we have to give you a dowry to support the whole of your family, that's quite a different kettle of fish! I want to give my daughter one husband only, and not five or six, and I don't want to saddle her with two families on her shoulders!"

In the next room Barbara was pretending not to listen and briskly turning her winder. But as soon as 'Ntoni appeared in the doorway she bent her head over her reel and pulled a long face too. The poor fellow turned yellow and green and all the colours of the rainbow, and did not know what to do, because Barbara, with those big, black eyes of hers, had him completely under her spell, and when her mother wasn't there she said to him: "It means that you care for me less than you care for your own family," and started crying into her apron.

"Blast it!" 'Ntoni exclaimed. "If only I were back in the navy!" He started tearing his hair and banging his head, but the blockhead couldn't make up his mind to do what he ought to have done. Venera Zuppidda said that everyone must look after his own interests, and her husband said he had told her all along that he didn't like entanglements.

"You go back to your work!" she replied. "You don't know anything about these things!"

Whenever 'Ntoni went to see them he found nothing but sour faces, and Venera Zuppidda invariably reminded him that the Malavoglia had asked Grazia to comb Mena's hair—and a fine combing it had been, she said, all for the sake of licking Piedipapera's boots because of that small sum of money they owed him; and Piedipapera had taken the house after all, and left them as naked as the new-born Jesus!

"Do you think I don't know what your mother, Maruzza, used to say when she still carried her head high?" she said. "Do you think I don't know that she used to say that Barbara wasn't good enough for her son 'Ntoni, because she was as spoiled as though she were a young lady and wasn't suited to be a fisherman's wife? The Mangiacarrubbe woman and Cicca both told me so at the wash-place!"

"The Mangiacarrubbe woman and Cicca are both bitches," 'Ntoni replied. "They say that because they're jealous because I didn't marry the Mangiacarrubbe girl!"

"As far as I'm concerned you can have her! Much good may you be to her!"

"Talking to me like that," said 'Ntoni, "is just the same as saying: don't set foot in my house again."

'Ntoni tried to act like a man, and didn't appear again for two or three days. But little Lia, who knew nothing about all this, kept coming to play in Venera Zuppidda's yard, as she had got into the habit of doing when Barbara gave her prickly pears and chestnuts because she liked her brother 'Ntoni. But now Barbara didn't give her prickly pears and chestnuts any more.

"Why do you keep coming to look for your brother here?" Venera Zuppidda said to her. "Is your mother afraid we want to steal him from her?"

La Vespa came to the Zuppiddi's yard too, with a stocking on her neck, to say some blistering things about men, who were worse than dogs; and Barbara said to the little girl: "I know I'm not as good a housekeeper as your sister!" And when Venera added: "Your mother, who takes in washing, would do better to rinse out those cheap rags you've got on your back, instead of standing about gossiping about other people's affairs at the wash-place!"

The little girl didn't understand most of this, but the little that she said in answer infuriated Venera Zuppidda, who told her that it was her mother, Maruzza, who put her up to saying the rude things that she said, and sent her there specially to annoy her. So in the end the little girl gave up going there, and Venera Zuppidda said it was better that she should stay away, for she didn't want any Malavoglia spies prying about the house to find out whether they were still trying to steal their precious Pumpkin.

Things reached such a pitch that Venera Zuppidda

and La Longa no longer spoke to each other, and if they saw each other in church they turned their backs on each other.

"You'll see that they'll end by putting their brooms out!" the Mangiacarrubbe woman said, crowing with delight. "My name's not Mangiacarrubbe if they don't end by putting their brooms out! That's a fine game that Venera Zuppidda has been playing with Pumpkin!"

Men generally don't meddle in these women's squabbles; if they did, there'd be a danger of their developing into something serious, and even ending in stabbing affrays. Women, after they have put their brooms out and turned their backs on each other and relieved their feelings by pulling each other's hair out and giving each other a piece of their mind, soon make it up again and kiss and make friends and gossip on the doorstep as before. 'Ntoni, bewitched by Barbara's black eyes, quietly slunk back to her window to make friends again, though sometimes Venera Zuppidda felt like emptying the bean soup over his head, and even Barbara shrugged her shoulders, now that the Malavoglia no longer had a penny to bless themselves with.

In the end, to get rid of the nuisance, because the fellow insisted on hanging about the doorstep like a dog, and because he'd spoil her chances if anyone else had a mind to pass that way because of her, she decided to have it out with him.

"Well, 'Ntoni," she said, "the fish in the sea are for those who can afford to eat them. Let us set our hearts at rest, and not think about each other any more!"

"You may be able to set your heart at rest, Barbara, but for me, falling in and out of love can't be done to order."

"Try, and you'll succeed! You won't lose anything by

trying! I wish you every luck and every good fortune, but let me look after my own affairs, because I'm twenty-two!"

"I knew that you'd say that to me, now that they've taken our house and everyone turns his back on us!"

"Listen, 'Ntoni, my mother may come at any moment, and it's not right that she should find me with you."

"That's quite true. It's not right, now that they've taken the house by the medlar tree!"

Poor 'Ntoni's heart was full, and he didn't want to leave her like this. But she had to go to the fountain for a jugful of water, and she said good-bye to him and tripped rapidly away, moving her hips in a way that was very attractive. Her name was Zuppidda—"lame" —because her grandfather had broken his leg in a collision between two carts at the fair at Trecastagni, but Barbara had two very fine legs, both in perfect condition.

"Good-bye, Barbara!" the poor chap answered, and so laid a stone over the past and went back to rowing like a galley-slave, for the life that he led from Monday to Saturday was nothing but a galley-slave's life, and he was tired of wearing himself out for nothing, because not even a dog has any use for you when you haven't any money, and there's no sense in toiling like a slave from morning to night. He was utterly sick of the life he was leading; he preferred doing nothing in earnest, and stayed in bed pretending to be ill, as he had done when he was fed up with the navy, with the added advantage that his grandfather didn't come and examine him carefully all over, as the medical officer had done in the frigate.

"What's the matter with you?" his grandfather asked.

"Nothing. What's the matter with me is that I'm a poor man!"

"And what are you going to do about it? We have to live as we were born."

Unwillingly he allowed himself to be loaded with more gear than a donkey would carry, and he didn't open his mouth all day long, except to grumble and curse. "If you fall in the water you can't help getting wet," he said. If his brother started singing while the boat was under sail, he'd say: "Go on, sing away! When you're old, you'll bark like grandfather!"

"You don't gain anything by barking in the meantime," the boy replied.

"You're quite right, it's such a fine life, isn't it?"

"Fine or not, we didn't make it what it is," his grandfather said to settle the matter.

In the evening 'Ntoni ate his soup with rage in his heart, and on Sundays he hung about the tavern, where people had nothing to do but laugh and enjoy themselves, without thinking that next day they would have to go back to doing what they had done the whole week before; or he would spend whole hours sitting on the steps of the church with his chin in his hand, watching the people go by and dreaming about jobs in which there was nothing whatever to do.

On Sundays he could at least enjoy the things that don't cost money—the sunshine, and sitting and doing nothing with his arms folded—and then he even grew tired of thinking about his unhappy state and of longing for the things that he had seen when he was a sailor, with the memory of which he passed the time on workdays. He liked lying in the sun like a lizard and doing nothing at all. And when carters passed, sitting on the shafts of their carts, he muttered that they had a fine job. "Just like going about in a carriage all day long!" And if he saw some poor, tired old woman coming back from town, bent under her load like a tired donkey and complaining all the way, as the old do, he'd say:

"I'd like to do what you're doing, sister. After all, it's just like going for a walk!"

TEN   Instead of going for walks, 'Ntoni went to sea every blessed day and had to bend his back at the oar. But when the sea was in an ugly mood and threatened to swallow them at a gulp, the lad showed that he had a heart greater than the sea. "It's the Malavoglia blood," his grandfather said. It was a sight to see the lad at work with his hair flying in the wind, while the boat tossed about on the waves like a mullet in love.

Now that the village had so many boats that the fishing was like sweeping the sea clean with a broom, they often hazarded the Provvidenza, old and patched as she was, on the open sea for the sake of the few fish that were to be found. Even on days when clouds hung over Agnone and the eastern horizon was black, the sail of the Provvidenza was always to be seen far out on the leaden sea, looking as small as a pocket handkerchief, and everyone said that Master 'Ntoni and his family went hunting for trouble with a candlestick.

Master 'Ntoni replied that he had a living to make, and when he was far out on the open sea, where the water was as green as grass, and the houses of Trezza looked like a white dot in the distance, and there was nothing but water all round them, and the corks that held up the nets disappeared one by one, he would start talking away to his grandsons out of sheer happiness. In the evening, as soon as the Provvidenza appeared between the Fariglioni, La Longa hurried down to the shore to meet them and look at the fish leaping in the baskets and filling the bottom of the boat as though with silver. Before anyone had time to ask what sort of a catch it was Master 'Ntoni would call out: "A hundredweight!" or "A hundredweight and a quarter!" and he never turned out to be more than a *rotolo* out; and then he would spend the whole evening talking, while the women pounded the salt among the pebbles. Then they would count the casks one by one, and Uncle Crocifisso would come and inspect the catch and make them an offer with his eyes shut, and Piedipapera would shout and curse until Uncle Crocifisso agreed to the right price. At these times they liked Piedipapera's shouting, because it's no use going on being angry with people in this world; and afterwards Piedipapera would bring them the money in a handkerchief and La Longa would count it out in her father-in-law's presence, and lay aside so much for the housekeeping and so much for the rent. Mena helped to pound the salt and fill the casks too. She wore her blue dress again now, and her coral necklace, which had been given as a pledge to Uncle Crocifisso, and the women were able to go to mass in the village again, because they were starting to get together a dowry for Mena again, in case some young man should set his eyes on her.

"All I want," said 'Ntoni, moving his oar slowly to prevent the current from causing the Provvidenza to drift away from the circle of nets, while his grandfather was thinking of all these things, "all I want is to see that bitch Barbara gnashing her teeth with rage when we've set ourselves on our feet again, and regretting that she ever slammed the door in my face!"

"The test of a good pilot is stormy weather," the old man answered. "When we're once more what we used to be, we'll be in good odour with everybody and all doors will be opened to us again."

"The one who didn't close her door to us was Nunziata," Alessi said, "and Cousin Anna as well."

"A friend in need is a friend indeed. That's why the Lord helps them, with all the mouths they have to feed."

"When Nunziata goes to the lava field for kindlings, or her bundle of washing is too heavy for her, I go and help the poor girl."

"Now pull over this way, because this time St. Francis has sent us the grace of God."

The boy stretched his legs and pulled, panting as though he were doing everything himself. Meanwhile 'Ntoni, who was lying flat in the bottom of the boat with his hands under his head against the stretcher, was gazing at the white gulls against the background of endless blue sky, while the Provvidenza rocked gently on the green waves, which came from as far out as the eye could see.

"Why is the sea sometimes green and sometimes blue and sometimes white and sometimes as black as lava? Why isn't it always the same colour, like the water which is all that it really is?" Alessi asked.

"It's the will of God," his grandfather answered. "It tells the seaman when it's safe to put to sea and when it's better to stay ashore."

"Those gulls have a fine life, flying about up there all the time, with nothing to fear from the waves if there's a storm."

"When there's a storm they don't have anything to eat either."

"So what we all need is fine weather, then, like Nunziata, who can't go to the fountain if it's raining."

"Neither good weather nor bad weather lasts for ever," the old man remarked.

But when the weather was bad, and a nor'wester blew and the corks bobbed up and down on the water all day long as though someone were playing the fiddle for them to dance, and the sea was as white as milk or seethed as though it were boiling, and the rain poured down on their backs all day long and they got soaked to the skin, because no coat could possibly keep it out, and the waves leapt all round them like fish in a frying pan, then it was a different kettle of fish altogether, and 'Ntoni, with his coat collar buttoned up to his nose, had no desire to sing, and he had to keep bailing the Provvidenza the whole time, and his grandfather kept saying that "a white sea means a sirocco" or "a choppy sea means a fresh wind," as though they were there to learn proverbs; and at home in the evening, when the old man stood at the window, looking out at the weather, he would produce another proverb. "A red moon means wind; a bright moon means fine weather; a pale moon means rain," he would announce.

"If you know it's going to rain, why should we go out tomorrow?" 'Ntoni asked. "Wouldn't it be better to stay in bed for an extra couple of hours?"

"Rain from Heaven means pilchards in the nets!" the old man would reply.

When the water in the boat came up to his knees 'Ntoni would curse and swear.

"Maruzza will have a good fire ready for us when we get home this evening, and we shall all get dry," his grandfather would tell them.

And at dusk, when the Provvidenza came in with her belly full of the grace of God and her sail billowing like Donna Rosolina's skirt, and with the lights in the houses winking to one another behind the black

Fariglioni rocks as though they were signalling, Master 'Ntoni would point out to his grandsons the beautiful fire blazing in La Longa's kitchen across the yard in the Strada del Nero, for the wall in front of the house was low, and from the sea you could see the whole house, with the four tiles which provided shelter for the chickens; and you could see the oven through the open door. "What did I tell you?" the old man would exclaim with delight. "Just look at the fire that La Longa has made for us!" And La Longa would be waiting for them on the shore with the baskets all ready. When they had to be carried back empty, nobody had any desire to talk, but when there were not enough of them, and Alessi had to run home for more, the old man would put his hand to his mouth and call out: "Mena! Mena!" Mena would know exactly what was wanted, and they would all come down in procession with more baskets—Mena, Lia, and even Nunziata, with her whole brood following behind her; and then there would be gladness and rejoicing, and the cold and the rain would be forgotten, and they would all sit up late round the fire, gossiping about the grace of God that St. Francis had sent, and about what they would do with the money.

But that sort of thing meant risking one's life for an extra *rotolo* of fish, and once the Malavoglia came within a hair's breadth of all losing their lives for the sake of gain, as Bastianazzo had done. One evening they were opposite Agnone, and the sky was so dark that even Etna was invisible, and the wind was blowing in great gusts that seemed as though they were trying to speak.

"Ugly weather!" said Master 'Ntoni. "The wind's as changeable as a minx today, and the sea looks just like

Piedipapera's face when he's going to play some dirty trick on you!"

Although the sun hadn't gone down yet, the sea was the same colour as the lava field, and every now and then it seethed round them as though a pot were boiling.

"The gulls must all have gone to sleep," Alessi remarked.

"The Catania light must have been lit by now, but you can't see it," said 'Ntoni.

"Keep the helm over to the nor'east, Alessi," his grandfather ordered. "In half-an-hour we shan't be able to see anything; it'll be as black as pitch."

"We'd be better off in Santuzza's bar on an evening like this," said 'Ntoni.

"Or tucked up in your bed asleep, eh?" his grandfather replied. "You ought to be a clerk, like Don Silvestro!"

The poor old man had been complaining of his pains all day long. "It means a change in the weather," he said. "I can feel it in my bones!"

All of a sudden it grew so dark that you couldn't even see well enough to curse. Only the waves sweeping past the Provvidenza gleamed as though they had eyes and wanted to swallow her up. In the midst of the roaring expanse of sea the Malavoglia lost any further desire to talk.

"I've an idea," 'Ntoni suddenly said, "that tonight we ought to consign our catch to the devil."

"Shut up!" said his grandfather, and his voice in the darkness made them all seem very small on their wooden seats.

The wind howled in the Provvidenza's sail and the rope was singing like a guitar-string. Suddenly the wind started whistling, just like the railway engine when it emerges from the tunnel in the mountain above Trezza, and a wave which nobody saw coming took hold of the Provvidenza and tossed her like a bag of nuts, making her timbers creak.

"Down with the sail! Down with the sail!" shouted Master 'Ntoni. "Cut it down! Cut it down quick!"

'Ntoni, with his knife between his teeth, was standing on the side, hanging over the sea to make a counter-weight. He was clinging to the yard like a cat, and the sea raged underneath him as if it wanted to devour him.

"Hold on tight! Hold on tight!" his grandfather shouted above the noise of the raging waters, which seemed to be trying to snatch him from his perch, and were tossing the Provvidenza about like a cork, while the wind made her heel right over. The water rushed in and came up to their knees.

"Damnation!" shouted 'Ntoni. "If I cut down the sail, what shall we do when we want it?"

"Don't swear! Because now we're in the hands of God!"

When Alessi, who was clinging to the tiller, heard his grandfather say this, he started shrieking: "Mother! Mother!"

"Shut up!" his brother, with the knife between his teeth, shouted at him. "Shut up, or I'll kick your arse!"

"Cross yourself and keep quiet," said his grandfather. After that the boy did not dare make a sound.

The sail was so taut that suddenly it collapsed, and in a flash 'Ntoni had hauled it in and furled it.

"You know your calling like your father did," his grandfather said to him. "You're a Malavoglia too!"

The boat righted herself; she made a great leap and then went on tossing about on the waves.

"Now we want a firm hand on the tiller; give it to

me!" said Master 'Ntoni. Although the boy clung to it like a cat too, some waves came which knocked both their chests against it.

"Use your oar, Alessi, use your oar!" 'Ntoni shouted. "You're fit to do a job too! The oars are worth more than the tiller now!" Alessi, pulling against the stretcher, plucked up what courage he could.

"Hold tight!" his grandfather called out. What with the howling of the wind, his voice could barely be heard from one end of the boat to the other. "Hold tight, Alessi!"

"Yes, grandfather, yes!" the boy replied.

"Are you frightened?" 'Ntoni asked him.

"No!" his grandfather answered for him, "but let us commend ourselves to God!"

"Heaven help us!" exclaimed 'Ntoni, whose chest was heaving. "What we need now is iron arms, like a steam-engine's. This sea's getting the better of us!"

His grandfather said nothing, and for a moment they stopped and listened to the howling of the wind.

"Mother must be on the shore, looking out for us," said Alessi.

"Forget about your mother," his grandfather answered. "It's better not to think about her now."

After another long interval, 'Ntoni, panting with exhaustion, asked: "Where are we?"

"In the hands of God," the old man replied.

"Let me cry, then," exclaimed Alessi, who was at the end of his tether; and he started shrieking and shouting for his mother at the top of his voice, in the midst of the roaring of the wind and sea; and this time no one had the spirit to tell him to be quiet.

Eventually his brother, in a changed voice that he did not recognise himself, said:

"It's all very well making that noise, but nobody can

hear you, and it's better to keep quiet. Keep quiet, because it's not right to act like that, either for your own sake or for ours!"

"Set the sail!" ordered Master 'Ntoni. "Hold her into the wind and let us trust ourselves to God."

The wind made the operation very difficult, but in five minutes the sail was set and the Provvidenza started leaping over the waves, heeling over like a wounded bird. The three Malavoglia clung to the windward side, and nobody spoke, because when the sea is in that mood you have no spirit to open your mouth.

Master 'Ntoni was the only one to speak. "They must be telling their beads for us at home by now," he said.

Night had come down as black as pitch. The Provvidenza scudded before the wind and waves, and they said no more.

"The light on the mole!" 'Ntoni shouted. "Do you see it?"

"To starboard! To starboard!" Master 'Ntoni yelled. "It's not the light on the mole! We're running on the rocks! Furl the sail! Furl the sail!"

"I can't furl the sail!" 'Ntoni replied, his voice stifled by the storm and his exertions. "The sheet's wet! The knife, Alessi, the knife!"

"Cut it down! Quick!"

A second later there was a crash. The Provvidenza, which had been heeling hard over, righted herself as suddenly as though a spring had been released and nearly flung them all into the sea. The broken yard, together with the sail, came crashing down into the boat. Then a voice was heard moaning "Ah! Ah!" as though someone was about to die.

"Who is it? Who's moaning?" asked 'Ntoni, who was using his teeth as well as his knife to cut the bolt-ropes of the sail, which had fallen on to the boat with the yard and was covering everything. A gust of wind suddenly seized it and carried it whistling away. Then the two brothers were able to clear the remnants of the yard and drop it into the sea. The boat righted herself, but Master 'Ntoni did not rise to his feet or answer when 'Ntoni called. Now, when wind and sea are in tumult together, nothing is more frightening than to get no answer from someone to whom you call. "Grandfather! Grandfather!" Alessi shouted too, and when no answer came both brothers' hair stood on end. The night was so black that you could not see from one end of the Provvidenza to the other, and Alessi was no longer weeping with terror. The old man lay in the bottom of the boat with a gaping wound in his head. 'Ntoni groped until he found him, and thought he was dead, because he was not breathing and did not move. The abandoned tiller swung this way and that, while the boat rocked and plunged amid the waves.

"St. Francis of Paola! Blessed St. Francis!" the two lads shrieked, no longer knowing what to do.

Merciful St. Francis, going about in the storm to rescue the faithful, heard them and extended his mantle under the Provvidenza just when she was about to be smashed like a nut-shell on the Pigeon Rock, just under the customs shed. The boat leapt the rock like a colt and landed nose downwards on dry land. "Courage! Courage!" the guards shouted from the shore, running hither and thither with lanterns and throwing them ropes. "Courage!" they shouted. "Here we are!" Finally a rope fell across the Provvidenza, which was quivering like a leaf. The rope cut across 'Ntoni's face like a whip, but at that moment it was more welcome than a caress.

"Help me! Help me!" he yelled, seizing the rope, which was slipping rapidly away, as if trying to escape from his hands. Alessi grasped it with all his strength, and the two managed to wind it two or three times round the tiller, and the customs guards hauled them ashore.

Master 'Ntoni, however, showed no sign of life, and when they brought the lantern they saw that his face was covered with blood, so that everyone thought he was dead, and his two grandsons started tearing their hair. But after a couple of hours Don Michele, Rocco Spatu, Vanni Pizzuto, and all the idlers who were at the tavern when the news came, arrived, and massage and cold water made the old man reopen his eyes. When he found out where he was, and that he was less than an hour from Trezza, he asked to be carried home on a ladder.

Maruzza, Mena and the neighbours, who were shrieking and beating their breasts in the village square, saw him being brought back on the ladder, as white as a corpse.

"It's nothing! It's nothing!" said Don Michele, who was leading the way, and he hurried to the chemist's for some "Seven Thieves" vinegar. Don Franco brought the bottle himself, and Piedipapera and his wife, the Zuppiddi, Master Cipolla and the whole neighbourhood turned up in the Strada del Nero, because on occasions like this the past is forgotten. La Locca turned up too. Whenever anything happened in the village she always followed the crowd, whether by day or night, as though she never closed her eyes and were still waiting for her Menico. People crowded into the street outside the Malavoglia house as though somebody had died, and there were so many of them that Cousin Anna had to slam the door in their faces.

Nunziata came rushing along half-dressed, and started banging on the door. "Let me in! Let me in!"

she shouted. "Let me find out what's happened at Maruzza's!"

"What was the use of sending us for the ladder if they won't let us into the house to see what's happening?" La Locca's son shouted.

Venera Zuppidda and the Mangiacarrubbe woman had forgotten all the insults they had exchanged and talked away busily outside the door, with their hands under their aprons.

"That's what it means to be a fisherman," said Venera Zuppidda. "In the end it costs you your life." If a woman married her daughter to seafaring folk, she said, one day she'd have her coming home again a widow, and with orphans on her hands into the bargain, because if it hadn't been for Don Michele, tonight would have seen the end of the Malavoglia. The best plan was to copy those who did no work, but made a living just the same, like that Don Michele, for instance, who was as fat and well-nourished as a canon, and always wore woollen cloth, and ate very well indeed, and was sought after by everybody. Even that Republican, the chemist, used respectfully to take off his big, black hat to him.

Don Franco came out and said: "It's nothing. We've bandaged him up. But if he doesn't get a fever, he's done for."

Piedipapera insisted on going in and seeing Master 'Ntoni, because he was a friend of the family's, and so did Master Fortunato, and as many others as could manage to elbow their way in.

"I don't like the look of him at all!" Master Cipolla solemnly announced, shaking his head. "How do you feel, Master 'Ntoni?"

Meanwhile Venera Zuppidda, who had been left outside, was saying:

"Now you see why Master Fortunato refused to give his son to St. Agatha! That man has a flair!"

"He whose wealth is at sea owns nothing," La Vespa added. "What you want is a good, solid piece of land!"

"What a night for the Malavoglia!" exclaimed Grazia Piedipapera.

"Have you noticed that this family's misfortunes always happen at night?" Master Cipolla remarked, leaving the house with Don Franco and Tino Piedipapera.

"And all the result of trying to make a living, poor souls!" said Grazia Piedipapera.

For two or three days Master 'Ntoni was more dead than alive. The fever came, as the chemist said it would, but it was so high that it nearly finished him off. The old man, with his bandaged head and his long beard, did not complain as he lay in his corner. But he had a terrible thirst, and when Mena or La Longa brought him something to drink he would snatch the jug with trembling hands, as though he were afraid they might steal it from him.

Don Ciccio came every morning, tended the wound, felt his pulse, made him put out his tongue and then went away again, shaking his head.

One night, after Don Ciccio had shaken his head more vigorously than usual, they left the candle burning all night. La Longa had put the picture of Our Lady beside it, and they told their beads at the sick man's bedside—he hardly seemed to be breathing and didn't even want water any more. No one went to bed, and Lia got so sleepy that she nearly broke her jaws with yawning. There was an ominous quiet about the house, and passing carts rattled the glasses on the table and startled the watchers at the bedside, and the neighbours stood at their doors, talking quietly to each other and peeping through the doorway at what was happening in the house. The light had gone out of Master 'Ntoni's eyes, and he asked what the doctor had said, and wanted to see all the members of his family, one by one. 'Ntoni was by his bedside and wept like a small boy, because he had a good heart.

"Don't cry like that!" his grandfather said to him. "Don't cry like that! You're the head of the household now. Remember that you've got the whole family on your shoulders now, and do as I did."

The womenfolk, including even little Lia, hearing him talk like that, started shrieking and tearing their hair, because women have no sense in these circumstances, and they didn't notice that at the sight of their distress the old man's face filled with so much dismay that it looked as if he were really going to die. But he went on in a weak voice:

"Don't spent a lot of money on the funeral. The Lord knows we have no money to waste, and will be satisfied with the beads that Maruzza and Mena will tell for me. Mena, you must do as your mother has always done, because she has been a saint, and has seen many misfortunes; and you must protect your sister, just as a hen protects her chickens. As long as you help one another, misfortunes will not seem so grave. 'Ntoni is grown-up now, and soon Alessi will be able to help you too."

"Don't talk like that!" the sobbing women implored him, as though he were dying on purpose. "For mercy's sake, don't talk like that!" He shook his head sadly, and replied:

"Now that I've told you what I wanted to tell you, it doesn't matter. I'm an old man. When the oil's finished, the lamp goes out. Now turn me round on the other side, because I'm tired."

Later he called 'Ntoni again and said to him:

"Don't sell the Provvidenza, old as she is. If you do, you'll be forced to work for others, and you don't know how hard it is when Master Cipolla or Uncle Cola says: 'No, I don't need anybody for Monday.' And there's something else I want to tell you too, 'Ntoni, and that is that when you've got some money together, the first thing you must do is to find a husband for Mena, someone who plied her father's trade; and I want to tell you this too, 'Ntoni; when you've married Lia too, if you can manage to save any money, put it aside for buying back the house by the medlar tree, because it has always belonged to the Malavoglia, and your father and Luca, God rest their souls, went away from it to die. Uncle Crocifisso will sell it to you if he can make a profit."

"Yes, grandfather, yes," 'Ntoni promised, weeping. Alessi was listening too, looking as grave as though he were already grown-up.

The women, hearing the old man talking and talking, thought he had delirium, and came and wanted to put cold poultices on his forehead.

"Don't," said Master 'Ntoni. "Don't. I'm in my right senses. Before I go I want to finish what I've got to say."

Meanwhile fishermen could be heard calling each other outside, and carts started passing again along the road. "In two hours it will be daylight," said Master 'Ntoni, "and you can fetch Don Giammaria!"

The poor people waited for the coming of daylight as though it were the Messiah, and kept going to the window to see if there were any sign of the dawn. At last the room started to grow light, and Master 'Ntoni said again:

"Now send for the priest, because I want to confess."

Don Ciccio arrived while the priest with the holy

oil was still there, and he was so annoyed that he wanted to turn his donkey's bridle and go away again. "Who told you there was any need of the priest?" he said. "Who told you that it was time for extreme unction? That's the doctor's business to decide! I'm surprised the priest came without a doctor's certificate! There's no need of extreme unction, I tell you, he's getting better!"

The neighbours were sure that they would be coming at any moment to take the body away, and were all waiting at their doorsteps to see it pass. "Poor man!" they muttered.

"That old man's tough," Venera Zuppidda was saying. "I tell you he's got nine lives, like a cat. You mark my words! I tell you he'll see us all into the grave!"

Meanwhile Nunziata arrived, carrying a jug on her head. "Out of the way, please," she said. "I'm in a hurry. They're waiting for water at Maruzza's, and if my children get up to mischief, they'll have everything in the middle of the street!"

Lia came to the door, looking as pleased as Punch.

"Grandfather's better," she announced. "Don Ciccio said he isn't going to die yet!"

She could hardly believe that the women actually listened to her as though she were a grown-up woman. Alessi came and said to Nunziata:

"Now that you're here, I'll hurry over and have a look at the Provvidenza."

"That lad has more sense than his big brother," said Cousin Anna.

"Don Michele will get a medal for throwing a rope to the Provvidenza," the chemist announced. "There's a small pension that goes with it. That's how they waste the people's money!"

Piedipapera stuck up for Don Michele, and said that

he deserved a medal and a pension for dashing into the water up to his knees with his boots on to save the life of the Malavoglia. Was it a trifle to have saved three lives? The man had been within an ace of losing his life himself! The result was that everyone started talking about Don Michele, and on Sunday, when he put on his new uniform, all the girls looked at him to see if he were wearing the medal yet.

"Now that Barbara Zuppidda has put the Malavoglia lad out of her mind, she won't turn her back on Don Michele any more," Piedipapera went about saying. "I saw her peeping out of the door when he walked down the street!"

When Don Silvestro heard this, he said to Vanni Pizzuto:

"A great deal of good you've done, getting rid of Master 'Ntoni's 'Ntoni, if Barbara has set her eyes on Don Michele!"

"If she has set her eyes on him, she'll have to take them off again, because her mother can't stand policemen or scroungers or strangers."

"We'll see, we'll see! Barbara is twenty-three, and once she realises that if she goes on waiting for a husband she may not get one at all, she'll take him, whether she likes it or not. Would you like to bet twelve *tarì* that they talk to each other through the window?" And he produced a brand new five-lire piece.

"I shall bet nothing," Pizzuto answered, shrugging his shoulders. "I don't care a fig one way or the other!"

Piedipapera and Rocco Spatu, who were listening, burst into loud laughter. "Very well, I'll bet you nothing, then," said Don Silvestro, who had been put in a good humour, and he went off with the others to exchange a few words with Uncle Santoro outside the tavern.

"Listen, Uncle Santoro, would you like to earn twelve

tarì?" he said, producing the new coin from his pocket, although Uncle Santoro couldn't see. "Mastro Vanni Pizzuto wants to bet twelve *tarì* that Don Michele goes and talks to Barbara Zuppidda in the evenings now. Wouldn't you like to earn twelve *tarì*?"

"Blessed souls in purgatory!" exclaimed Uncle Santoro, kissing his beads. He had been listening intently, but he obviously felt uneasy, and was moving his lips this way and that, just as a hunting dog moves its ears when it hears footsteps.

"Don't worry, they're all friends," Don Silvestro explained with a laugh.

"They're Tino Piedipapera and Rocco Spatu," the blind man announced, after listening carefully for a little while longer.

He always recognised everybody who passed, whether they were barefooted or wearing boots. "You're Tino Piedipapera," he would say, or: "You're Cinghialenta." And as he was always there, passing the time of day with somebody or other, he always knew everything that was happening in the village. When the children came to fetch the wine for dinner, he called them and asked them questions for the sake of earning the twelve *tarì*. "Alessi!" he would call out, or "Nunziata!" or "Lia! Where are you going?" or "Where have you been?" or "What have you been doing today?" or "Have you seen Don Michele? Has he been walking down the Strada del Nero?"

'Ntoni, poor fellow, had run hither and thither tirelessly and had been distraught with anxiety as long as there had been any need of it, but, now that his grandfather was getting better he spent his time loafing round the village, with his arms crossed, waiting for it to be possible to bring the Provvidenza back to Mastro Zuppiddo to be patched up a second time; and he

would go to the tavern for a chat, as he had no money
in his pockets, and tell everybody how the Malavoglia
had seen death face to face. That was how he passed
his time, talking and spitting. When anyone bought
him a glass or so of wine, he would start grumbling at
Don Michele, who had stolen his girl and now went
and talked to her every evening—Uncle Santoro had
seen him, for he had asked Nunziata if Don Michele
used to walk down the Strada del Nero now.

"By the blood of Judas, my name isn't 'Ntoni Malavoglia if I don't get my own back on him," he said.

People found his vindictiveness amusing, and so they
bought him drinks. Santuzza, while she rinsed the
glasses, always used to turn away so as not to hear the
bad language in the bar, but she forgot to do so when
she heard Don Michele mentioned, and stayed and
listened with wide-open eyes. She had grown inquisitive too, and she was all ears when they talked about
him, and when Nunziata's little brother or Alessi came
to fetch the wine she would bribe them with apples
or green almonds to tell her who had been walking
down the Strada del Nero. Don Michele swore by everything that's holy that there wasn't a word of truth
in what they said, and in the evening, after the tavern
was shut, there would be the very devil of a row behind
the closed door. "Liar!" Santuzza would shriek at him.
"Murderer! Atheist! Thief!"

It ended in Don Michele's giving up going to the
tavern. He satisfied himself with sending for his wine
and sitting alone with his bottle in Pizzuto's shop, for
the sake of peace.

When 'Ntoni went to the chemist's for his grandfather's medicine, Don Franco would say to him:
"You're the people. As long as you're as patient as a
beast of burden, you'll get beaten like one." To change

the subject the Lady, knitting stockings behind the
counter, would ask: "How is your grandfather?" 'Ntoni
dared not open his mouth in the Lady's presence, and
went away muttering, with the glass in his hand.

His grandfather was better now, and they put him
outside in the sunshine, wrapped in a cloak and with a
handkerchief round his head. It made him look like a
revived corpse, so much so that people went to look at
him out of sheer curiosity. The poor old man would nod
at his acquaintances, like a parrot, and smile, quite
happy at being seated by the door wrapped up in his
cloak, with Maruzza continually going in and out and
the sound of Mena's loom coming from inside the house
and the chickens scratching in the street. Now that
he had nothing else to do, he learned to recognise all
the chickens individually, and he would watch what
they were doing; and he would pass the time by listening to the neighbours' voices, and say: "That's Venera
Zuppidda telling her husband off," or "That's Cousin
Anna coming back from the wash-place." Then he
would watch the lengthening shadow of the houses,
and when the sun no longer shone on the door they
would put him against the wall opposite, because he
was like Mastro Turi's dog, which always chose the sun
to lie down in.

Eventually he started to be able to walk a little
again, and they would take him down to the shore,
supporting him under the arm-pits, because he liked to
curl up and snooze on the stones, opposite the boats,
and he said that the smell of salt water did him good;
and he enjoyed watching the boats, and listening to
what sort of a day so-and-so and so-and-so had had.
The men would talk to him occasionally as they went
about their business. "There's still some oil left in the
lamp, isn't there, Master 'Ntoni?"

In the evening, when the whole family was at home and the door was shut and La Longa told her beads, he enjoyed having them all round him, and he would look at their faces one by one, and then look all round the room, and at the chest of drawers with the statue of the Good Shepherd on it, and the little table with the lamp on it. "It doesn't seem true that I'm still here with you," he would say.

La Longa said she had been so upset by the fright he had given her that she no longer seemed to have her dead husband and son constantly before her eyes, though previously they had been like two thorns perpetually in her side. She was so worried by this that she went and confessed to Don Giammaria. But the priest gave her absolution, because one trouble drives away another, and the Lord does not desire that we should be afflicted with them all at the same time, because if that happened our hearts would break and we should die. Her husband and her son were dead, and she had been driven from her house; but at least she had the satisfaction of having been able to pay the doctor and the chemist, and she no longer owed anybody anything.

In the end the old man said he couldn't stand idleness any longer, and said he wanted something to do. He started mending nets and making lobster pots; and he started walking with a stick as far as Mastro Turi's yard to see how the Provvidenza was getting on, and he would stay there basking in the sun. Eventually he actually went out fishing again with his grandsons.

"He's just like a cat!" said Venera Zuppidda. "If a cat doesn't fall on its nose it never dies!"

La Longa had put a table outside the door and had started selling oranges, nuts, hard-boiled eggs and black olives. "You just wait and see," said Santuzza.

"They'll end by selling wine! I'm very pleased, because they're God-fearing people." And Master Cipolla, when he walked down the Strada del Nero, shrugged his shoulders when he passed the house of the Malavoglia, who were now trying to set themselves up as traders.

Trade was good, because Maruzza's eggs were always fresh, a d Santuzza, now that 'Ntoni came to her bar, would end over for olives when her customers weren't thirs y. So they managed to scrape together the money to pay Mastro Turi Zuppiddo, and the Provvidenza was patched up again, though now she really looked like an old shoe; they even managed to save a few lire. They laid in a good stock of casks, and salt for the anchovies, in case St. Francis should send them good fortune, and they bought a new sail for the boat, and a little money was laid aside in the chest of drawers. "We manage like the ants," said Master 'Ntoni; and every day he would count the money and go and look at the house by the medlar tree; he would stand and gaze at it with his hands behind his back. The door was shut, sparrows twittered on the roof, and the vine was dangling over the window. Then he would go and look over the garden wall, where onions had been sown; it looked like a sea of white plumes; and then for the hundredth time he would go and see Uncle Crocifisso. "You know, Uncle Crocifisso, if we manage to save enough money to buy the house, you must sell it to us," he would say, "because it has always belonged to the Malavoglia. Every bird to its own nest, as the saying is, and I want to die where I was born. Blessed is he who dies in his own bed." Uncle Crocifisso would grunt, to avoid committing himself; he had some new tiles put on the roof and a coat of lime put on the wall in the yard to send up the price.

"Don't worry, don't worry," Uncle Crocifisso would

reassure him. "The house is there, and it won't run away. All you have to do is to keep your eye on it. Everyone keeps his eye on the things he really cares about!" Once he added:

"Why don't you marry your Mena?"

"I'll marry her in God's good time," Master 'Ntoni answered. "I'd be only too pleased to marry her tomorrow!"

"If I were in your shoes, I'd give her to Alfio Mosca. He's a good chap, honest and hard-working. His only fault is that he spends his time hunting high and low for a wife. Now they say he's coming back to the village, and he seems just the man for your granddaughter."

"Don't they say that your niece La Vespa wants him?"

"So you say that too!" Dumbbell started shouting. "So you say that too! Who says so? It's nothing but lying gossip! He's after my niece's plot of land, that's what he's after! How would you like it if I sold your house to somebody else?"

At this Piedipapera joined in the conversation. As soon as two people started talking in the square, he always turned up in the hope of picking up some business. "La Vespa's after Brasi Cipolla now," he said. "I saw them with my own eyes, walking down the footpath by the stream together, after his engagement to St. Agatha was broken off. I was looking for a couple of smooth stones for repairing the cattle trough, which doesn't hold water any more. She was looking at him coyly, with the corner of her handkerchief over her mouth, and saying: 'By this blessed medallion that I wear on my breast, it isn't true! Pooh! How sick you make me when you remind me of that old fool of an uncle of mine!' She was talking about you, Uncle Crocifisso!"

At this Uncle Crocifisso created a terrible commotion, and the whole village heard about it. He actually wanted Don Michele and the customs guards to take La Vespa in charge. After all, she was his niece, and he was responsible for her, and surely Don Michele was paid for looking after honest people's interests. Everyone was amused to see Master Cipolla running around in a terrible state of alarm too. People were delighted that Brasi, that imbecile of a son of his, had fallen for La Vespa, after behaving as though not even Victor Emmanuel's daughter were good enough for him, and jilting the Malavoglia girl without even so much as saying good afternoon.

Mena, however, had not gone into mourning after being jilted by Brasi. On the contrary, she had started singing again while working at the loom or helping to salt anchovies on fine summer evenings. This time St. Francis really sent good fortune. There was an anchovy season such as had never been known before, and it meant money for the whole village. The boats returned laden to the brim, with the men singing and waving their caps from a distance to their wives standing and waiting for them with their children on the shore.

Dealers came in swarms from Catania, on foot, on horseback and in carts, and Piedipapera was left with no time even to scratch his head. Towards even-song the village was like a market-place, with shouting and noises of every kind. In the Malavoglia yard the lamp was kept burning till midnight, as though it were a festival. The girls sang, and the neighbours and Cousin Anna's daughters and Nunziata's sisters came and helped too, because there was money for everybody, and there were four rows of casks, already filled and with stones on top of them, standing along the wall.

"I wish Barbara Zuppidda were here now!" said 'Ntoni, sitting on the stones, with his arms crossed, to provide additional weight. "Now she'd see that we're worth something too, and that we don't care a fig for Don Michele and Don Silvestro!"

Dealers followed Master 'Ntoni about with money in their hands, and Piedipapera drew him aside by the sleeve and told him that now was the time to take his profit. But Master 'Ntoni replied obstinately that they could talk it over again at All Saints, when anchovies would be worth something. "No, I don't want a deposit," he said, "I don't want my hands tied! I know the way things go." And he would tap the casks and say to his grandchildren: "Here's your house and Mena's dowry. St. Francis has granted me the grace of letting me die content."

They had also laid in all their provisions for the winter, grain and beans and oil; and they had paid Massaro Filippo a deposit for their Sunday wine.

Now they had no more anxieties. The old man and his daughter-in-law counted over the money in the stocking and the casks lined up in the yard, and worked out how much more they needed to buy back the house. Maruzza knew where every single coin had come from. These came from the sale of oranges and eggs, those Alessi had earned on the railway, these Mena had earned at her loom. "All of us have helped," she would say, and Master 'Ntoni would add: "Didn't I tell you that to handle an oar the five fingers of the hand have to help one another? We don't need much more now!" And off he would go into a corner with Maruzza, and they would look at St. Agatha, who deserved to be talked about, poor girl, because she had no will of her own, but was content to work, singing to herself like the birds in their nests before daybreak.

Only when she heard carts passing in the evening did she think of Alfio Mosca, who was going about the world the Lord knew where; and then she stopped singing.

Throughout the village nothing was to be seen but people carrying nets and women sitting at the threshold, pounding stones. Outside every door there was a row of casks, so that it did your nose good to walk down the street, and a mile before you reached the village you could smell that St. Francis had sent a grace; and all over the village there was talk of nothing but pilchards and brine, even at the chemist's, where they settled the affairs of the world in their own way. Don Franco wanted to teach the village a new way of salting anchovies that he had read about in books. When they laughed at him he shouted: "Fools that you are! What's the good of talking about progress and Republicanism to people like you!" People turned their backs on him and left him shouting away like a maniac. Ever since the world began, anchovies have been salted and pounded with bricks.

"It's the way my grandfather did it! That's what they all say!" the chemist went on shouting behind their backs. "You're a lot of donkeys—all that's missing is the tail! What can you do with people like that? They're satisfied with Mastro Croce Giufà, because he's always been mayor! They'd be capable of saying that they don't want a republic because they've never had one!" Later on he repeated all this to Don Silvestro, when he followed up a certain private conversation they had had recently—though, as a matter of fact, Don Silvestro hadn't opened his mouth on that occasion, but had contented himself with listening quietly. Don Silvestro was known to be at daggers drawn with Mastro Croce's Betta, because she wanted to be mayor, and her father had allowed her skirt to be tied round his neck, with the result that one day he said one thing and next day another, just as Betta dictated. When he was remonstrated with, he replied: "I'm the mayor!" just as his daughter had told him to, and when Don Silvestro went and talked to her she placed her hands on her hips and said to him:

"Do you suppose you'll always be allowed to lead my poor father by the nose and feather your own nest? Even Donna Rosolina says that you're gobbling up the whole village! But you won't gobble me up, that you won't, because I've no desire to get married, and I look after my father's interests!"

Don Franco declared that without new men nothing whatever could be done; it was useless to rely on village bigwigs like Master Cipolla, who said that, thanks be to God, he had his own affairs to look after, and had no need to serve the public for nothing; or like Massaro Filippo, who had no thoughts for anything but his land and his vines, and had only taken an interest when there had been talk of taking off the tax on new wine. "All those people are behind the times," Don Franco concluded, with his beard in the air. "They all belong to the camarilla age! In these times new men are needed!"

"Then let us send to the foundry and have them specially made," Don Giammaria replied.

"If things were as they ought to be, we should be swimming in money," Don Silvestro remarked. That was all he said.

"Do you know what are needed?" the chemist said in a whisper, with a cautious glance in the direction of the backshop. "What are needed are people like ourselves!"

After whispering this secret into their ears, he went over to the shop door on tiptoe, where he stood with his beard in the air, swaying to and fro on his little legs with his hands behind his back.

"Fine people your new men would be," muttered Don Giammaria. "You'd find as many as you needed at Favignana, or in the other prisons, without having to send to the foundry. Go and talk to Tino Piedipapera, or that drunkard Rocco Spatu, because they're the people with your modern ideas! I've been robbed of twenty-five *onze*, and nobody has been sent to Favignana or to any other prison. Those are your new men and your new times!"

At this moment the Lady came into the shop, with her stocking in her hand, and the chemist hastily gulped down what he had been going to say and went on muttering into his beard, pretending he was watching the people going to the fountain. Eventually Don Silvestro, who wasn't afraid of the chemist's wife, seeing that nobody was going to say anything else, said outright that the only new men were 'Ntoni Malavoglia and Brasi Cipolla.

"Don't you start meddling in these things!" the Lady started scolding her husband. "They've nothing whatever to do with you!"

"I'm not saying anything," Don Franco answered, stroking his beard.

Now that Don Franco's wife was there, the priest had the upper hand, for she was a wall from behind which he could throw stones in safety. So he started amusing himself by saying things to infuriate the chemist. "Fine fellows, those new men of yours!" he said. "Do you know what Brasi Cipolla's doing, now that his father is looking for him to box his ears because of La Vespa? He's going about hiding everywhere, just like a naughty boy! Last night he slept in the sacristy; and yesterday my sister had to send a plate of macaroni

out into the fowl-house where he was hiding, because
the young blockhead had had nothing to eat for twenty-
four hours, and was all covered with chicken lice. And
'Ntoni Malavoglia! There's another fine type of new
man for you! His grandfather and all the rest of the
family are straining and sweating to set the family on
its feet again, but whenever he can find an excuse he
spends his time loafing round the village and hanging
about the tavern, just like Rocco Spatu!"

The gathering dissolved as it always did, without
anything being settled, and as usual everyone was of
exactly the same opinion as before, and, to make matters worse, this time the Lady had put in an appearance, which meant that Don Franco had been de-
prived even of the satisfaction of speaking his mind.

Don Silvestro laughed, cackling like a hen; and as
soon as the conversation ended he went away too, with
his hands behind his back, deep in thought.

"Don't you see that Don Silvestro is much more sensible than you?" the Lady said to her husband as he
closed the shop. "He's a man with something to him!
If he has something to say, he shuts it up inside him
and doesn't say a word! The whole village knows that
he cheated Donna Rosolina of twenty-five *onze*, but
no one has the courage to say it to the face of a man
like that! You'll never be anything but a fool, unable
to manage your own affairs; an idiot barking at the
moon! A useless, idle chatterbox!"

"But what have I done? What have I said?" said the
chemist, following her up the stairs with the lamp in
his hand. Did she know what he had said? He never
dared to make any of his speeches, which had no rhyme
or reason, in front of her. All she knew was that Don
Giammaria had gone away, crossing himself as he
walked across the square and muttering: "A fine type

of new man, indeed, like that 'Ntoni Malavoglia, wandering round the village at this time of night!"

ELEVEN One day, when he was loafing round the village, 'Ntoni Malavoglia met two young men who had sailed from Riposto a few years before to seek their fortune, and were now returning from Trieste, or from Alexandria in Egypt, or at any rate from somewhere a long way away, and had more money to spend at the tavern than Peppi Naso even, or Master Cipolla. They sat astride the narrow table in the bar-room and cracked jokes with all the girls, and had silk handkerchiefs stuffed in all their pockets. The result was that they set the whole village in a commotion.

All 'Ntoni found when he got home in the evening was the women changing the brine in the casks or gossiping with the neighbours; or passing the time telling stories or asking each other riddles, which were all very well for the children, who sat up sleepy-eyed to listen to them. Master 'Ntoni would listen too, keeping one eye on the brine draining from the casks and nodding with approval when somebody told a particularly good story or when the children showed that they were quite as good at answering riddles as the grown-ups.

"The best story," 'Ntoni announced, "is about the two strangers who arrived here today, with so many silk handkerchiefs that it doesn't seem true! They slap their money down on the counter without even bothering to count it. They've seen half the world, they say, and Trezza and Aci Castello are nothing in comparison. That's something I've seen for myself. There are people in those places who spend their whole time enjoying themselves instead of salting anchovies; and women, dressed in silk, and with more rings on their fingers

than Our Lady of Ognina, walk about the streets looking for handsome sailors!"

The girls opened their eyes wide, and Master 'Ntoni
pricked up his ears too, just as he did when the children
were playing at their guessing games. Alessi was slowly
emptying the casks and passing them to Nunziata.
"When I'm grown-up," he said, "if I get married, I want
to marry you."

"There's time for that yet," Nunziata answered, perfectly seriously.

"There are towns as big as Catania, so big that if
you don't know your way about them you get lost,"
'Ntoni went on. "You can walk on and on between the
rows of houses until you lose your breath, without ever
seeing the sea or the country!"

"Master Cipolla's grandfather went to those places,"
said Master 'Ntoni. "That was where he made his
money. He never came back to Trezza; he only sent
back his money to his children."

"Poor man!" said Maruzza.

"See if you can guess this one," said Nunziata. "I've
two that shine, two that prick, four hooves and a brush.
What am I?"

"An ox!" Lia answered at once.

"You must have known it, you guessed it so quickly!"
her brother exclaimed.

"I should like to go to those places and get rich too,
like Master Cipolla," 'Ntoni went on.

"I should forget it if I were you," said his grandfather, who was full of satisfaction because of the rows
of casks standing in the yard. "Now we've got the anchovies to salt." But La Longa looked at her son anxiously, and said nothing, because whenever he talked
about going away she was reminded of the two who
had gone and not returned.

The rows of casks along the wall grew longer and longer, and Master 'Ntoni, putting another one in its place, with the stones on top, said: "Here's another. At All Saints all this will be money!"

'Ntoni laughed, like Master Fortunato when he talked about other people's money. "A fine sum of money!" he muttered, and went on thinking about the two strangers, who spent the day loafing about wherever they liked and lay on the benches at the tavern and rattled the money in their pockets. His mother looked at him as though she could read his thoughts, and the stories that they were telling in the yard did not make her laugh.

"He who eats these anchovies," said Cousin Anna, "will be the son of a crowned king, as handsome as the sun. He will ride on his white horse for a year, a month and a day until he reaches an enchanted fountain, flowing with milk and honey. There he will get off his horse to drink, and pick up a thimble, which my daughter Mara, who was taken there by the fairies, dropped when she was filling her pitcher. The king's son will use her thimble to drink out of, and fall in love with her; and then he'll ride for another year and a month and a day until he gets to Trezza, and his white horse will take him straight to the wash-house, where my daughter Mara will be spreading out her washing to dry; and the king's son will marry her, and put a ring on her finger; and then he'll put her behind him on his white horse and take her back to his kingdom!"

Alessi gaped as he listened, as though he could actually see the king's son on his white horse, galloping away with Cousin Anna's Mara on the crupper.

"And where will he take her to?" asked Lia.

"Far, far away, to his own country far beyond the sea, from which no one ever returns."

"Just like Alfio Mosca," said Nunziata. "I shouldn't like to go away with the king's son if I were never to return!"

"Your daughter hasn't got a dowry, so the king's son will never come and marry her," said 'Ntoni. "Everybody will turn his back on her, just as they do to people who have lost all their money."

"That's why my daughter is working here now—she's working to earn herself a dowry. After working all day at the wash-place, she comes here to earn a little extra. Isn't that right, Mara? Even if the king's son doesn't come, somebody else will. I know well enough what the way of the world is, and we have no right to complain. Why didn't you fall in love with my daughter, 'Ntoni, instead of falling for that Barbara, whose complexion's as yellow as saffron? Wasn't it because Barbara Zuppidda is well provided for? And when misfortune came and you lost what you owned, Barbara threw you over, as was perfectly natural!"

"You put up with everything," 'Ntoni replied sulkily. "They're right to call you Happy Heart!"

"Would it change anything if I wasn't Happy Heart? When you're penniless, the best thing to do is to go away, like Alfio Mosca."

"That's just what I say!" 'Ntoni declared.

"Leaving your own village, where even the stones know you, is worse than anything," said Mena. "It must be heartbreaking. Blessed the bird that makes its nest where it was born!"

"Bravo, St. Agatha!" her grandfather said. "That's what I call talking sense!"

"Yes," muttered 'Ntoni, "and in the meantime, while we toil and sweat to build your nest, no doubt we'll have to go short of food. When we do manage to buy back the house by the medlar tree, we'll still have to go on wearing ourselves out from Monday to Saturday. We shall be no better off than we were before!"

"What would you like to be, 'Ntoni, since you don't want to work? A lawyer?"

"I don't want to be a lawyer," 'Ntoni growled, and went off sulkily to bed.

But after this he thought of nothing but the gay and carefree life that other people lived; and in the evening, to avoid listening to the stupid talk, he stood outside the door, leaning against the wall, watching the people go by and meditating on his unhappy lot; at least he got a little rest that way for the following day, when he would have to begin doing the same thing all over again, just like Alfio Mosca's donkey, which swelled its back when it saw Alfio coming with the pack-saddle, actually waiting to be harnessed. "That's what we are!" he muttered. "Donkeys! Beasts of burden!" It was obvious that he was utterly fed up with the life he was leading, and could think of nothing but going away and making his fortune, like the two strangers. His mother, poor woman, put her arms round his shoulders, spoke to him endearingly, with tears in her eyes, and looked at him searchingly, trying to read and touch his heart. He said it would be better, both for him and for them, if he went away, and when he came back they would all be happy. The poor woman did not sleep a wink all night, and wetted the pillow with her tears. In the end his grandfather noticed it, and called 'Ntoni outside the door, next to the little shrine, and asked him what was the matter.

"Well, what is it? Tell your grandfather!"

'Ntoni shrugged his shoulders. His grandfather went on nodding his head and spitting and scratching his head, searching for words.

"It's no use denying it, you've got something on your

mind, my boy; something that wasn't there before! He who associates with cripples ends by limping!"

"What's the matter is that I'm a poor man!"

"Well? What is there new about that? So were your father and your grandfather before you. The fewer your desires, the richer you are! It's better to put up with your lot than to complain."

"That's a fine consolation!"

This time the old man found the words, because his heart sprang to his lips.

"At least don't talk like that in front of your mother!"

"My mother? It would have been better if she had never borne me!"

"Yes!" replied Master 'Ntoni. "Yes! If she had known you were going to talk like this, it would have been better if she had never borne you!"

For a moment 'Ntoni was at a loss for words.

"Well," he said eventually. "What I'm going to do is for her sake, for your sake, and for everybody's sake. I want to make my mother rich, that's what I want to do! Now we're working ourselves to the bone to buy back the house and for Mena's dowry. Next Lia will grow up, and with a few bad seasons we'll be back where we were before. I'm sick and tired of this life! I want to change my condition, my own and the whole family's. I want mother and you and Mena and Alessi and all of us to be rich!"

Master 'Ntoni's eyes opened wide. He seemed to want to chew over the words he had just heard before he could swallow them.

"Rich!" he exclaimed. "Rich! And what shall we do when we are rich?"

'Ntoni scratched his head and started racking his brains, trying to think what they would do when they were rich.

"We shall do what the others do," he said. "We shan't do anything at all! . . . We shall go and live in town, and do nothing, and eat macaroni and meat every day!"

"Very well, go and live in town, then. I want to die where I was born." Master 'Ntoni's head fell on his chest at the thought that the house in which he was born was no longer his. "You're young, and you don't understand . . . you don't understand. You'll see what it's like when you no longer sleep in your own bed and you don't see the sun shining through your own window! You'll see! I'm telling you, and I'm an old man!" The poor, bent old man started coughing, as though he were going to suffocate. He shook his head sadly. "Every bird is happy in its own nest. Do you see those sparrows? Do you see them? They've always nested there, and they always will, and they'll never want to go away."

"I'm not a sparrow," 'Ntoni answered. "I'm not a bird, and I'm not an animal; and I don't want to live like a dog on a chain, or like Alfio Mosca's donkey, or a mule on a chain-pump, turning the same wheel all the time, and I don't want to starve to death in the gutter, or end up as a meal for the dogfish."

"Instead you ought to thank God that you were born here, and shun the idea of going away and dying far away from the stones that know you. He who changes the old for the new changes for the worse! You're afraid of having to earn the bread you eat, that's what's the matter with you. When your great grandfather left me the Provvidenza and five mouths to feed, I was younger than you, and I wasn't afraid! I did my duty without grumbling, and I do it still; and I pray God to help me to do it as long as I live, just as your father did before you, and your brother as well, God rest his soul, who wasn't afraid to go and do his duty. Your mother, confined to the four walls of the house, did her duty too, poor woman, and you don't know how much she has wept, and how much she weeps now that you want to go away. In the morning your sister finds the sheet wet with her tears. But she keeps silent and does not talk of the things that you propose to do; and she too has worked and struggled like a poor ant all her life. All her life she has worked and struggled—even before she had cause for tears, when she gave you the breast, and before you knew how to button up your own trousers, and before you felt tempted to move your legs and roam the world like a gipsy!"

'Ntoni ended by breaking down and crying like a baby, because at bottom he had a good heart; but by the next day he had made up his mind to go away again. In the morning it was with the greatest reluctance that he allowed himself to be loaded up with gear, and he carried it down to the sea grumbling all the way. "Just like Alfio Mosca's donkey!" he muttered. "As soon as it gets light it stretches its neck to see if he's coming with the pack-saddle!" After they had dropped the nets he let Alessi do the gentle rowing necessary to keep the boat on its course, and sat with his arms crossed, gazing at the distant horizon, where lay the big cities where people had nothing to do except enjoy themselves all day long, or thinking about the two sailors who had been in those places and returned, and had now left the village again. He thought they had nothing to do in the world except go from one tavern to the next, spending the money in their pockets. In the evening, after the boat had been tidied and the gear put away, to avoid having to look at his long face, the family let him roam round the village like a stray dog, without a penny in his pockets.

"What's the matter, 'Ntoni?" La Longa would say to

him, looking him timidly in the face, with her eyes bright with tears, because the poor woman guessed what was on his mind. "Surely you can tell your mother!" He either did not reply or replied that nothing was the matter. But in the end he told her what was on his mind. His grandfather and the others wanted to be the death of him, he said, and he couldn't stand it any longer. He wanted to go away and make his fortune, as others had done.

His mother listened, and had no spirit to speak. Her eyes were full of tears, so painful to her were the things that he said, weeping and stamping his feet and tearing his hair. The poor woman would have liked to speak and throw her arms round his neck and weep too, to prevent him from going; but when she tried to speak her lips trembled and she couldn't.

"Listen," she said. "Go away, if you want to, but you won't find me here when you come back; because I'm old and tired now, and I shan't be able to stand this new sorrow!"

'Ntoni tried to reassure her; he would soon be back, he said, with his pockets full of money, and then they would all be happy. Maruzza, still looking him in the eyes, shook her head sadly and said no, no, when he came back she would no longer be there.

"I feel old," she said. "I feel old. Look at me, 'Ntoni! I no longer have the strength to weep as I did when they brought me the news of your father and your brother. When I go to the wash-house I come back in the evening exhausted; it used not to be like that. No, my son, I'm no longer young and strong. When your father and your brother were alive, I was young and strong. The heart gets worn out, too, you see, like old clothes, which wear out bit by bit in the wash. I lack spirit now, and I'm afraid of everything; everything's too much for me now, just as though I were in the sea and every wave passed over my head. Go away, if you want to; but let me close my eyes first!"

Her face was wet with tears; but she didn't know she was weeping, and she thought she could see her son Luca and her husband before her, when they went away never to return.

"So I shall never see you again," she said. "One by one the house is emptying; and who will there be to look after the poor orphans when your poor old grand-father goes too? Oh! Our Lady of the Sorrows!"

She held her son's head on her breast, as though he were leaving immediately, and kept feeling his face and his shoulders. 'Ntoni couldn't stand it any longer, and started kissing her and talking to her with his face close to hers.

"All right!" he said. "If you don't want me to go, I shan't go! Don't talk to me like that, don't! All right, I'll go on working like Alfio Mosca's donkey, which they'll push into a ditch to die when it can't pull the cart any longer! Does that satisfy you? For heaven's sake stop crying like that! Look how grandfather has slaved all his life! And now he's old, and he's still slaving away as though it were the first day! He's still try-ing to drag himself out of the mire! That's what our lot is!"

"Don't you believe that everyone has his troubles? There's a nail for every hole, a new one if not an old. Look how Master Cipolla has to chase after his Brasi to prevent him from throwing away God's good gifts, for which he has worked and sweated all his life, into La Vespa's apron! And just look at Massaro Filippo, rich as he is, who gazes at the sky and tells his beads and prays for rain for his vineyard every time a cloud passes! And Uncle Crocifisso, who goes without food to save money, and is always quarrelling with someone or other! Do you suppose those two strange sailors haven't got their troubles too? Who knows whether they'll find their mothers still alive when they get back home? . . . And as for ourselves, if we manage to buy back the house by the medlar tree, when we've got grain in the attic and beans for the winter and we've married off Mena, what shall we lack for then? When I'm buried, and your poor old grandfather is dead too, and Alessi is grown-up and can earn his own living, you can go away and do what you like! But then you won't go, I tell you, because then you'll understand what we all felt when we saw your heart set on leaving home, although we all went about our business without saying anything. Then you won't have the spirit to leave your village, where you were born and grew up, and your dead, buried under the marble over there, which has been worn smooth by all the knees that have knelt on it on Sundays, in front of the altar of Our Lady of the Sorrows!"

After this 'Ntoni gave up talking about leaving home and going away to make his fortune, because every time his mother saw him sitting at the threshold looking a little glum she started devouring him with her eyes. The poor woman really had grown so pale and tired and exhausted that as soon as she had nothing to do she sat down, with her hands in her lap and her back as bent as that of her father-in-law, so that it was a pitiful sight to see. But she little suspected that she herself was about to leave for a destination in which she would rest for ever, under the smooth marble in the church, leaving behind all whom she loved, all those who in turn tormented her poor, distracted heart.

At Catania the cholera had broken out, with the result that everyone who could left the town and went to live in the villages or the country round about. All these strangers with money to spend brought good fortune to Trezza and Ognina. But if anyone mentioned selling a dozen casks of anchovies, the dealers pulled a long face and said that because of the cholera there was no money about. "Don't people eat anchovies any more?" Piedipapera asked them. But he told Master 'Ntoni, and anyone else with anchovies for sale, that because of the cholera people no longer wanted to ruin their digestion with anchovies and such disgusting stuff; they preferred eating meat and macaroni, so it was advisable to be reasonable about the price. This was something that the Malavoglia had not taken into account. So in order not to be caught napping, La Longa, while her menfolk were at sea, started going and offering eggs and new bread for sale at the cottages where the strangers lived, and managed to make a little money that way. But you had to be very careful whom you spoke to, and not even accept a pinch of snuff from anyone you didn't know. You had to walk in the very middle of the road, and keep well away from the walls, for you never knew what you might pick up; and you had to take care not to sit on stones or on low walls. Once, when coming back from Aci Castello with her basket on her arm, La Longa felt so tired that her legs felt like lead and started trembling, and she gave in to the temptation of sitting down for a few minutes' rest on the four smooth stones which stand in a row in the shadow of the fig tree near the shrine just outside the village. She did not notice it at the time, but afterwards she realised that a stranger, who looked tired too, poor fellow, had been sitting there a few moments earlier, and had left on the stones some traces of something that looked like filthy oil. In short, she caught the cholera too. She reached home almost in a state of collapse, looking as yellow as a votive tablet to Our Lady, and with black rings under her eyes. Mena, who was alone in the house, burst into tears at the sight of her, and Lia ran to gather some rosemary and mallow leaves. Mena trembled like a leaf while making her bed, though her mother, sitting on the high chair, with her yellow face and the black rings under her eyes, was careful to say: "It's nothing! Don't be nervous! I shall be all right when I'm in bed!" She tried to help, but her strength failed her, and she had to sit down again.

"Holy Mother of God!" Mena kept muttering. "Holy Mother of God! And the men are at sea!" Lia burst into tears.

When Master 'Ntoni came home with his grandsons and saw the door half-closed and the light burning, he started tearing his hair. Maruzza was in bed by this time, and her eyes, in the semi-darkness and at that time of day, looked as though the life had already been sucked out of them, and her lips were as black as pitch. At that time neither the doctor nor the chemist went out after sunset, and even the neighbours barred their doors and filled every nook and cranny with pictures of the saints for fear of the cholera. So poor Maruzza got no help, except from her family, who dashed frantically about the house at seeing her departing like this; they did not know what to do, and pounded their heads against the wall in their despair and grief. Then La Longa, seeing that there was no more hope, asked them to put on her breast the piece of cotton dipped in holy oil that she had bought at Easter, and asked them to leave the candle alight, as they had done when Master 'Ntoni had been dying, because she wanted to see her whole family round her bed, and give herself the satisfaction of looking at them one by one with those wide-open eyes of hers from which the sight had nearly departed. Lia wept in a heart-breaking manner, and all the others, who were as white as a sheet, looked at each other as though appealing for help, and they forced themselves not to break down and weep in the presence of the dying woman, though Maruzza was perfectly well aware of their sorrow, though she could no longer see it, and she was sorry that her going left those poor people so grief-stricken. She kept calling them one by one, in a hoarse voice and, though she could no longer move her hand, she tried to raise it to bless them, as though she knew she were leaving them a treasure. " 'Ntoni," she kept saying in a barely audible voice, " 'Ntoni, you're the eldest, and you must look after these orphans." Hearing her talk like this while she was still alive, the others could not help breaking down and sobbing.

They spent the whole night like this in front of the little bed, in which Maruzza now lay motionless, until the candle flickered and went out, when she departed too, and the dawn came in through the window, as pale as the dead woman; her face was drawn and had grown sharp like a knife, and her lips were black. But Mena could not stop kissing her on the lips, and talking to her as though she could still hear. 'Ntoni sobbed and beat himself on the breast. "Oh, mother," he cried, "I wanted to leave you, but you went first!" Alessi, even when he grew old and had white hair himself, never forgot the sight of his mother lying on her death-bed, with her white hair and yellow face, which had grown sharp, like a knife.

Towards evening they came in a great hurry to take the body away, and no one thought of paying a visit of condolence, because everyone thought of his own skin, and even Don Giammaria, when he came to sprinkle the holy water, stayed outside on the threshold, carefully gathering up his Franciscan habit and holding it so that it did not touch the ground. The chemist told everybody that this was typical of the selfish priest that he was. He, the chemist, wasn't afraid of the cholera, and if he had been brought a prescription he would have opened his shop, even at night. He said it was nonsense to believe that the cholera was sprinkled in the streets and behind doors. "That shows that it must be he who spreads it," Don Giammaria went about whispering. This made everyone in the village want to murder the chemist; but he only laughed, cackling like a hen, just like Don Silvestro, and said: "What! I, who am a Republican, spreading the cholera? Mind you, if I were a clerk, or a Government toady, I don't say I wouldn't!" But the Malavoglia were left alone, with Maruzza's empty bed.

For a long time after she was taken away they did not open the door. It was lucky that Master 'Ntoni, like the prudent squirrel, had laid in stocks in good time, and that they had beans and wood and oil; otherwise they would have died of hunger, because no one went to see whether they were alive or dead. Then they put black handkerchiefs round their necks and gradually started venturing out into the street again, pale-faced and still dazed by what had happened. Maruzza had been one of the first in the village to go down with the cholera, and all the women asked them from a distance how it had happened; but when Don Michele passed, or anyone else who ate the King's bread and wore a gold-braided hat, they would cast a terrified glance at him and hurriedly shut themselves up again in their houses. There was a great accumulation of filth throughout the village, and not so much as a chicken was to be seen in the street. Even Mastro

Cirino never showed himself, and didn't ring for matins and vespers, for he too ate Government bread, because of the twelve *tarì* a month he received as communal beadle, and he feared he might be murdered as a Government toady.

Now that Vanni Pizzuto, Don Silvestro and the rest had gone to ground like rabbits, Don Michele was the undisputed master of the streets, and except for him there was no one to walk up and down outside the Zuppiddi's closed door. Unfortunately there was no one to see him, except the Malavoglia, who had no more to lose and therefore sat motionless on the threshold, with their chins in their hands, looking to see who was passing by. As all other doors were shut, Don Michele would look at St. Agatha. He also looked at her to show 'Ntoni that he wasn't afraid of anyone, and besides, Mena, pale as she was, really did look like St. Agatha; and her young sister, wearing her black handkerchief, was growing up into a very pretty girl too.

Poor Mena suddenly felt twenty years older. She started treating Lia as La Longa had treated her. She felt she must watch over her like a hen, and that the whole responsibility for the house rested on her shoulders. She got used to remaining alone with her sister when the men were at sea, with that empty bed always before her eyes. When she had nothing to do she sat with her hands in her lap, staring at it, and then she felt that her mother had really left her; and when she heard them saying in the street that so-and-so or so-and-so had died, she said to herself that that was how they must have spoken when La Longa died—La Longa, who had left her alone with her orphaned sister, who wore a black handkerchief just as she did.

From time to time Nunziata or Cousin Anna would drop in, with a long face and without saying anything, and would stand at the door, looking up and down the deserted street, with their hands under their aprons. Men coming back from the sea would walk past hurriedly and cautiously, carrying their nets; and passing carts did not even stop at the tavern.

Who knew where Alfio Mosca might be going with his cart at that moment? Or whether, being all alone in the world, he had been flung in a ditch to die of the cholera? From time to time Piedipapera passed, gazing all around him and looking as though he were starving; and Uncle Crocifisso, to whom people all over the village owed money, would pass on his way to find out what state of health his debtors were in, because if they died it meant that he would lose his money. Even Don Giammaria, going to give extreme unction, was always in a great hurry, walking with his cassock tucked up, accompanied by a barefooted boy ringing the bell, because there was no sign of Mastro Cirino. The sound of that bell in the deserted streets, in which not so much as a dog was to be seen—even Don Franco kept his door half-shut—was heartrending.

The only person who went about as usual, both by day and night, was La Locca, with her white, dishevelled hair; she went and sat outside the house by the medlar tree as before, or waited on the shore for the boats to come in. Not even the cholera wanted her, poor soul.

The strangers had disappeared from the village like the birds in winter time, and there were no customers for fish, and everybody said that after the cholera there would be famine. Master 'Ntoni had to dip into the money laid aside for buying back the house, and little by little it started dwindling away. But all he could think of was that Maruzza had not died in her own house, and he could not get it out of his mind. When

'Ntoni saw the money going he shook his head too.

When the cholera at last disappeared, and barely half the money they had scraped together with so much effort was left, he started saying that things could not go on like this, that he couldn't stand these continual ups and downs any more, and that it would be better to have one good try to get out of the mire for good and all, and that he couldn't stand these poverty-stricken surroundings in which his mother had died.

"Don't you remember that your mother asked you to look after Mena?" Master 'Ntoni asked.

"What good can I be to Mena if I stay here? Tell me that!"

Mena looked at him timidly, but with eyes which read his heart, like his mother had done, and dared not say anything. But once, clinging to the doorpost, she said to him:

"It doesn't matter about helping me, provided only that you don't leave us alone! Now that mother is no longer here, I feel lost in the world, and I no longer care about anything. But I'm sorry for Lia, who will be left without anyone in the world if you go away, like Nunziata when her father went away!"

"It's no use!" 'Ntoni answered. "It's no use! I can't help you if I haven't got any money. The proverb says God helps him who helps himself. When I've earned some money I'll come back, and then we shall all be happy!"

Lia and Alessi opened their eyes wide and looked at him in dismay, and his grandfather's chin dropped on his chest. But at last Master 'Ntoni said:

"Now that you've got neither father nor mother, you can do what you like. As long as I'm alive, I'll look after these children, and when I'm dead the Lord will provide for them."

As 'Ntoni insisted on going, Mena got all his things ready, as his mother would have done, and she thought to herself that while her brother was away he would be just like Alfio Mosca, and have no one to look after him. And while she mended his clothes and sewed his shirts her thoughts ran on so many things that her heart was full.

"I can't bear to pass the house by the medlar tree any more," she said to her grandfather when she sat beside him. "It upsets me too much, after all the things that have happened since we left it."

She wept as she got her brother's things ready, as though she would never see him again. At last, when everything was ready, his grandfather took the lad aside to give him some parting advice, for when he was out in the world on his own he would have only himself to rely on, because no member of the family would be there to tell him what to do or to share his troubles; and he gave him a little money, in case he should ever have need of it, as well as his leather-lined coat, for which he had no more use, now that he was an old man.

The children, seeing the preparations for their elder brother's departure, followed him timidly about the house, hardly daring to talk to him any more, as though he were already a stranger.

"It's just like when my father went away," said Nunziata, standing at the doorway when she came to say good-bye. Nobody else said anything after this.

The neighbours came one by one to say good-bye to 'Ntoni Malavoglia, and then stood and waited in the street to watch him go. He put his bundle on his back and picked up his boots, but then kept putting off his departure, as though his heart and his legs were failing him at the last moment. He looked about him, as

though to impress the house and the village and everything firmly on his mind, and his face was as distraught as those of the others. His grandfather took his
stick to accompany him as far as Catania, and Mena
wept quietly in a corner. "Come on then!" 'Ntoni said
at last. "I must be off! After all, I'm going to come back!
I came back once before when I went away to be a
sailor." Then he kissed Mena and Lia and said good-
bye to the neighbours and made as if to go, but Mena
ran after him, sobbing loudly at the top of her voice,
quite beside herself, and shrieking: "Now what will
mother say? Now what will mother say?"—as though
her mother could still see and speak; and she told him
once more how, when he had wanted to go away before, her mother had wept all night, so that in the
morning, when she had made the bed, she had found
the sheet all wet. For this was something that had
stuck in her mind more than anything else.

'Ntoni had gone some distance before Alessi plucked
up courage to shout: "Good-bye, 'Ntoni!" and wave to
him; and then Lia started shrieking.

"That's just how my father went away," said Nunziata, who had stayed by the door.

Before turning the corner of the Strada del Nero,
'Ntoni, who had tears in his eyes too, turned and
waved. Then Mena closed the door and went to sit in a
corner with Lia, who was sobbing at the top of her
voice. "Now there's one more missing from the house,"
she said. "If we were in the house by the medlar tree, it
would seem as empty as a church!"

As one by one all those who loved her departed, she
really felt lost in the world. And Nunziata, who was
there with her little ones about her, kept saying:

"That's just how my father went away!"

TWELVE   Now that Master 'Ntoni had no one left but Alessi to help him manage the boat, he had to take on hired help, either Uncle Nunzio, who had an enormous number of children and whose wife was ill, or La Locca's son, who came and complained at the door that his mother was dying of hunger, and that his Uncle Crocifisso refused to give him anything, saying that he had been ruined by the cholera, because so many people had died, and so cheated him of his money, with the result that he had caught the cholera himself—though he had not died of it, La Locca's son added, shaking his head sadly. "If he had died, my mother and I and the whole family would have had enough to eat," he said. "We spent two days looking after him, with La Vespa, and he looked as though he were going to die at any minute, but he got better instead!"

But often the Malavoglia didn't earn enough to pay Uncle Nunzio's or La Locca's son's wages, and then they had to dip into the money they had so laboriously scraped together towards buying back the house by the medlar tree. Each time Mena took the stocking from under the mattress, she and her grandfather sighed. La Locca's son wasn't to blame, poor chap. To earn his pay he would have been willing to cut himself in pieces; it was all the fault of the fish that refused to be caught; and when the Provvidenza came slowly home in the evening, with the sail flapping idly and the men using their oars because the wind was slack, La Locca's son would say to Master 'Ntoni: "Give me wood to chop or vine-branches to tie up. I can go on working till midnight if you want me to, as I used to do for Uncle Crocifisso. I don't want to take my pay if I haven't earned it!"

Master 'Ntoni, after thinking it over for a time, decided with an aching heart to talk things over with Mena. She was as sensible as her mother had been, and she was the only one left with whom he could talk things over. It would be best, he said, to sell the Provvidenza, which was no longer profitable, and indeed was a drain on them now, because of the money that had to be paid out to Nunzio or La Locca's son. If they didn't sell her, little by little she would eat up all the money they had laid aside for the house. The Provvidenza was old, and money had continually to be spent on her to patch her up and keep her afloat. Later, if 'Ntoni came back and things grew better again, as they had been when they had managed to save some money, they would buy another boat and christen her the Provvidenza again.

On Sunday, after mass, he went to the village square to talk to Piedipapera about it. Piedipapera shrugged his shoulders, shook his head, said that the Provvidenza was good for nothing but firewood and, talking all the time, led him down to the shore, from where the Provvidenza's patches were visible under the new pitch; and he kicked her with his lame leg, as he had done before. Besides, he said, the fishing business was in a bad way. People were thinking of selling their boats, and newer ones than the Provvidenza at that, rather than of buying new ones. In any case, who was there who could possibly buy the Provvidenza? Master Cipolla wouldn't be interested in an old wreck like that. It was a matter for Uncle Crocifisso, but just now Uncle Crocifisso had other things on his mind, what with that crazy La Vespa, who was running after all the single men in the village and driving him to distraction. In the end Piedipapera agreed, in the sacred name of friendship, to find a suitable moment to mention the matter to Uncle Crocifisso, that is to say, if Master 'Ntoni had really made up his mind to get rid of the Provvidenza at all costs and was willing to let her go for a song; for he, Piedipapera, knew how to handle Uncle Crocifisso.

However, when Piedipapera drew Uncle Crocifisso aside by the cattle trough and finally broached the matter, Uncle Crocifisso shrugged his shoulders and shook his head and wanted to go away without even discussing it. Poor Piedipapera had to hold him by the coat and force him to stop and listen. He shook him, and held him firmly by the coat with his arm round his shoulders, and talked into his ear. "You're a fool if you let a chance like this slip!" he said. "You can get the Provvidenza for a song. Master 'Ntoni's only selling her because he can't carry on, now that his grandson has left him. You could have her run by Nunzio or La Locca's son; they are dying of hunger, and they'd work for you for practically nothing, and you'd have all the profit! I tell you it's the chance of a life-time, and you're a fool if you don't take advantage of it. The boat's still as good as new. Master 'Ntoni knew what he was doing when he had her built. Listen to me! It's a golden opportunity, I tell you, just like the lupin deal!"

Uncle Crocifisso wouldn't listen. His face was yellow from the cholera, and he nearly had tears in his eyes. He tried to shake free from Piedipapera's embraces, nearly leaving his coat behind in the process. "I'm not interested!" he kept saying. "I'm not in the least interested! You don't know what troubles I've got on my mind, Piedipapera. Everyone's after my property; they're all trying to suck my blood, like a lot of leeches. Pizzuto's running after La Vespa now!"

"Why don't you marry La Vespa yourself? She's your flesh and blood, isn't she, she and her plot of land? If you married her, she wouldn't be like an extra mouth to feed, because she's a fine housekeeper, and the bread you gave her to eat wouldn't be thrown away. She'd be an unpaid servant in the house, and you'd have her plot of land into the bargain. Listen to me, Uncle Crocifisso, I tell you this is a golden opportunity, just like the lupin deal!"

Meanwhile, Master 'Ntoni was waiting outside Pizzuto's shop like a soul in torment, watching Piedipapera and Uncle Crocifisso, and trying to guess what the outcome of their talk would be, for they seemed to be quarrelling. Eventually Piedipapera came over and reported Uncle Crocifisso's first offer, and then he went back and started talking to him all over again; and he went on darting to and fro across the square, like a shuttle on the loom, dragging his lame leg behind him, until he had succeeded in getting them to agree. He told Master 'Ntoni that he had got a very good price for the Provvidenza, and assured Uncle Crocifisso that he had got her for a song. Then he arranged for the sale of all the gear in the same way, for now the Malavoglia had no more use for it. But when they came to take away the lobster pots and the nets and the rods and gaffs and all the rest Master 'Ntoni felt as though his insides were being torn out.

"Don't worry," Piedipapera said to him. "I'll see about getting work for you and Alessi. But you'll have to be satisfied with very little, you know. You know the proverb—a young man's strength and an old man's wisdom. I leave to your generosity the question of what you owe me for arranging the sale!"

"In hard times one has to live on crusts," Master 'Ntoni replied. "Necessity clips the wings of generosity."

"All right, all right, let's leave it at that," said Piedipapera, and he actually went off to talk to Master

Cipolla at the chemist's shop, to which Don Silvestro had once more succeeded in luring him, as well as Massaro Filippo and one or two other village bigwigs, to discuss the affairs of the commune; after all, it was their money which was at stake, and there was no sense in counting for nothing in the village when you were well off and paid higher taxes than other people. "With all your money you could help poor Master 'Ntoni to make a living," Piedipapera said to Master Fortunato. "You could easily find work for him and his son Alessi. You know that there's nobody who knows more about fishing than he does, and he'd be satisfied with very little, because they haven't a crust to eat. And you'd do very well out of it into the bargain, Master Fortunato, you take it from me!"

Master Fortunato, being tackled at such a moment, could hardly refuse, and he and Piedipapera started haggling about what the rate of pay should be, because times were hard and Master Fortunato's men had very little to do, and it was really an act of charity to take on Master 'Ntoni at all.

"Very well, I'll take him on, then," Master Fortunato eventually said, "but only on condition that he comes and asks me himself. Would you believe it? I'm told that he has actually borne me a grudge ever since I broke off my son's engagement to Mena! A fine marriage that would have been! And on top of it the Malavoglia have the impudence to bear me a grudge!"

Don Silvestro, Massaro Filippo and Piedipapera, all who were present, in fact, hastened to say that Master Fortunato was, of course, perfectly right. Brasi had done nothing but run after women ever since the idea of marriage had been planted in his head. It was a continual worry to his poor father; and now the Mangiacarrubbe girl had set her cap at him, since he was the kind of young man at whom women set their caps. At least she was a pretty girl, with a good pair of shoulders, and not old and losing her hair, like La Vespa. But La Vespa owned a plot of land, and the Mangiacarrubbe girl, so they said, owned nothing but her black tresses.

Now that Brasi's father had him once more firmly anchored to the house because of the cholera—he no longer went and hid himself in the lava field or at the chemist's or in the sacristy—the Mangiacarrubbe girl knew very well how to set about fascinating him. In the crowd coming out of church after mass she would quickly brush past him, grazing him with her elbow; or she would wait for him demurely at the door, with her hands folded and her silk handkerchief over her head, and throw him a look of the kind that young men find devastating, and then she would turn and adjust the corners of the handkerchief under her chin to see if he were following her; or when he appeared at the end of the street she would conceal herself behind the basil in the window-box and look at him with her big, irresistible black eyes. But if Brasi stopped to gape at her she would turn her back and lower her head, blushing deeply, and put the corner of her apron in her mouth. In the end, since Brasi could not pluck up courage to speak to her, she took matters into her own hands and spoke to him.

"Listen, Brasi," she said, "why won't you leave me in peace? I know that I'm not for you. It's better that you should give up passing this way, because the more I see you the more I should like to see you, and it's making me the talk of the whole village! Venera Zuppidda puts her head out of the window every time she sees you pass, and then she goes and talks about it to everybody, though she'd do better to keep her eyes on that little minx of a daughter of hers, Barbara, who has turned the street into a public square, what with all the people who come this way because of her. Her mother never mentions how many times Don Michele walks up and down in front of the house to see Barbara at the window!"

After this Brasi was no longer to be shaken off. He couldn't have been driven from the street even with cudgels. He was perpetually hanging about, with his arms dangling from his shoulders, his nose in the air and his mouth wide open, just like Giufà. The Mangia-carrubbe girl changed her silk handkerchief or wore a different glass bead necklace every day, just as though she were a queen. Venera Zuppidda said she was putting all her goods in the shop window; but that half-wit Brasi took it all for solid gold, and he was reduced to such a state that he wouldn't even have been afraid of his father, if he had come to box his ears. People said it was the hand of God, come to chastise Master Fortunato for his pride; and that Master Fortunato would have done a hundred times better to have married his son to the Malavoglia girl, who at least had a small dowry and didn't fritter it away on handkerchiefs and necklaces. Mena, however, never so much as showed her nose at the window, because it didn't seem right, now that her mother was dead, and she always wore a black handkerchief. Besides, she had her young sister to look after and be a mother to, and she had no one else to help her about the house. She had to go to the wash-place and fetch water from the fountain and take their food to the men when they were out at work. She was no longer like St. Agatha, who was never seen because she was always at the loom; she had little time to spend at her loom now. Don Michele, ever since Venera Zuppidda had announced from her balcony, with her distaff in her hand, that she would tear his eyes out with it if he went on hanging about the street after her Barbara, used to walk up and down the Strada del Nero ten times a day, to show that he wasn't afraid of Venera Zuppidda and her distaff; and when he passed the Malavoglia house he used to slow down to have a look at the pretty girls who were growing up in it.

When the menfolk came back from the sea in the evening, they always found everything ready; the table was always laid and the pot simmering over the fire. The table was too big for them now, and they felt lost sitting round it. They would shut the door and eat their meal in peace. Then they would sit at the door, clasping their knees in their hands, and rest after the day's work. At least they weren't short of anything, and they no longer had to dip into the money laid aside for the house. Master 'Ntoni always had the house before his eyes, because it was only a few yards away, with the windows shut and the medlar tree standing against the wall in the yard. Maruzza had not died in the house by the medlar tree; and perhaps he wouldn't die in it either; but their savings were slowly starting to mount again, and now that Alessi was growing up—he was a good lad, of the real Malavoglia stamp—one day they would go back to it. When they had married the girls off and bought back the house, and if they could buy a boat as well, they would lack for nothing, and he would be able to die content.

Nunziata and Cousin Anna used to come and sit with them on the stones after dinner and talk; for they had been left alone and abandoned in the world, just like the Malavoglia; it made them feel almost like relatives. Nunziata, who arrived with her little ones like a hen surrounded by her brood, seemed to be completely at home. Alessi would sit next to her and say: "Did you finish your bundle today?" or "Will you be helping Massaro Filippo with the vintage on Monday? Now that the olive season's coming, you'll be able to earn money even if you don't get any washing; and you'll be able to take your brother with you, because they'll give him two soldi a day now." Nunziata would gravely discuss all her plans with him and ask his advice, and they would go aside and talk things over as solemnly as though they already had white hair. "They've learned young, because they've seen so many misfortunes," said Master 'Ntoni. "Misfortunes teach one sense." Sometimes Alessi, sitting and clasping his knees just like his grandfather, would say to Nunziata:

"Will you marry me when I'm grown-up?"

"There's time yet," she would reply.

"Yes, I know there's time, but it would be better to make up your mind now, because then I shall know what to do. Lia's starting to wear long dresses and handkerchiefs with roses on them, and you've got your boys to think about as well. We must manage to buy a boat; having a boat will help us to buy back the house. Grandfather wants the house back, and so do I, because I can find my way about it in the dark. There's a fine, big yard for the gear, and the sea's right at hand. When my sisters are married, we can put my grandfather in the big, sunny room leading out into the yard. When the poor old man can't go to sea any longer, he'll be able to stay by the door in the yard, and in summer he'll be quite near the medlar tree, to give him some shade. Our room will be the one facing the kitchen garden, don't you agree? You'll have the kitchen next door. Like that we shall have everything at hand, shan't we? When my brother 'Ntoni comes back we'll give the room to him, and go upstairs to the attic. You'll have the kitchen or the garden right at the bottom of the stairs."

"The fireplace in the kitchen wants mending," said Nunziata. "The last time I cooked the supper there, when poor Maruzza was in no state to do anything, the pot had to be propped up with stones."

"Yes, I know," Alessi answered, nodding his head with his chin in his hands. His eyes were far away, as though he could see Nunziata in front of the hearth and his mother sitting in despair beside the bed. "You know the house by the medlar tree so well that you could find your way about it in the dark too. Mother always said you were a good girl."

"They've sown onions in the garden now, and they've grown as big as oranges."

"Do you like onions?"

"I have to. When we've no money, the children and I always eat them. They help the bread down, and they're cheap."

"That's why there's such a big sale for them. Uncle Crocifisso didn't want to sow cabbages and lettuces at the house by the medlar tree because he's got them at his own house, so he had nothing but onions sown. But we'll sow broccoli, and cauliflowers. . . . They're good, aren't they?"

The girl, sitting at the threshold clasping her knees, was staring into the distance too; and then she started singing, while Alessi listened intently.

"But there's time yet," she said eventually.

"Yes," said Alessi. "First we must marry Mena and then Lia, and your brothers have got to be placed. But it would be better to make up your mind now!"

"When Nunziata sings," said Mena, appearing in the doorway, "it's a sign that it'll be fine tomorrow, and that she'll be able to go to the wash-place." Cousin

Anna was in the same situation, because the wash-place was her farm and her vineyard, and her delight was to have plenty of washing, particularly now that her son Rocco was spending more time than ever at the tavern, getting over being jilted by the Mangia-carrubbe minx.

"Not every evil comes to harm us," observed Master 'Ntoni. "Perhaps it will result in your Rocco learning sense. In the same way it will do my 'Ntoni good to be away from home for a time; because when he comes back he'll be tired of roaming the world, and he'll see everything here in a new light and will stop grumbling at everything. And if we ever manage to have a boat at sea and move into that house over there again, he'll realise what a fine thing it is to sit at the doorway in the evening after you've come home tired and had a good day, and to see a light in the room where you've seen it so often, the room in which you've seen the faces of all those who were dear to you in the world. But now so many have departed, one by one, and the room is dark and the door is shut, as though they put the key in their pockets when they went away for ever."

After an interval the old man went on: "'Ntoni shouldn't have gone. He should have known that I'm an old man, and that if I die these children will have nobody left."

"If we buy back the house by the medlar tree while he's away, he will have a surprise when he comes back," said Mena. "He'll come and look for us here!"

Master 'Ntoni shook his head sadly.

"There's time yet," he said eventually, just like Nunziata.

"If 'Ntoni comes back with a lot of money, he'll buy the house," Cousin Anna remarked.

Master 'Ntoni made no reply. The whole village had decided that 'Ntoni, having been away seeking his fortune for such a long time, was bound to come back with a lot of money, and there were many who were already envious of him, and wanted to leave everything and go away in search of fortune, too. You couldn't altogether blame them, because, when all was said and done, they had nothing to leave but a lot of whining children and complaining women; the only one who lacked the spirit to leave his complaining woman was that fool, La Locca's son—you know what kind of a mother he had—and Rocco Spatu, whose heart was set on the tavern.

But, fortunately for the complaining women's sake, one day the news spread that Master 'Ntoni's 'Ntoni had come back at night with a Catania ship, and that he was ashamed to show himself with no boots to his feet. His clothes were so tattered and torn that if he had come home with any money he would have had nowhere to put it. But his grandfather and his brother and sisters welcomed him and made a fuss of him, and were as delighted to see him as if he had returned with a fortune, and his sisters hung round his neck, laughing and crying, and Lia had grown so tall that 'Ntoni hardly recognised her. "Now you won't leave us again, will you?" they said.

His grandfather blew his nose too, and muttered: "Now that these children won't be left stranded, I can die in peace!"

But for a week 'Ntoni didn't have the courage to show himself in the street. Everybody laughed in his face when they saw him, and Piedipapera went about saying: "Have you seen the fortune that Master 'Ntoni's 'Ntoni came back with?" Those who had dallied a little over packing their bundles before setting out on the crazy adventure of going out into the world and seeking their fortune laughed loudest of all.

Anyone who sets out to make his fortune and fails is inevitably regarded as a fool. Don Silvestro, Uncle Crocifisso, Master Cipolla and Massaro Filippo were not fools; and everyone paid them court, because those who are penniless always gape in admiration and envy at the rich and fortunate, and work for them for a handful of straw, just like Alfio Mosca's donkey, instead of kicking the cart to pieces and lying down on the grass and kicking its hooves in the air. The chemist was perfectly right when he said that the world needed to be kicked to pieces and put together again in an entirely different fashion; but even he, with his big beard and his everlasting preaching of revolution, was one of those who had managed to seize fortune and keep it in the glass cases in his shop; all he had to do was to enjoy God's good gifts, standing at the door of his shop and talking to people, and when he had finished pounding dirty water in the mortar with his pestle he had done his work. His father had taught him a fine trade, making money out of well water. But the trade that 'Ntoni had been taught by his grandfather was that of breaking his back and wearing out his arms all day long, and risking his life and dying of hunger into the bargain, and of never having a day to lie down in the sun like Alfio Mosca's donkey. By the Holy Mother of God, he was fed up with it, and he would prefer to do like Rocco Spatu, who at least did no work. He had completely lost interest in Barbara Zuppidda and Mother Tudda's Sara and all the other girls in the world. All they cared about was finding a husband who would work like a dog to provide them with food and buy them silk handkerchiefs, so that they could show themselves off at the front door on Sundays with their

hands over their full bellies. He would rather remain
with his hands over his own belly, on Sundays and
Mondays and, indeed, for the rest of the week, because
there was no point in exerting oneself for nothing.

'Ntoni had turned preacher, just like the chemist; so
at any rate he had learned something on his travels.
His eyes had been opened, just like a kitten's on the
fourth day. When a chicken can walk it comes home
with its belly full. 'Ntoni had filled his belly with arguments, if with nothing else, and he went all over the
place repeating them, in the village square, at Pizzuto's
shop, and at Santuzza's bar. Being grown-up now,
he no longer had to go to Santuzza's tavern secretly;
after all, he was too old now for his grandfather to pull
his ears; and he knew what answer to make if he were
rebuked for seeking what little enjoyment he could.

His grandfather, poor old chap, instead of pulling
his ears, appealed to his better nature. "Now that you're
here, we'll soon manage to get together the money for
the house. Uncle Crocifisso has promised not to give it
to anyone else," he said. He kept on harping on his
everlasting theme of buying back the house. "Your
mother, alas! did not die in it. The house will enable us
to provide a dowry for Mena. Then, with God's help,
we shall fit out another boat. I must say that at my age
it's very hard to have to work for others, and to have
to take orders after being one's own master all one's
life. You boys were born to be your own masters too.
Would you like us to use the money for the house to
buy a boat first? Now that you're grown-up, you must
give your opinion, because you ought to have more
sense than an old man like me. What do you want to
do?"

'Ntoni didn't want to do anything. What did he care
about the house or a new boat? Another bad season

would come, or a cholera epidemic, or some other misfortune, and they would lose their house and their
boat all over again, and they would be back where
they started from, slaving away like ants. A fine prospect! When they had their house and their boat, would
it mean that they would be able to give up work and
eat meat and macaroni every day? In the places where
he had been; there were people who always went about
in carriages, that's what they did; people in comparison
with whom Don Franco and the communal secretary
slaved like donkeys, filling up forms or pounding dirty
water. At least he would like to know why there were
people in the world who were born lucky and were
able to enjoy themselves all day long without doing
any work, while others were born penniless and had to
spend their lives pulling wagons with their teeth.

Besides, he had been born his own master, as his
grandfather had said, and this business of going out
to work for others didn't suit him at all. The idea of
having to take orders from people who, as everybody
in the village knew, had sprung up from nothing, la-
bouring and sweating and scraping their money together a halfpenny at a time! He still went to work,
because his grandfather took him—he didn't yet have
the courage to refuse. But when the skipper started
bullying, and shouted from the stern: "Now then, boys,
what are we playing at?" he felt like hitting him over
the head with an oar. So he preferred sitting on the
shore, mending nets, stretching his legs and resting his
back against the stones. If he stopped work and sat
with his arms folded for a few moments, at least there
was nobody to say anything to him.

Rocco Spatu, when he had nothing else to do, used
to come and stretch his arms too, and so did Vanni
Pizzuto, between shaving one customer and the next,

as well as Piedipapera, whose job was going about and talking to everybody on the chance of picking up some business. They discussed everything that went on in the village, including the story of how Donna Rosolina, during the cholera epidemic, had told her brother under the seal of the confessional that Don Silvestro had cheated her of twenty-five *onze*, and that she could not go to the police because she had stolen the twenty-five *onze* from her brother herself.

"You see?" remarked Pizzuto. "Where did she get the twenty-five *onze* from? Stolen goods don't last!"

"At least they were in the house," Spatu replied. "If my mother had twelve *tarì* and I took them, would I pass for a thief?"

Talking about thieves naturally led them to the subject of Uncle Crocifisso, who, they said, had lost more than thirty *onze*, what with all the debtors who had died of the cholera and left their pledges on his hands. Dumbbell, not knowing what to do with all the rings and earrings that he was left with, was now going to marry La Vespa. There was no doubt about it, for they had actually been seen going to the municipal offices to arrange for the publication of the banns, and Don Silvestro had been there at the time.

"It's not true that he's marrying her because he's got so many earrings," said Piedipapera, who was in a position to know. "After all, the earrings and necklaces are solid gold and silver, and he could easily go to town and sell them; he could actually make a hundred per cent. on what he gave for them. He's only marrying La Vespa because she showed him in black and white that, as the Mangiacarrubbe girl had lured Brasi Cipolla into the house, she was going to the notary to arrange her marriage settlement with Rocco Spatu. Excuse my mentioning it, won't you, Rocco?"

"Certainly, Tino, certainly," Rocco replied. "I don't care a damn. Women are bitches. Anyone who trusts them is a fool!"

"They're all the same!" said 'Ntoni. "They only look for a husband because they want to be kept by him."

"Uncle Crocifisso rushed to the lawyer's like a maniac as soon as he found out about it," Piedipapera went on. "That's why he's marrying La Vespa."

"The Mangiacarrubbe girl's very lucky, isn't she?" 'Ntoni remarked.

"If Brasi Cipolla lives for a hundred years after his father dies, he'll still be as rich as a pig," said Rocco Spatu.

"His father is kicking up the devil of a fuss, but he'll have to give in in the end. He has no other sons, and the only thing he could do to prevent the Mangiacarrubbe girl from enjoying his wealth would be to get married himself."

"I'm delighted," said 'Ntoni. "The Mangiacarrubbe girl hasn't got a penny. Why should Master Cipolla be the only one to be rich?"

Here the chemist, who came down to the shore to enjoy his after-lunch pipe, joined in the conversation, and started plugging away at his usual theme that the present state of the world was all wrong, and that everything ought to be scrapped and started again from scratch. But talking to such people was as useless as pounding water with a pestle. The only one who understood anything was 'Ntoni, who had been out in the world, and had had his eyes opened a little, like a kitten. During his naval service he had been taught to read, so he used to go to the door of the chemist's shop to hear what was in the newspaper and to talk to the chemist, who was decent to everybody and did not worry about his wife's scoldings. "Why do you meddle in affairs that don't concern you?" she used to shout at him.

"One must let women talk and quietly go one's own way," Don Franco would say as soon as the Lady had gone back to her room. He was perfectly willing to talk, even to people who had no boots on, provided they did not soil his high-backed chairs. He would point to what the newspaper said, explaining the words one by one, for he was convinced that the world ought to be run in the way that the newspaper recommended.

When Don Franco came down to the stream-bed where the friends were talking he would wink at 'Ntoni Malavoglia, who would be mending nets, leaning against the stones with his legs outstretched, and make signs to him with his head, waving his big beard. A fine state of affairs it was when some men had to break their backs against the stones while others could sit in the sun smoking, though in reality all men ought to be brothers. . . .

THIRTEEN   When his grandson came home drunk in the evening Master 'Ntoni tried his hardest to get him to bed without the others' noticing it, because this was something which had never happened in the Malavoglia family before, and it brought tears to his eyes. In the early hours of the morning, when he called Alessi to get ready to go to sea, he let 'Ntoni sleep on, because he wouldn't have been fit for anything in any case. At first 'Ntoni felt ashamed afterwards, and when they came back in the evening he would be waiting for them on the shore with bent head. But gradually he grew hardened, and said to himself that by going to the tavern he would be able to make next day another Sunday.

The poor old man did everything he could to touch his heart, and even took his shirt secretly to Don Giammaria and spent three *tarì* to have the evil exorcised. "Look, 'Ntoni," he would say. "This is something which has never happened in the Malavoglia family before. If you follow the evil ways of Rocco Spatu, your brother and sisters will follow your example. One rotten apple spoils all the rest, and all the money we've scraped together with so much effort will be frittered away. Because of one fisherman the boat was lost, and then what shall we do?"

'Ntoni bent his head and muttered, but next day he started all over again. Once, when his grandfather remonstrated with him, he actually said: "What do you expect? At least when I'm drunk I forget my sorrows!"

"What sorrows? You're young, you're healthy and you know your calling. What more do you want? Your brother, who is still a boy, and I, who am an old man, have managed to drag ourselves out of the mire. If you were willing to help us, we could work ourselves back to being what we used to be. Even if we could never again be as happy as we were, because of those who have departed, at least we should have no other troubles; and we should all be united, like the fingers of the hand, and we should have enough to eat. What will happen to you all when I die? As it is, I feel afraid every time we set out on a long trip; and I'm an old man!"

When his grandfather succeeded in touching his heart, 'Ntoni would break down and weep. As soon as they heard him coming, his brother and sisters, who knew what was going on, would huddle into a corner, as though he were a stranger or they were afraid of him; and his grandfather, with his beads in his hand, would murmur: "Oh! blessed soul of Bastianazzo! Oh!

soul of my daughter-in-law Maruzza! You perform the miracle!" When Mena saw 'Ntoni coming home with pale face and shining eyes, she would say: "Come this way! Grandfather's at home!" and bring him in through the kitchen door. Then she would start weeping quietly beside the fireplace. Eventually 'Ntoni announced one day that he wouldn't go to the tavern any more, even if it meant the death of him, and he went back to work again with a will, as he had done in the past. He actually started getting up earlier than the others, and he would be waiting for his grandfather on the shore, two hours before dawn, when the Three Kings were still high over the church tower and you could hear the crickets chirping in the fields, almost as though they were at your feet. His grandfather could hardly contain himself with delight, and he talked to 'Ntoni continually, to show him how fond of him he was; and he said to himself that it was the blessed souls of 'Ntoni's mother and father who had performed the miracle.

The miracle lasted the whole week, and on Sunday 'Ntoni refused to go as far as the village square, to avoid seeing the tavern even in the distance and hearing his friends calling him. But all day long he had nothing whatever to do; it seemed as though it would never end, and he nearly broke his jaw with yawning. He was no longer a boy to spend his time picking broom in the lava field, singing like his brother Alessi and Nunziata, and he wasn't a girl to sweep the house like Mena, or an old man, like his grandfather, to use the time mending broken casks or lobster pots. He stayed all day sitting in the doorway in the Strada del Nero, down which not so much as a chicken passed, and from which you could hear the distant voices and laughter from the tavern. In the end, out of sheer boredom, he

went to bed, and on Monday morning he started pulling his long face again. "It would be better for you if
Sunday never came," his grandfather remarked, "because next day you're in a terrible state." So it would
be better for him if Sunday never came! At the thought
of every day being a Monday his heart sank to his boots,
and in the evening, when he came back from sea, he
had no desire even to go to bed. So to relieve his
feelings he started roaming round the village to talk
about his misfortunes, with the result that he drifted
back to the tavern again.

Before, when he had come staggering home, he had
always come in quietly, making himself as small as
possible, and either muttering excuses or not saying
anything at all. But now he started raising his voice,
and if he found his sister, looking pale and swollen-
eyed, waiting for him, and if she whispered to him to
come in by the kitchen door because his grandfather
was in, he would reply: "I don't care if he is!" Next day
he would get up distraught and in a bad temper, and
he swore and shouted from morning to night.

One day the poor old man, at his wits' end for what
to do to touch his heart, drew him into the corner of the
little room, shut the door, so that the neighbours should
not hear, and said to him, weeping like a child: "Oh!
'Ntoni, don't you remember that it was in this room
that your mother died? Why do you inflict on her the
sorrow of letting her see you going the way of Rocco
Spatu? Don't you see how poor Cousin Anna toils and
sweats because of that drunkard of a son of hers? And
how she weeps sometimes when she has no bread to
give her other children, and a happy heart is not
enough? He who consorts with wolves grows like one,
and he who associates with cripples ends by limping.
Don't you remember the night when your mother

was dying of the cholera and we were all in this room,
gathered round her bed, and she commended Mena
and the children to your care?" 'Ntoni moaned like a
weaned calf, and said he would like to die too. But then
he gradually drifted back to the tavern again, and instead of coming home he would roam the streets with
Rocco Spatu and Cinghialenta, stopping in the doorways and leaning against the walls, dead tired, and
to drive away melancholy the three would start to sing.

Eventually things grew to such a pitch that Master
'Ntoni no longer dared show himself in the street for
shame. 'Ntoni would come home looking grim and
truculent, to prevent his devotions from being inter-
rupted by the old man's preaching. He did all the
preaching in a low voice to himself; the cause of the
whole trouble was the state in which he was born.

To relieve his feelings he would go and talk to the
chemist, and others who had sufficient time to discuss
the shocking injustices of the world. If one went to
Santuzza's bar to forget one's troubles, for instance, one
was called a drunkard; but how many were there who
got drunk on good wine at home, although they had
no troubles to forget? No one reproached them, or
preached them sermons about working for their living,
because they didn't have to work for their living and
were rich enough for two, though in reality all men
were God's children alike and everything ought to be
shared out fairly. "That lad has brains!" the chemist
observed to Don Silvestro and Master Cipolla and
anyone else who would listen. "He sees things crudely
and in the round, but the essence is there. It's not his
fault that he isn't able to express himself better. It's
the fault of the Government, which leaves him in
ignorance."

To educate him Don Franco would bring him the

Secolo and the *Gazzetta di Catania*, but 'Ntoni didn't like reading. For one thing, it was an effort; and for another there was the fact that in the navy he had been forced to learn to read. Now that he was free to do whatever he liked, he had somewhat forgotten how the words are put together in print. In any case it didn't put a penny in his pocket. What did all the stuff in the newspapers have to do with him? Don Franco tried to explain what it had to do with him; and when Don Michele walked across the square he would point to him with his big beard and wink significantly at 'Ntoni, and whisper to him the current gossip that Don Michele, having heard that Donna Rosolina had some money and was giving it away to people who promised to find her a husband, was after her himself.

"The first thing to do is to make a clean sweep of all the braided hats. We must make a revolution," Don Franco said.

"And what will you give me for making a revolution?"

'Ntoni's reply annoyed Don Franco. He shrugged his shoulders and went off to pound dirty water with his pestle. Talking to people like that really was as useless as pounding water with a pestle, he said. As soon as 'Ntoni had taken his departure, Piedipapera whispered:

"If he wants to kill Don Michele, he ought to do so for quite a different reason; because Don Michele's after his sister." Piedipapera had had his knife into Don Michele ever since he had started glaring at him and Rocco Spatu and Cinghialenta whenever he met them. That was why he wanted to get rid of him.

Because of 'Ntoni, the poor Malavoglia had become the talk of the village; so low had their fortunes fallen. Everybody knew that Don Michele was continually

walking up and down the Strada del Nero to annoy
Venera Zuppidda, who stood guard over her daughter
with her distaff in her hand. However, Don Michele,
so that his walks should not be entirely wasted, had
cast his eyes on Lia, who had grown up into a very
pretty girl, and had no one to look after her, except
her sister, who used to blush for her and say: "Let's
go back into the house, Lia, because it's not right to
stay at the door, now that we're orphans."

But Lia was even vainer than her brother 'Ntoni,
and she liked standing at the door and showing herself
off in her rose-pattern handkerchief, which made
everyone say: "How pretty you look with that handkerchief, Lia!" And Don Michele devoured her with
his eyes.

Poor Mena, standing at the door waiting for her
brother to come home drunk, would have liked to have
dragged her sister inside the house whenever Don Michele passed, but she felt so tired and humiliated that
her hands dropped helplessly to her side. "Are you
afraid that he'll eat me?" Lia said to her. "No one wants
to have anything to do with us, now that we're penniless. You see what's happened to 'Ntoni! Not even the
dogs want him!"

Piedipapera went about whispering that if 'Ntoni
had any spirit he would get rid of Don Michele.

'Ntoni, however, had a different reason for wanting
to get rid of Don Michele. After Santuzza had broken
with Don Michele, she had taken a fancy to 'Ntoni, because of the jaunty angle at which he wore his cap,
and the way he swung his shoulders as he walked,
which he had picked up in the navy. She put all the
left-overs from her customers' plates aside for him, and
in one way and another managed to keep his glass
filled too. The result was that the tavern kept him as

plump and sleek as the butcher's dog. 'Ntoni repaid the obligation by dealing with any customers who were awkward and started shouting and cursing when the time came for paying the reckoning. With the good customers, however, he was always gay and cheerful, and when Santuzza went to confession he used to look after the bar. He was treated as one of the house, and everyone liked him, except Uncle Santoro, who regarded him as a bird of ill-omen, and grumbled.

That was how 'Ntoni earned his living. When his grandfather reproached him for not working and his sister gazed sadly at him he would reply: "Do I cost you anything, by any chance? I don't spend any of your money, and I earn my own keep!"

"It would be better if you were dying of hunger," his grandfather replied, "and if we all died this very day."

This kind of conversation usually ended in a general silence, with everybody's back turned to everybody else. To avoid quarrelling with his grandson, Master 'Ntoni was reduced to not opening his mouth; and, when 'Ntoni couldn't stand the moralising atmosphere any longer, he would leave them to their snivelling and go off in search of Rocco Spatu or Vanni Pizzuto, who were always thinking up something new, and with whom you could be cheerful.

One of the best things they had thought up lately had been to serenade Uncle Crocifisso on his wedding night. They had gathered everybody in the village to whom Uncle Crocifisso would no longer lend any money, formed up under his window, armed with old pots and pans and cowbells from the butcher's and a large variety of whistles, and kicked up an infernal din until midnight. When La Vespa got up next morning, looking greener than ever, she promptly went and had

a row with that odious Santuzza creature, at whose bar
the plot had been hatched because, needless to say,
she was jealous that La Vespa had found herself a husband.

When people saw Uncle Crocifisso all dressed up in
his wedding suit in the village square, looking like a
death's head because of the fright that La Vespa had
given him by making him spend money on buying it,
they all laughed in his face. La Vespa was always
wanting to spend money, and if she had had her way
the cupboard would have been bare in a week. She
said that she was the mistress of the house now, and
the result was that there was the very devil of a row at
Uncle Crocifisso's every day. His wife scratched his
face and said that, being the mistress of the house, she
must have the keys, and that she had no intention of
being worse off than she had been when she was single,
having to ask every time she wanted a piece of bread
or a new handkerchief. If she had known beforehand
what being married to Uncle Crocifisso was going to
be like, she would never have done it, and would have
preferred keeping her plot of land and her medallion
as a Daughter of Mary . . . etc., etc. Uncle Crocifisso
declared that he was ruined, that he was no longer
master in his own house, that it was like having the
cholera in the home, and that La Vespa was trying to
make him die of despair before his time by cheerfully
squandering the money that he had so laboriously accumulated. If he had known beforehand how the marriage was going to turn out, he would have consigned
both La Vespa and her plot of land to the devil, for he
had no need of a wife, and he had been blackmailed
into the marriage by having been made to believe that
La Vespa had hooked Brasi Cipolla, and that he was
going to be cheated of that accursed plot of land.

At this point it became known that Brasi Cipolla had
committed his crowning act of folly by running away
with the Mangiacarrubbe girl, and that Master Fortunato was hunting for them everywhere, in the lava
field and under the bridge and all along the valley,
fuming with rage and swearing by all that's holy that
when he found them he would give them both a terrible drubbing and pull his son's ears so hard that they
would come away in his hand. Uncle Crocifisso started
tearing his hair when he heard this, and declared that
the Mangiacarrubbe girl had been the ruin of him by
not running away with Brasi a week earlier. "It was
the will of God," he went about saying, beating himself on the breast, "it was the will of God that La Vespa
should be inflicted on me as a punishment for my sins!"
His sins must have been enormous, because La Vespa
spoiled even the taste of bread in his mouth, and made
him suffer the pains of purgatory night and day. To
make matters worse, La Vespa boasted that she would
be faithful to him and would never look at any other
man, even if he were as young and handsome as 'Ntoni
Malavoglia.

'Ntoni Malavoglia now carried his head high, and if
his grandfather so much as breathed a word to him he
merely laughed. It was his grandfather who now had
to humble himself, as though he were in the wrong.
'Ntoni said that if he weren't wanted in the house he
had somewhere else to go; he could go and sleep in
Santuzza's stable; and he pointed out that they were
saving money by not having to provide him with food.
As for the money that Master 'Ntoni and Alessi and
Mena earned by fishing and weaving and washing and
so forth, they could lay it aside for that famous St.
Peter's bark of theirs, and wear themselves out in it
every day for a *rotolo* of fish; or they could buy back

the house by the medlar tree, and cheerfully starve to death in it. In any case, he wouldn't ask them for a penny. Being a poor devil anyhow, he preferred enjoying a bit of ease while he was still young, and he didn't spend his nights bewailing his misfortunes like his grandfather. There was the sun to be enjoyed by everybody, and the shade of the olive trees for coolness, and the square to stroll in and the steps of the church on which to sit and talk; and there was the highway on which to watch people pass and pick up the news, and the tavern for eating and drinking in with your friends; and if you felt bored and had a yawning fit you could play *morra* or *briscola*; and finally, if you felt really sleepy, there were the fields where Master Naso's rams were pastured to lie down in by day and Sister Mariangela's stable to sleep in by night.

Eventually his grandfather, with lowered head and bent back, went and sought him out at Santuzza's. He drew him by the sleeve behind the stable, so that nobody should see, and wept like a child.

"Aren't you ashamed of living this life, 'Ntoni?" he said. "Have you no thought for your home, and for your brother and sisters? If only your father and La Longa were alive! 'Ntoni! 'Ntoni!"

"But are you people by any chance any better off than I am, for all your toiling and moiling?" 'Ntoni answered. "The whole thing's just our rotten, bad luck! You've spent your whole life working like a cart-horse, and now you're old and bent like a fiddle-bow, and what have you got to show for it? You people don't know the world! You're like kittens with your eyes still closed. Do you by any chance eat the fish you catch? You're reduced to a state in which they wouldn't even accept you at the poor-house, but do you know for whom you sweat all the week? You work for a lot of people who never do a stroke themselves and count their money by the shovelful!"

"You have no money and neither have I. We have never had any money, and we have earned our living as God willed. That's why we must all help one another; otherwise we shall die of hunger."

"Earned our living as the devil willed, you mean, because our state is all the work of Satan. You know what to expect when your hands are all doubled up with the rheumatics like a withered vine root and you can't use them any longer! You can go away and die like a dog in the valley under the railway bridge!"

"No! No!" the old man exclaimed, throwing his arms, which were shrivelled like an old vine root, round 'Ntoni's neck. "If you'll help us, we can earn the money to buy back the house!"

"Yes, the house by the medlar tree! You've never been out in the world, so you believe it's the most beautiful palace in the world!"

"I know it isn't the most beautiful palace in the world! But it's not for you, who were born in it, to say so, particularly as your mother didn't die in it."

"Nor did my father. Our fate is to end as a meal for the dogfish. In the meantime I want at least to take advantage of what little pleasure I can get, as there's no point in wearing myself out for nothing. When you've got your house and your boat, what next? What about Mena's dowry? And Lia's? What a prospect, by the blood of Judas!"

The old man went away with bent back, mournfully shaking his head. If a piece of rock had fallen on him he could not have been more crushed than he was by his grandson's bitter words. He had no more spirit left, and his hands fell limply to his sides, and he wanted to weep. His only thought was that Bastianazzo and Luca had never had 'Ntoni's ideas, and had always done their duty without complaining; and it tortured him to think that it was useless to think about a dowry for Mena or Lia, because it was beyond their reach.

Poor Mena was so downcast that she seemed to know it too. The neighbours now kept away from the Malavoglia, as though they still had the cholera in the house, and left her with no one to talk to, except her sister, with her rose-pattern handkerchief, or Nunziata or Cousin Anna, when they did her the kindness of dropping in for a chat. For Cousin Anna had her troubles too, with that drunkard Rocco on her hands, and everybody knew about it now; and so had Nunziata, who had been so small when that vagabond of her father had abandoned her and gone away to seek his fortune. That was the reason why the three of them understood each other so well when they talked quietly, with bent heads and their hands under their aprons, and also when they remained silent, not looking at each other, each thinking about her own affairs. "When you're reduced to the state that we're in," said Lia, who spoke like a grown-up woman, "you have to help yourself as best you can!"

From time to time Don Michele stopped to pass the time of day or crack some joke with Mena and Lia, who had gradually grown used to his gold-braided hat and no longer felt afraid of it. Lia sometimes actually made a joke herself, and laughed at it. Mena didn't dare scold her, or go into the kitchen and leave her alone with him, now that she no longer had a mother; so she stayed there, withdrawn into herself, looking up and down the street with tired eyes. Now that it was obvious that the neighbours had dropped them, they were really grateful that Don Michele, in spite

of his gold-braided hat, condescended to stop for a chat
at the Malavoglia door; and, if Don Michele found Lia
alone, he would look her in the eyes, twirling his
moustaches and with his braided hat at a jaunty angle,
and say: "What a pretty girl you are, Lia!"

No one had ever said that to her before, so she grew
as red as a beetroot.

"How is it that you're not married yet?" Don Michele
went on.

She shrugged her shoulders and said she didn't know.

"You ought to be dressed in wool and silk and wear
long earrings. Upon my word of honour, you'd put
many ladies in the city to shame!"

"Wool and silk dresses are not for me, Don Michele,"
Lia answered.

"Why? Hasn't Barbara Zuppidda got them? And
won't the Mangiacarrubbe girl be having them, now
that she's hooked Master Cipolla's Brasi? And won't La
Vespa be having them too, if she wants them?"

"They're rich, they are!"

"How unfair life is!" Don Michele exclaimed, smack-
ing his sabre with the palm of his hand. "I'd like to have
some luck in the lottery, Lia, just to show you what
I'm capable of!"

Sometimes, when Don Michele had nothing else to
do, he would take off his hat and ask permission to sit
on the stones beside her. Mena thought he came to the
Strada del Nero because of Barbara Zuppidda, so she
didn't say anything. But Don Michele swore to Lia
that it wasn't for Barbara's sake that he came that way,
and that Barbara had never so much as entered his
head, upon his word of honour. He had quite different
ideas in his head, in case Lia didn't know!

He stroked his chin, twirled his moustaches and
looked at the girl like a basilisk. She turned all the

colours of the rainbow and got up to go away. But
Don Michele took her hand and said: "Why do you
want to treat me like this, Lia? Stay here, because nobody's going to eat you!"

That was how they passed the time while waiting
for the menfolk to come back from sea; the girl at the
door and Don Michele sitting on the stones beside her,
snapping twigs between his fingers for lack of anything
else to do.

"Would you like to live in town?" he asked her.

"What would I do in town?"

"Town is the place for you. Upon my word of honour,
you're not meant to live here among these yokels!
You're goods of fine quality, Lia, and you ought to be
well-dressed, as I know how, and live in a nice little
house, and go for walks along the esplanade and in the
Villa Bellini gardens when the band's playing. With a
fine silk handkerchief on your head and an amber necklace. Upon my word of honour, to think of you staying
here amid all the pigs! They've promised to transfer
me in the New Year. I can't wait for my transfer to
come through!"

Lia, who hardly knew what amber necklaces or silk
handkerchiefs were like, found this an excellent joke,
and she laughed and shrugged her shoulders. Another
time Don Michele, with a great air of mystery, produced a lovely red and yellow handkerchief, wrapped
in a beautiful piece of tissue-paper, which he had got
from some confiscated contraband, and he wanted to
make her a present of it.

"No! No!" she exclaimed, blushing deeply. "I won't
take it, not if you kill me!" Don Michele insisted. "I
didn't expect this, Lia," he said. "I don't deserve to be
treated like this!" But he had to wrap the handkerchief
in the tissue-paper again and put it back in his pocket.

After this, as soon as she saw Don Michele appearing in the distance, Lia would disappear into the house, for fear that he would offer her the handkerchief again. No matter how often he walked up and down the street, making Venera Zuppidda fume with rage, and no matter how often he craned his neck to peep into the Malavoglia doorway, no one was ever to be seen. In the end he decided to go in. When the two girls saw him they were aghast, and did not know what to do. They started trembling as though they had the ague.

"You wouldn't accept the silk handkerchief, Lia," he said to the girl, who had grown as red as a beetroot, "but I came back because of the good will that I have for you all. What is your brother 'Ntoni doing?"

When she was asked what her brother was doing, Mena reddened too, because he wasn't doing anything. Don Michele went on:

"I'm afraid your brother 'Ntoni may be the cause of some anxiety to the family. I'm a friend, and I shut my eyes; but, when another sergeant comes here in my place, he'll want to know what your brother 'Ntoni does in the evening, out in the direction of Il Rotolo, with Cinghialenta and that other good type, Rocco Spatu, when they go for walks in the lava field, as though they had good boot-leather to waste. Open your eyes to what I'm saying now, Mena; and tell him not to be seen so often with that snake-in-the-grass Piedipapera at Pizzuto's shop, because everything is known, and he'll be the one left to take the consequences. The others are old foxes, and it would be as well if your grandfather didn't let your brother 'Ntoni go for walks in the lava field, because the lava field is not the best place for going for walks in; and tell him that the rocks at Il Rotolo have ears, and that, even without field-glasses, you can see the boats that come quietly slipping along towards dusk, as though they were out fishing for bats! Tell him this, Mena, and tell him also that this warning comes from a friend who wishes you well. As for Cinghialenta and Rocco Spatu, and also Vanni Pizzuto, they are being watched. Your brother trusts Piedipapera, and doesn't know that the customs guards get a percentage on all contraband they seize, and that the way to catch a gang of smugglers red-handed is to offer one of them a share to give away his accomplices. As for Piedipapera, remember that Jesus Christ said to John: 'Beware of marked men.' The proverb says so too!"

Mena's eyes opened wide and she grew pale, though she did not fully understand what Don Michele said; but she was filled with alarm at the idea of her brother's being involved in some way with the men in braided hats. To comfort her Don Michele took her hand and went on:

"If it became known that I'd told you this, I should be done for. I'm risking my braided hat because of my liking for you Malavoglia. But I don't want any harm to come to your brother. Upon my word of honour, I shouldn't like to meet him in a tight corner one dark night, not even for the sake of seizing a thousand lire-worth of contraband!"

After Don Michele had startled them like this, the two girls had no more peace. Instead of going to bed, they sat up late, waiting for their brother, while he roamed the streets with Rocco Spatu and other members of the gang, singing. The two girls couldn't get out of their minds the firing and the shouting they had heard on the night of the shooting of the two-footed quail. It rang in their ears all night.

"Go to bed!" Mena said to her sister. "There are certain things that you're too young to know about!"

She said nothing to her grandfather, not wishing to cause him more suffering, but the first time she found 'Ntoni in a quiet mood, sitting sadly at the door with his chin in his hand, she plucked up courage and spoke to him.

"What is it you do with Rocco Spatu and Cinghialenta?" she said. "Be careful, because you've been seen on the lava field and in the direction of Il Rotolo. Beware of Piedipapera. You know that according to the old proverb Jesus Christ said to John: 'Beware of marked men!'"

"Who told you that?" said 'Ntoni, jumping to his feet as though he had been stung. "Who told you that?"

"Don Michele," she answered, with tears in her eyes. "He told me to warn you against Piedipapera, because to catch smugglers you have to offer a share to one of the gang!"

"Is that all he said?"

"Yes."

'Ntoni swore that there wasn't a word of truth in all this, and made Mena promise not to say anything to her grandfather. Then he went hurriedly away and sought refuge in the tavern to get over the shock. If he saw anyone in a braided hat coming, he made a long détour to avoid meeting him. He assured himself that Don Michele knew nothing, but was only talking wildly to intimidate him, because of the grudge he bore him because of Santuzza, who had turned him out of the house like a mangy dog. Don Michele was well paid for sucking the blood of the poor, and he wasn't afraid of him, in spite of his gold braid. It was monstrous for him to behave like this, fat and prosperous as he was! His only job was to try and lay his hands on poor devils who were trying to earn a twelve-*tarì* piece as best they could; and it was monstrous that if you wanted to bring in something from abroad you had to pay duty on it, as though it were stolen property! And Don Michele and his spies had to come and stick their noses into what you were doing! They could lay their hands on anything they pleased and keep it for themselves; but if anyone else chose to risk his life by doing what he was entitled to do and unloading a bit of stuff, he passed for a thief and was hunted with carbines and pistols, as though he were a wolf or worse. But stealing from thieves had never been a sin. Don Giammaria had said so himself at the chemist's shop, and Don Franco had nodded his head and his big beard in complete agreement, because as soon as a republic had been established all that sort of thing would be done away with. "And clerks, those limbs of Satan, will be done away with too," the priest had added. The disappearance of those twenty-five *onze* from his house was still rankling in Don Giammaria's mind.

Donna Rosolina had not only lost twenty-five *onze* but the use of her senses as well; she was now running after Don Michele, in an attempt to throw away the rest of her money. When she saw him walking down the Strada del Nero she thought he was after her; so she was perpetually busy on her balcony with her bowls of capsicums or making tomato purée, to show what she was capable of; for even with a pair of pincers it would have been impossible to extract from her head the idea that Don Michele, with his paunch, was not looking for a sensible woman who was a good housekeeper, as she understood the term. So she stood up for Don Michele when her brother abused the Government and all the idlers who lived at its expense, and said: "You're certainly right about Don Silvestro, who sponges on the village without doing anything. But you must have customs duties to pay for our soldiers, who look so well in their uniforms; without them we should all devour each other like wolves!"

"They're idlers, paid to carry a rifle and nothing else," sneered the chemist. "They're like priests, who charge three *tarì* for saying a mass. They finish their day's work in half-an-hour, and then they're free to enjoy themselves for the rest of the day, like Don Michele. Ever since he gave up warming the benches at Santuzza's, he has done nothing but loaf around the village."

"That's why he's got his knife into me!" 'Ntoni chimed in. "Just because he wears a sabre, he thinks himself entitled to rage like a mad dog and throw his weight about. But one of these days I'll bash his face in with his sabre, just to show what I think of him!"

"Bravo!" exclaimed the chemist. "Now you're talking! The people must show its teeth! But please don't do it here, because I don't want any trouble in my shop. The Government would be delighted to compromise me, but I don't like the idea of having anything to do with judges or police!"

'Ntoni Malavoglia raised his fists to heaven and cursed and swore by Jesus Christ and the Virgin Mary that he meant what he said, even if it meant going to prison; for he had nothing to lose. Since Massaro Filippo had stopped supplying the tavern with wine, what with all the things that her old skinflint of a father, whining away between one Ave Maria and the next, had said about 'Ntoni, Santuzza no longer felt so well-disposed towards him. Her father had told her that, now that her customers couldn't get Massaro Filippo's wine, to which they had grown as used as a baby to the breast, they were vanishing like flies after St. Andrew's Day. He kept asking her why she wasted

her time on a worthless good-for-nothing like 'Ntoni
Malavoglia.

"Don't you see that he'll eat you out of hearth and
home," he said, "and that all you'll get for your pains,
after you've fattened him up like a pig for market, is
that he'll go and make love to La Vespa or the Mangiacarrubbe girl, now that they're rich? You're losing all
your customers, now that he's always hanging on to
your apron strings and they never have a chance of
cracking a joke with you." Or he would say: "It's a
shame to have such a ragged and dirty fellow hanging
about the place, turning it into a pig-stye, and it turns
people's stomachs to drink from the glasses. Don Michele was all right. It looked well to have him at the
door with his gold-braided hat. People who pay for
their wine like to drink it in peace, and they like to see
somebody wearing a sabre about the place. Everyone
used to raise his hat to Don Michele, and when he was
about nobody ever argued about what he owed, if it
was chalked up on the wall. Now that he doesn't come
any longer, Massaro Filippo doesn't come either. The
last time he passed this way I tried to get him to come
in. But he said there'd be no point in coming in, because, now that you've quarrelled with Don Michele,
he can't smuggle his new wine any more!"

Santuzza held out for some time yet, because she
liked to be mistress in her own house and was not to be
dictated to by anybody. But she regarded everything
her father said as gospel, and her eyes began to be
opened, and she no longer treated 'Ntoni in the same
way as before. She stopped putting aside the left-overs
from the customers' plates for him and slopped dirty
water in the dregs from the customers' glasses that she
left for him. The result was that 'Ntoni started pulling
a long face and grumbling, and Santuzza told him that

she didn't like idlers, and that she and her father had
always worked for their living, and that he ought to do
the same; he ought to help a little about the house
and chop wood or look after the fire, instead of hanging
about like a beggar, doing nothing but making a din,
or dozing with his head in his hands, or spitting all
over the place, putting the floor into such a disgusting
state that there was nowhere left to put your feet.

After the delivery of these home-truths 'Ntoni was
forced to think about finding ways and means of paying for the food that they gave him at the tavern, because he no longer dared go home, where they no
longer even laid the table for meals, but ate with the
plate between their knees, and without appetite, because they were thinking about him, as though he too
were dead. "This is the last blow for an old man like
me," said Master 'Ntoni; and those who saw him trudg-
ing to work with his nets on his shoulder said: "This
is Master 'Ntoni's last winter. Soon the orphans will
be left in the middle of the street." And Lia, if Mena
told her to come inside when Don Michele passed, answered with a touch of defiance:

"Yes, I must come inside as though I were a treasure!
Don't worry, because even the dogs don't want treasures
like us!"

"You wouldn't talk like that if your mother were
alive," said Mena.

"If my mother were alive, I shouldn't be an orphan,
and I shouldn't have to think about helping myself;
and 'Ntoni wouldn't be wandering the streets either,
making it a disgrace to be a sister of his. No one will
want to marry a sister of 'Ntoni Malavoglia's!"

Now that 'Ntoni was up against it, he had no more
hesitation about being seen with Rocco Spatu and Cinghialenta in the lava field or out towards Il Rotolo, and

you would see the three of them talking in whispers, with a sinister expression on their faces, looking like a pack of hungry wolves. Don Michele once more warned Mena that he was afraid that 'Ntoni would be the cause of anxiety to the family.

To find her brother, Mena had to go and look for him in the lava field or in the direction of Il Rotolo or at the tavern door. She would weep and sob and pull him by the sleeve. But he would refuse to listen, and answer that Don Michele had his knife into him. Don Michele, he said, was always saying the most scurrilous things about him to Uncle Santoro. He had heard in Pizzuto's shop that Don Michele had said to Uncle Santoro: "And if I went back to your daughter's, what sort of a figure should I cut?" And Uncle Santoro had answered: "Nonsense! The whole village would be wild with envy!"

"But what are you going to do?" Mena asked him with a pale face. "Think of your mother, 'Ntoni, and think of us, who are alone and abandoned in the world!"

"Nonsense! I'll shame him and Santuzza in front of the whole village on the way to mass! I'll tell everything, and make people laugh! Even the chemist over there will hear me! I'm not afraid of anything any more!"

When people heard that Don Michele was back at Santuzza's again, they said: "The dogs and cats have made peace. They must have had some good reason for squabbling!"

It was a bitter pill for 'Ntoni to be turned out of the tavern like a mangy dog. Not having a penny in his pockets, he couldn't even go to the bar and order a drink under Don Michele's nose and stay there all day long with his elbows on the counter, just to spite them.

Instead, he had to stay outside in the street like a stray dog, with his head down and his tail between his legs, muttering: "By the blood of Judas, one fine day I'll make him pay for this!"

Rocco Spatu and Cinghialenta, who always had money, stood at the tavern door, laughing in his face and making the cuckold sign at him; and they came and whispered to him, and led him by the arm towards the lava field, talking in his ear. The fool still hesitated before falling in with what they said, so they told him that obviously he didn't mind starving to death outside the tavern door and being openly cuckolded by Don Michele.

"Don't talk like that!" 'Ntoni shouted, raising his fists. "Don't talk like that! Or by the blood of Judas one of these fine days something nasty'll happen!"

Rocco Spatu and Cinghialenta grinned, shrugged their shoulders and left him with a sneer. But in the end they goaded him to such a pitch that he could stand it no longer; and he walked right into the very middle of the tavern, looking like a death's head, with his hand on his hips and his old coat thrown over his shoulders, swaggering as though he were clothed in velvet and glaring all round him to provoke Don Michele. For the sake of his gold braid Don Michele pretended not to notice, and made an attempt to go away; but this cowardly behaviour made 'Ntoni's blood boil; and he laughed and sneered in his and Santuzza's faces, and spat in the wine he was drinking, saying it was poison, of the kind given to Jesus on the cross; and that it was baptized into the bargain, having been watered by Santuzza, and that it was folly to allow oneself to be robbed by coming to a filthy drinking den like this, which was the reason why he had given it up. This stung Santuzza to the quick, and she could no longer contain herself. She told him that the reason why he had been turned out was that they were tired of keeping him for the sake of charity, and that they had been forced to chase him out with a broomstick because he was a starving good-for-nothing and down-and-out. At this 'Ntoni started creating an uproar and breaking the glasses, shouting that he had been turned out to make room for a codfish with gold braid on his hat, but that he wasn't afraid of anybody, and that if he chose he'd draw wine from Don Michele's nose. Don Michele's hat was all askew, and he had turned as yellow in the face as 'Ntoni. "Upon my word of honour," he was muttering, "this time things'll turn out nasty!" Meanwhile Santuzza was raining glasses and bottles on both of them, so they ended by coming to blows and rolling over each other on the floor, under the benches, with the customers kicking and striking them to separate them. Eventually Peppi Naso took off his leather belt and started using it impartially on both of them. That belt took off the skin wherever it landed, and it separated them.

Don Michele brushed his jacket, put on his sabre, which he had lost in the scuffle, and went away, muttering to himself. Because of his gold braid he didn't do anything else. A stream of blood was pouring from 'Ntoni Malavoglia's nose, but, seeing Don Michele scuttling away like that, he couldn't be prevented from hurling a stream of abuse after him from the tavern door, shaking his fist and wiping the blood away with his sleeve. He swore he'd give Don Michele the rest of what he owed him the next time they met.

FOURTEEN   When 'Ntoni Malavoglia met Don Michele to give him the rest of what he owed him, it was an ugly business. It happened late one night, when it was pouring with rain and so dark that even a cat couldn't have seen, at the corner of the lava field nearest to Il Rotolo, where the boats that pretended to be fishing for mullet at midnight used quietly to tack, and where 'Ntoni used to hang about with Rocco Spatu and Cinghialenta and other unpleasant customers who smoked pipes, the faint gleam of which enabled the customs guards, crouching among the rocks with their carbines in their hands, to pick them out one by one.

Don Michele, walking down the Strada del Nero, had again warned Mena to tell her brother not to go to Il Rotolo at night with Rocco Spatu and Cinghialenta.

But a hungry belly won't listen to reason, and 'Ntoni had turned a deaf ear. After struggling with Don Michele under the benches of the tavern, he felt he no longer had any reason to be afraid of him; and besides, he had sworn to give him the rest of what he owed him the next time they met, and he had no wish to pass for an idle boaster and a coward in the eyes of Santuzza and everyone else who had heard him make the threat. "I've said I'll give him the rest of what I owe him wherever I meet him. If I meet him at Il Rotolo, I'll give it him at Il Rotolo," he repeated to his gang of friends, among whom La Locca's son was now included. They spent the evening at Santuzza's bar, drinking and making an uproar, and Santuzza had not been able to throw him out, now that he had money to burn in his pocket. Don Michele had passed on his rounds, but Rocco Spatu, who knew the law, spat, and said that so long as there was a lamp at the door they had a perfect right to stay where they were, and he leaned against the wall to steady himself. Santuzza was nearly falling asleep behind her glasses, and 'Ntoni Malavoglia was enjoying keeping her from her bed and making her yawn.

Meanwhile Uncle Santoro had groped his way in with the lamp and was closing the door. "Now go away, because I'm sleepy," said Santuzza. "I don't want to be fined because of you, if they find the door open at this time of night!"

"Who'll come and take the fine off you? That police spy, Don Michele? Bring him here and I'll pay him the fine! Go and tell him 'Ntoni Malavoglia's here!"

Meanwhile Santuzza had taken him by the shoulders and pushed him out of the door. "Go and tell him yourself!" she said. "Go and get into trouble away from here! I don't want to get mixed up with the police because of you!"

'Ntoni, finding himself thrown out into the muddy street like this, with the rain coming down in bucketsful, started drawing his knife and cursing and swearing that he'd do away with Santuzza as well as with Don Michele, but Cinghialenta, who was the only one of the gang who was in full possession of his senses, dragged him away by his coat and said: "That's enough for this evening! Don't you know what we've got to do tonight?"

At this La Locca's son was overcome with a great desire to break down and weep in the dark.

"He's drunk!" exclaimed Rocco Spatu, who was standing under the eaves. "Bring him over here, it'll do him good!"

'Ntoni, somewhat calmed by the water which poured down on him from the eaves, allowed himself to be led away by Cinghialenta, and he splashed through the puddles, still swearing and muttering that if he met Don Michele he'd give him what he'd promised. Suddenly he found himself face to face with Don Michele, who happened to be wandering about that part of the village too, with his pistol on his paunch and his trousers tucked into his boots. At this 'Ntoni became completely calm, and the gang quietly moved away towards Pizzuto's shop.

Outside Pizzuto's shop they started whispering in the shelter of the wall, and the noise of the downpour drowned their words. Suddenly the clock chimed, and all four stopped to listen.

"Let's go in," said Cinghialenta. "He can keep his door open as long as he likes, and without having a lamp outside!"

"It's so dark, you can't see," said La Locca's son.

"In weather like this we must have a drink," said Rocco Spatu. "Otherwise we'll break our necks in the lava field."

At this Cinghialenta started grumbling that they were behaving as though they were going out on the spree. "I'll get Mastro Vanni to give you some lemon water," he said.

"I don't need any lemon water!" 'Ntoni replied indignantly. "You'll see whether I can't do my stuff better than the lot of you!"

Vanni Pizzuto didn't like letting them in at this time of night, and said he was in bed. But as they went on knocking, and threatened to wake the whole village and cause the guards to come and poke their noses into what was going on, he made them give the countersign and came down and opened the door in his pants.

"Are you mad to kick up such a row?" he exclaimed. "I've just seen Don Michele pass!"

"Yes, we saw him too."

"Do you know where he was coming from?" Pizzuto asked, looking at 'Ntoni. 'Ntoni shrugged his shoulders.

Vanni, standing to one side to let them in, winked at
Rocco and Cinghialenta.

"He'd been to the Malavoglia's. I saw him come out
with my own eyes!"

"What do you expect me to do about it?" said 'Ntoni,
with a thick tongue.

"Nothing, it's not a matter for this evening."

"If it's not a matter for this evening, why the devil
did you drag me from the tavern and get me drenched
to the skin?" said Rocco Spatu.

"We were talking to Cinghialenta about something
else," Vanni Pizzuto explained. "It's all right, the man
from Catania came. He said the stuff will be there for
this evening, but it'll be a terrible business unloading it
in this weather."

"All the better; there'll be no one to see us."

"Yes, but the customs guards have long ears, and I
believe I've seen them hanging about the shop and
peering inside!"

A moment's silence followed, and to get rid of them
Vanni Pizzuto went and filled four glasses of herb beer.

"I don't care a fig for the customs guards," said Rocco
Spatu, after he had drained his glass. "If they meddle
in my affairs, so much the worse for them! I've got a
little knife here that doesn't make so much noise as
their pistols."

"We earn our living as best we can, and don't wish
harm to anyone," Cinghialenta added. "Why can't we
be allowed to land what we like where we like any
longer?"

"They go about spying like a lot of thieves to see that
duty's paid on every pocket-handkerchief that anyone
tries to bring ashore, and no one meets them with rifle
bullets," said 'Ntoni Malavoglia. "Do you know what
Don Giammaria said? He said that robbing thieves is no

sin. And the worst thieves are the men with gold braid, who eat us all alive!"

"The thing to do is to carve them into small pieces," said Rocco Spatu, with eyes shining like a cat's.

At this La Locca's son put his glass back on the table without touching it with his lips. He looked as yellow as a corpse.

"Are you drunk already?" Cinghialenta asked him.

"No," he answered. "I haven't been drinking."

"Let's go. The fresh air'll do us good. Good-night to those staying behind!"

"Just a moment," said Pizzuto, with his hand on the door. "No, there's no need to pay for the herb beer. I'm not asking you to pay for it, because you're friends. But if all goes well, please don't forget me! You know I've got a room behind there, with space for a whole mass of stuff, and no one ever peeps into it, because I'm as thick as thieves with Don Michele and his guards. I don't trust Piedipapera, because he played a dirty trick on me last time, and took the stuff to Don Silvestro's house. Don Silvestro can never be satisfied with the share you give him, because it means risking his job. But with me you needn't have that anxiety, and I know you'd give me my fair share. True, I've never denied Piedipapera his due, and I give him a drink every time he comes here, and I shave him for nothing. But by heaven, if he plays a dirty trick like that on me another time, I won't allow myself to be made a fool of, and I'll tell Don Michele everything!"

"All right, Vanni, all right, there's no need to tell Don Michele anything! Has Piedipapera been about this evening?"

"No, he wasn't even in the square! He was at the chemist's shop, talking Republicanism with the chemist. Whenever there's anything on, he's always miles away, to show that he has absolutely no connection with anything that might happen. He's an old fox, he is, and the guards' bullets will never get him, although he's as lame as the devil. Next morning, when it's all over, he turns up and claims his share as bold as brass. But he leaves the bullets to others!"

"It's still raining," said Rocco Spatu. "Is it never going to stop tonight?"

"There won't be anyone at Il Rotolo in this weather," said La Locca's son. "We'd better go home!"

'Ntoni, Cinghialenta and Rocco Spatu were standing in the doorway. The rain was coming down in torrents, and they remained quiet for a moment, staring out into the dark.

"Don't talk like a fool!" Cinghialenta said to La Locca's son, to give him courage, and Vanni Pizzuto quietly closed the door behind them, after whispering:

"Listen, if anything goes wrong, remember you haven't seen me this evening! I gave you a drink for the sake of friendship, but you were never at my house! Don't give me away, because I've got no one in the world!"

The four went quietly away, creeping along the wall to get what protection they could from the driving rain. "There's another who talks against Piedipapera, and says he has no one in the world," Cinghialenta muttered. "At least Piedipapera has a wife; and I've got a wife too, but I'm one of those who don't leave the bullets to others!"

At that moment they quietly passed Cousin Anna's door, and Rocco Spatu said he had a mother who, bless her soul, would now be fast asleep.

"Anyone who can stay in bed certainly doesn't go about on a night like this," said Cinghialenta.

'Ntoni signalled to them to be quiet and to go round by the path to avoid passing his house, because Mena or his grandfather might be waiting up for him, and might hear them.

"Your sister won't be waiting up for you," said that drunkard, Rocco Spatu. "If she's waiting for anybody, it'll be for Don Michele!"

'Ntoni went livid with rage and started feeling for his knife, but Cinghialenta asked if they were drunk to start a stupid quarrel while they were on their way to doing what they were going to do.

Mena really was waiting for her brother behind the door, with her beads in her hand, and Lia was with her; Lia did not say what she knew, though she was as pale as death. It would have been better for them all if 'Ntoni had gone down the Strada del Nero instead of going round by the path. Don Michele really had been to the house that night, and he had knocked at the door.

"Who is it at this time of night?" said Lia, who was secretly embroidering a silk handkerchief which Don Michele had at last managed to get her to accept.

"It's I, Don Michele! Let me in, because I've got something urgent to tell you!"

"I can't, because everyone's in bed, and my sister's waiting up for 'Ntoni behind the door."

"It doesn't matter if your sister hears, because it's 'Ntoni that I've come to talk about, and it's urgent! I don't want 'Ntoni to go to prison! But let me in, because if I'm seen here it'll cost me my job!"

"Holy Mother of God!" said the girl. "Holy Mother of God!"

"Keep your brother at home tonight when he comes in! But don't tell him it was I who said so. Tell him he must stay at home! He *must* stay at home!"

"Holy Mother of God! Holy Mother of God!" the girl repeated, clasping her hands.

"He's at the tavern now, but he's bound to come this way. Wait for him at the door; it will be better for him."

Lia was weeping quietly, with her face buried in her hands, so that her sister should not hear, and Don Michele, with his pistol on his paunch and his trousers tucked into his boots, saw her weeping.

"There's no one to worry about me tonight, Lia," he said, "but I'm in danger too, just like your brother. If anything should happen to me, remember that I came to warn you, and that I risked my livelihood for your sake."

Lia raised her face from her hands and looked at him with eyes full of tears. "May the Lord reward you, Don Michele, for your act of mercy," she said.

"I don't want any reward, Lia. I did it for your sake, and because I'm fond of you."

"Now go away, because everybody's asleep! For the love of God, Don Michele, go away!"

Don Michele went away, and she stayed by the door, telling her beads for her brother; and she prayed the Lord that He might send him that way.

But the Lord did not send him that way. All four of them, 'Ntoni, Cinghialenta, Rocco Spatu and La Locca's son, slipped quietly down the path in the shelter of the wall, and when they reached the lava field they took off their boots and listened anxiously for a few moments.

"There's not a sound!" said Cinghialenta.

The rain kept on falling, and all that could be heard in the lava field was the roaring of the sea below.

"You can't even see well enough to curse!" said Rocco

Spatu. "How will they make the Doves' Rock if it's as dark as this?"

"They know what they're doing," Cinghialenta answered. "They know every inch of this coast with their eyes shut."

"I can't hear anything," said 'Ntoni.

"Of course you can't!" said Cinghialenta, "but they must have been down there for some time."

"Then it would be better to go home," said La Locca's son.

"Now that you've eaten and drunk, you think of nothing but of going home," said Cinghialenta. "If you don't shut up, I'll kick you into the sea!"

"I don't intend to spend the night here with nothing to show for it," muttered Rocco Spatu.

"Now we'll find out whether they're there or not!" said Cinghialenta. He started hooting like an owl, and the others imitated him.

"If Don Michele hears that," said 'Ntoni, "they'll come here straight away, because owls don't go about on nights like this."

"There's no answer," whined La Locca's son, "so we'd better go home!"

All four looked at each other, though they couldn't see, and thought about what Master 'Ntoni's 'Ntoni had said.

"What shall we do?" said La Locca's son again.

"Let's go down to the road," Cinghialenta suggested. "If there's nobody there either, it'll mean they haven't come." On the way down to the road 'Ntoni said:

"Piedipapera is capable of giving us all away for a glass of wine!"

"Now that you haven't got a glass of wine in front of you," Cinghialenta said to him, "you're afraid too!"

"Go on, damn you!" 'Ntoni answered. "I'll show you whether I'm afraid or not!"

As they quietly climbed down the rocks, holding on like grim death for fear of breaking their necks, Rocco Spatu remarked in a whisper that Vanni Pizzuto, who had been grumbling at Piedipapera for taking his share without risking his neck, was now safely tucked up in bed himself.

"All right!" said Cinghialenta. "If you don't want to risk your neck, you should stay at home in bed too!"

After this no one breathed a word, and 'Ntoni, groping with his hands for secure footholds, thought that Cinghialenta might have refrained from saying that, because at moments like this it was impossible for a man not to be thinking about his home and his bed, and Mena snoozing behind the door.

After an interval Rocco Spatu said: "Our lives are not worth a farthing on a night like this!"

Suddenly there came a shout from behind the wall running along the road.

"Halt! Who goes there? . . . Stop there, all of you!"

"We're betrayed! We're betrayed!" they started shouting, running back across the lava field, this time without troubling about finding secure footholds.

But 'Ntoni had climbed the wall and had found himself face to face with Don Michele, whose pistol was in his hand.

"By the blood of the Virgin Mary!" 'Ntoni shouted, drawing his knife. "I'll show you if I'm afraid of your pistol!"

Don Michele's pistol went off, but he had been stabbed in the chest and fell like an ox. 'Ntoni turned and tried to escape, leaping like a deer, while bullets flew like hail. But the guards were soon on top of him and threw him to the ground.

"Now what will happen to my poor mother?" La Locca's son, whom they were binding like Jesus, was whining.

"By the blood of the Virgin Mary, don't pull so tight!" 'Ntoni yelled. "Don't you see that I can't move?"

"Come on, come on, Malavoglia," they answered. "Your account's nicely settled." And they pushed him in front of them at the point of their carbines.

While they led him back to their barracks, bound like Jesus too, with Don Michele carried on the guard's shoulders behind him, he searched with his eyes to see what had become of Cinghialenta and Rocco Spatu. They've got away, he said to himself. They've got away; and now they've no more to worry about than Vanni Pizzuto and Piedipapera, who are snugly tucked up in their beds at this time of night. It's only in my house that they'll be awake, because they'll have heard the firing.

The Malavoglia were awake, sure enough, waiting outside the door in the rain, as though they had a premonition, while their neighbours turned over in bed and yawned, and said to themselves that in the morning they would find out what had happened.

Later on, when the dawn was barely beginning to break, a crowd gathered outside Pizzuto's shop, where the lamp was still burning, and started excitedly talking about what had happened.

"They caught the smugglers red-handed," Pizzuto said, "and Don Michele was stabbed." People looked towards the Malavoglia door and made significant gestures. At last Cousin Anna arrived at the Malavoglia house, with dishevelled hair and looking as white as a sheet, not knowing what to say.

"What about 'Ntoni? Do you know where 'Ntoni is?" asked Master 'Ntoni, as though he had a premonition.

"He was arrested last night in the smuggling affray, with La Locca's son," replied Cousin Anna, who was completely beside herself. "They killed Don Michele!"

"Holy Mother of God!" said the old man, putting his hand through his hair. "Holy Mother of God!" Lia clutched at her hair too. All that Master 'Ntoni could say, still clutching at his hair, was: "Holy Mother of God!"

Towards afternoon Piedipapera arrived, looking very worried and tapping his brow. "Have you heard, Master 'Ntoni, of the terrible misfortune that has happened? I was terribly shocked when I heard the news!" His wife Grazia was there already, really weeping, poor woman, because of the disasters that rained on the Malavoglia. Her husband drew her aside towards the window and said: "What the devil are you doing here? You keep out of this! Coming to this house now means attracting the attention of the police!"

For this reason no one appeared at the Malavoglia door. Only Nunziata, who had not yet reached the age of discretion, asked her neighbour to keep her eye on the house and told her eldest child to look after the others and rushed to weep with Mena. Other people stayed in the street and watched the scene from a distance, or gathered like flies outside the barracks to see what Master 'Ntoni's 'Ntoni looked like behind the grating after stabbing Don Michele; or hung about Pizzuto's shop, where Vanni was selling herb beer and shaving people and telling in detail the whole story of what had happened.

"The blockheads!" the chemist exclaimed. "The blockheads! Fancy letting themselves be caught!"

"It'll be an ugly business," Don Silvestro added. "Penal servitude's something they won't be able to laugh off!"

"Those who deserve penal servitude don't get it," Don Giammaria pointedly remarked.

"Of course they don't!" replied Don Silvestro, as bold as brass.

"Nowadays," Master Cipolla remarked bitterly, "the real thieves rob you in broad daylight in the middle of the public square! They force their way into your house without bothering to break in by the door or window."

"That's just what 'Ntoni Malavoglia wanted to do in my house!" said Venera Zuppidda.

"That's exactly what I always said," her husband remarked.

"You keep quiet!" his wife told him. "What do you know about it? Look what a day it would have been for my daughter Barbara if I hadn't kept my eyes open!"

Her daughter Barbara was standing at the window, waiting to see 'Ntoni being taken away by the police.

"He won't be coming back again," everybody said. "Do you know what it says outside the Vicaria at Palermo? 'However far you run, I wait for you here,' and 'Bad metal wears out on the wheel.' Poor devils!"

"Smuggling's a thing that decent people don't go in for!" said La Vespa. "People who go about looking for trouble, find it. Look at the kind of people who go in for it—good-for-nothings with no fixed trade, like 'Ntoni Malavoglia and La Locca's son!"

Everybody agreed, and said it would be better for your house to collapse over your head than to have a son like that. La Locca was the only one who went about looking for her son. She planted herself outside the guards' barracks, shrieking to them to give him back to her, and wouldn't listen to reason; and then she started pestering her brother, Uncle Crocifisso, and planted herself on his balcony steps with her white, dishevelled hair flying in the wind.

"I wish I were in your shoes!" Uncle Crocifisso said to her. "I'm serving penal servitude here in my own house! What do you want from me? Even when your son was here, he never gave you any food!"

"La Locca will be better off as a result of this," remarked Don Silvestro. "Now that there's no one to provide for her, they'll take her to the poor-house, and she'll have macaroni and meat to eat every day. Otherwise she'll be a burden on the commune!"

When they once more reached the conclusion that bad metal wears out on the wheel, Master Fortunato added:

"Master 'Ntoni will be better off as the result of this too! Don't you realise that that good-for-nothing of a son of his must have eaten up his money? I know what it is to have a son who turns out like that! Now the King will have to keep him!"

But Master 'Ntoni, instead of thinking of the money he could save, now that his grandson was no longer in a position to squander it, actually started throwing away good money on him. The money he had earned with so much sweat and toil, and laid aside to buy back the house by the medlar tree, started flowing like water on lawyers and legal expenses. "Now we have no more need of the house or of anything," he said, with a face as pale as 'Ntoni's had been when the whole village had turned out to see him taken away by the police in handcuffs, and with a bundle under his arm—the bundle of shirts that Mena had tearfully taken him one evening, so that nobody should see. Her grandfather had been to see the lawyer, for he felt afraid, having also seen Don Michele being taken away to hospital in a carriage, looking yellow too, and with his uniform unbuttoned. All he cared about was that his grandson should be freed and allowed to come home again, and this time he did not quibble about expense or anything else. For he felt that after this earthquake, 'Ntoni would come home again and stay with them always, like when he was a boy.

Don Silvestro did him the kindness of going with him to the lawyer's, because he said that when disaster overtook your neighbour, as it had overtaken the Malavoglia, you must do all in your power to help him, even though he were a gaol-bird, and do everything possible to get him out of the hands of justice, for we were all Christians, and it was our duty to help one another. The lawyer, after listening to the whole story, and having further explanations given to him by Don Silvestro, rubbed his hands, and said it was a good case, and that but for him the outcome would certainly be penal servitude. Master 'Ntoni nearly collapsed at the mention of penal servitude, but Dr. Scipioni slapped him on the back, and said that if he didn't get 'Ntoni off with four or five years' hard labour he was no lawyer.

"What did the lawyer say?" Mena asked when her grandfather came back with that expression on his face, but she started crying without waiting for the answer. The old man tore the few white hairs he had left, and roamed about the house like a maniac, muttering: "Why aren't we all dead? Why aren't we all dead?" Lia, looking as white as a sheet, gaped at everyone who spoke to her, without being able to speak. Very soon subpoenas arrived for Barbara Zuppidda, Grazia Piedipapera, Don Franco, the chemist, and, in fact, everyone who ever gossiped in the square or at Vanni Pizzuto's shop. This set the whole village in an uproar, and people rushed about with pieces of stamped paper in their hands, swearing by God's truth that they knew nothing whatever about the affair, because they didn't want to have anything to do with justice. Curses on 'Ntoni and the Malavoglia, who insisted on involving them in their troubles! Venera Zuppidda went about shrieking like a maniac that she knew nothing whatever about the whole business, that she stayed shut up in her own house from morning to night, and that she wasn't one of those who stood gossiping at the front door with policemen or customs guards.

"Down with the Government!" exclaimed Don Franco. "They know I'm a Republican, and they would like to find an excuse to make me vanish from the face of the earth!"

People racked their brains to think what evidence Venera Zuppidda and Grazia Piedipapera and the others could possibly give, because they had only heard the shooting from their beds. But Don Silvestro rubbed his hands, just as the lawyer had done, and said he knew why they had been called to give evidence, and that it made things much more hopeful for the accused. Whenever the lawyer went to see 'Ntoni Malavoglia in prison, Don Silvestro went with him, when he had nothing else to do. No one now went to the municipal offices, and the olives had all been gathered in. Master 'Ntoni tried to go and see 'Ntoni two or three times too. But when he reached the prison gate, and saw all the barred windows, and the soldiers on guard with rifles outside, and the way they looked at everyone who went in, it made him feel ill, and he waited outside, sitting on the pavement in the midst of the chestnut and prickly-pear vendors, and he could not really believe that his 'Ntoni was behind those bars, with soldiers guarding him. Then the lawyer would come back, rubbing his hands and looking as fresh as a daisy after talking to 'Ntoni, and he would tell him that his grandson was well, and had actually put on weight. This made the poor old man think that his grandson must be one of the soldiers.

"Why don't they let him go?" he kept repeating like a parrot, or like a child that won't listen to reason. He also wanted to know whether 'Ntoni was still kept in handcuffs. "Don't worry about him," the lawyer said. "Let him be where he is for a while. In these affairs it's better to allow a little time to pass. As I've told you, he's not short of anything, and he's getting as fat as a capon. Don Michele's wound has nearly healed, and that's a good thing for us too. Don't worry, I tell you, and go out fishing and leave this affair to me!"

"I can't go out fishing while 'Ntoni's in prison—it's impossible! Everybody would look at us as we passed, and now that 'Ntoni's in prison my head doesn't seem in the right place any more!"

He continually repeated the same refrain. Meanwhile the money was running away like water, and the Malavoglia spent the whole time outside the house, with the door shut.

At last the day of the trial arrived, and all those who had been subpoenaed had to walk to court, unless they preferred being fetched by the carabinieri. Even Don Franco went, though he didn't dare wear his black hat to appear in the court of justice, and he looked even paler than 'Ntoni Malavoglia, who was there in the prisoner's cage, like a wild beast, with carabinieri on either side of him. Don Franco had never had anything to do with justice, and he was worried to death at having to appear for the first time in his life before this handful of judges and police, who could put you behind the bars like 'Ntoni Malavoglia in the twinkling of an eye.

The whole village crowded into the court room to

see what Master 'Ntoni's 'Ntoni looked like sitting behind the bars between the carabinieri. He looked as
yellow as candle light, and didn't even dare blow his
nose under the eyes of all his friends and acquaintances, who stared and stared at him. While the president, in his black robe and with the white tabs under
his chin, reeled off all the misdeeds he had done—they
were all written down in full, and nothing whatever
was omitted—he kept twisting his cap in his hands. Don
Michele was there, looking yellow too, sitting opposite
the jury, who were yawning and fanning themselves
with their handkerchiefs. Meanwhile the lawyer was
chatting in whispers to his neighbour, as though the
whole thing were no concern of his.

Venera Zuppidda, listening to all the terrible things
that 'Ntoni had done, whispered to her neighbour that
he certainly wouldn't escape penal servitude this time.

Santuzza was there too, to explain to the court where
'Ntoni had been that night, and how he had passed
the evening.

"But what do they want to know from us?" asked
Grazia Piedipapera.

"The lawyer told me they want to know if it's true
that Lia was carrying on with Don Michele, and that
'Ntoni wanted to kill him because of Santuzza."

"May you both be stricken with the cholera!" the
chemist whispered, glaring at them. "Do you want us
all to be sent to prison? Don't you know that in a court
of justice you must always deny everything, and not
admit that you know anything at all?"

Venera Zuppidda preened herself in her cape, but
went on muttering. "It's the truth!" she said. "I saw
them with my own eyes, and the whole village knows
it!"

There had been a terrible scene in the Malavoglia

house that morning, for when the old man saw that the whole village was going to hear 'Ntoni condemned, he insisted on going too, and Lia, with ruffled hair and wild eyes and chattering chin, wanted to go too, and looked all over the house for her cape without saying anything, though her face was distraught and her hands were trembling. Mena, who was pale too, seized her hands and said: "You mustn't go! You mustn't go!" without saying anything more. Their grandfather said they must stay at home and pray to the Virgin Mary; and their wailing was heard all along the Strada del Nero. Almost the first thing the old man saw when he reached the town was his grandson being taken past, surrounded by carabinieri. The old man's legs bent under him as he walked, and he went and sat on the steps outside the court building, in the midst of the people going up and coming down, all bent on their own affairs. He thought that all those people were going in to hear his grandson being condemned in the presence of all the soldiers and the judges, and this made him feel as though he had abandoned 'Ntoni in the middle of a public square or on a rough sea; so he went up with the crowd and entered the court room, and raised himself on tiptoe and saw the cage, and the carabinieri's hats, and the gleaming bayonets. But he couldn't see 'Ntoni among all those people, and the poor old man still imagined that he must be one of the soldiers.

Meanwhile the lawyer was talking and talking, as though he were never going to stop. Listening to him was like waiting for the bucket to come up from the bottom of a deep well. He denied all the misdeeds that the president of the court had attributed to 'Ntoni—the president had invented them in order to condemn the unfortunate young man, because that was his job. How could the president possibly say such things? Had

he by any chance seen 'Ntoni Malavoglia that night,
pitch-black as it was? Anything anyone chose to say in
the house of a poor man was right, and the gallows
were built for the unfortunate! The president, with his
elbows on his books, looked at Dr. Scipioni through his
spectacles without showing any sign of agreement. Dr.
Scipioni went on to say that he would like to know
where the alleged contraband was. Couldn't an honest
man go for a walk wherever he liked and at whatever
time of night he liked, particularly if he had a little
wine in his head and wanted to walk it off? At this
Master 'Ntoni nodded his head in agreement, and
muttered: "Yes! Yes!" with tears in his eyes, and he
could have kissed the lawyer, who was saying that
'Ntoni was a drunkard. Master 'Ntoni raised his head
again. This was fine! What the lawyer said next was
worth fifty lire in itself. He said they were trying at all
costs to prove that 'Ntoni had been caught red-handed
with a knife in his hand, and that stupid-looking Don
Michele had been brought before them to swear that
he had been stabbed in the stomach with a knife. But
how did they know it was 'Ntoni Malavoglia who had
stabbed Don Michele? Who was there to prove it? How
could they tell that Don Michele hadn't stabbed himself deliberately, in order to send 'Ntoni Malavoglia to
penal servitude? Did they want to know the truth?
Smuggling had nothing whatever to do with this case!
Between Don Michele and Master 'Ntoni's 'Ntoni there
had been a long-standing feud. It had to do with
women. Master 'Ntoni went on nodding his head, because the whole village knew the story of Don Michele
and Santuzza, and how Don Michele had been mad
with jealousy after Santuzza had taken a fancy to
'Ntoni. Master 'Ntoni could have sworn on the crucifix
to the truth of this story. The meeting between 'Ntoni

and Don Michele had taken place at night, the lawyer went on, after the boy had been drinking. Everyone knew what was likely to happen when you couldn't see quite straight any more; and they could ask Barbara and Venera Zuppidda, and a hundred other witnesses, the lawyer went on, once more to corroborate the fact that a love affair had been in progress between Don Michele and Lia, 'Ntoni Malavoglia's sister, and that Don Michele hung about the Strada del Nero every evening because of the girl. He had actually been seen there on the night of the stabbing.

After this Master 'Ntoni couldn't hear, because there was a whistling in his ears, and for the first time during the trial he saw 'Ntoni, who had risen to his feet in the cage and was tearing at his cap. There was a wild expression in 'Ntoni's eyes, and he wanted to speak, and he was making desperate gestures of denial. The old man was carried out of court by those standing near him, who thought that something had happened to him; and carabinieri laid him on the big table in the witnesses' room and splashed water in his face. Later, when he tottered down the steps with carabinieri holding him up on either side, people were streaming out of court, and he heard them saying that 'Ntoni had been sentenced to five years' hard labour. At that moment 'Ntoni emerged from another little door, surrounded by carabinieri, and bound like Christ.

Grazia Piedipapera set off back to the village as fast as her legs would carry her, because bad news always travels on wings. When she saw Lia, who was waiting at the door like a soul in torment, she seized her hands and shouted at her, quite beside herself:

"What have you done, you wicked girl! They told the judge you were having a love affair with Don Michele,

and now something has happened to your grandfather!"

Lia said nothing, and behaved as though she had
not heard, and went on gazing at Grazia Piedipapera,
wide-eyed and open-mouthed. Then she slowly collapsed on to a chair, as though both her legs had given
way. Then, after staying like that, without moving and
without speaking, for such a long time that Grazia Piedipapera went and splashed water in her face, she
started muttering: "I must go away, I can't stay here
any longer!" She started moving round the room like a
mad woman, repeating the same words to the chest of
drawers and to the chairs. In vain her sister followed
her, weeping and saying: "I warned you! I warned
you!" and trying to seize her by the hands. That evening, when their grandfather was brought home on a
cart and Mena ran to meet him, for she was no longer
ashamed in front of people, Lia walked out of the yard
and into the street and went away, and was not seen
again.

FIFTEEN   People said that Lia had gone to live with
Don Michele; for the Malavoglia no longer had anything to lose, and Don Michele would at least have
given her food. Master 'Ntoni had become a complete
graveyard bird, and did nothing but walk about, bent
up double, perpetually reeling off proverbs that had
no rhyme or reason. "Fetch the axe for the stricken
tree!" he would say; or: "You can't fall in the water
without getting wet!" or: "Flies buzz round a skinny
horse!" If anyone asked him why he was everlastingly
wandering about, he would answer: "Hunger drives
the wolf from the forest!" or: "A starving dog doesn't
fear the stick!" But, now that he was reduced to this

state, nobody wanted to listen to his troubles; people told him their own instead. If by any chance anyone took the trouble to ask him what on earth he was doing, leaning against the wall under the church tower as though he were Uncle Crocifisso waiting for someone to lend money to, or sitting in the shelter of the boats drawn up on the shore as though he were Master Cipolla waiting for his boat to come in, he would reply that he was waiting for death, which lingered, however, for "long are the days of the wretched." No one in the house talked about Lia, not even St. Agatha, who, when there was no one in the house, relieved her feelings by weeping secretly by her mother's bed. The house now felt as big as the ocean, and they felt lost in it. All the money had gone on 'Ntoni; Alessi was always away, working in one place or another, and in the evening, when she had to go and find her grandfather and take him by the hand and lead him home like a child, because in the dark he was as blind as a bat, Nunziata did her the kindness of coming and lighting the fire.

Now that the old man was no longer good for anything, Don Silvestro and the rest of the village said that Alessi ought to send him to the poor-house; but that was the one thing the old man dreaded. He had grown so childish that whenever Mena led him by the hand and put him out in the sun, where he stayed all day long waiting for death, he imagined he was being taken to the poor-house. "Death never comes," he would mutter. Some people actually asked him with a laugh how far it had got, then.

On Saturdays Alessi came home, and counted out the week's money in Master 'Ntoni's presence, as though the old man were still in his senses. He always nodded his head approvingly, and told them to hide the money under the mattress, and to cheer him up Alessi would say that not much more was needed to get together the money for the house by the medlar tree again, and that in a year or two they would manage it.

But the old man shook his head stubbornly, and said there was no more need of the house by the medlar tree, and that, now that the Malavoglia were scattered, it would have been better if the Malavoglia house had never been.

Once, when nobody else was about, he called Nunziata aside under the almond tree, as though he had something very important to say. But his lips moved silently, and he searched a long time for the words, looking this way and that. At last he said:

"Is it true what they said about Lia?"

"No!" replied Nunziata, crossing her hands. "No! By Our Lady of Ognina, no!"

He started shaking his head, with his chin on his breast.

"Then why did she run away? Why did she run away?"

He pretended to have lost his cap, and started looking for it all over the house. He touched the bed and the chest of drawers, and started sitting at the loom, without speaking.

"Do you know where she has gone?" he asked eventually, though to Mena he never mentioned the subject.

But Nunziata hadn't the slightest idea where Lia had gone; and nobody else in the village had either.

One evening Alfio Mosca stopped in the Strada del Nero, with his cart, to which there was now attached a mule, for the sake of which he had caught the fevers at La Bicocca and had nearly died of them. The fevers had left him with a yellow face and a stomach distended like a wineskin; but the mule was plump and its coat was glossy.

"Do you remember when I left for La Bicocca?" he said, "and you were still living in the house by the medlar tree? Everything's changed now, for the world is round and some sink and some swim!"

This time they couldn't even offer him a glass of wine to welcome him. Alfio knew where Lia was. He had seen her with his own eyes, and it had been like seeing Mena when he had stood at his window and talked to her across the way. He looked this way and that, as uncomfortably as though he had the weight of his cart on his stomach, and sat down silently at the empty table, at which they no longer had dinner in the evening.

"Now I must go," he said, seeing that nobody spoke. "If one leaves one's village one should never return, because while one's away everything changes; and you change yourself, and when you come back you look at things with different eyes!"

Mena went on sitting in silence. Alessi started telling him that when he had scraped a little money together he was going to marry Nunziata, and Alfio answered that he was quite right, if Nunziata had a little money too, because she was a good girl, and was known to everyone in the village. Thus even relatives forget the departed, and everyone in the world has to think about pulling the cart that God has given him to pull. That was what Alfio Mosca's donkey had had to do—God knows what it was doing, now that it had passed into other hands!

Now that her brothers were starting to earn a little money, Nunziata had a dowry, and she would buy herself neither gold nor white dresses, because, she said, these things were for the rich, and it wasn't right to have white dresses while you were still growing.

She had grown as tall and thin as a broomstick, with black hair and gentle eyes, and when she sat at the door, with all her children about her, she seemed still to be thinking about her father, on the day he had gone away and abandoned her with them, and all the troubles she had got through since that time, with her little brothers and sisters clinging to her skirts. Seeing how she had faced up to all her misfortunes and dragged herself out of the mire with all her young brothers and sisters on her hands, though she wasn't strong and was as thin as a broomstick, everyone had a good word for her and used to like to stop and have a chat with her.

"We've got the money," she said to Alfio Mosca, whom she had known for such a long time that he almost seemed a relative. "At All Saints my eldest brother starts work for Massaro Filippo, and the younger one will take his place at Master Cipolla's. When I've placed Turi too, we shall get married. But I must wait till I'm old enough, and have my father's consent."

"I wonder if your father thinks that you're still alive!" said Alfio.

"If he came back now," Nunziata answered, with that gentle, calm voice of hers and her arms resting on her knees, "he wouldn't go away again, because now we have the money."

Alfio again told Alessi that, if he had a little money, he was doing well to marry Nunziata.

"We shall buy back the house by the medlar tree," Alessi went on, "and grandfather will stay with us. When the others come back, they can stay there too. If Nunziata's father comes back, there'll be room for him as well!"

Nobody mentioned Lia, but all three thought of her

as they sat with their hands on their knees, gazing at the lamp.

Alfio Mosca eventually got up to go because his mule was shaking its bells, as though it too had recognised the girl whom Alfio had seen from the street, the girl for whom it would be idle to wait in the house by the medlar tree.

For some time Uncle Crocifisso had been waiting for the Malavoglia to approach him about buying back the house by the medlar tree, because a curse seemed to lay over it, and it was a drug on the market and remained idle on his hands. As soon as he heard that Alfio Mosca, whose bones he had wanted to break when he had thought he was after La Vespa, was back in the village, he went and asked him if he would mention the matter to the Malavoglia, in the hope of arranging a sale.

Alfio came and broached the matter, but Master 'Ntoni shook his head and said no. "We have no use for the house," he said, "because Mena can't get married any more, and there are no Malavoglia left. I'm still here, because the wretched live long. When I'm dead Alessi will marry Nunziata and leave the village!"

It seemed that he too was on the point of departing. He spent most of the time in bed, like a lobster hidden under the rocks, groaning and lamenting. "What business have I got here?" he would mutter, and he thought it a sin to accept the food they gave him. Alessi and Mena tried in vain to convince him that it was no sin. He insisted that he was causing them endless trouble and wasting their time and money. He made them count out the money hidden under the mattress, and whenever he discovered it had diminished a little he muttered: "At least if I weren't here you wouldn't be spending so much. There's nothing more I can do here, and I ought to go!"

Don Ciccio, who came to feel his pulse, also said it would be better if he were sent to the poor-house, because where he was he was uselessly consuming his own substance and that of his family. The old man watched them talking with tired eyes, and was terribly afraid that they would send him to the poor-house. But Alessi wouldn't hear of it, and said that, so long as there was bread in the house, there was bread for everybody, and Mena agreed, and in fine weather she put the old man out in the sunshine and, when she didn't have to go to the wash-place, she stayed beside him with her distaff and told him stories, like a baby. To cheer him, she told him what they intended to do when fortune smiled on them a little again. On St. Sebastian's Day they were going to buy a calf, and Mena intended paying for its winter hay herself; and in May they would sell it at a profit; and she showed him the chickens she was rearing, and the chickens would come and scratch in the dust at their feet. With the profit on the chickens they were going to buy a pig, which they would feed on the prickly-pear skins, which were now wasted, and the water in which the food was cooked, and by the end of the year it would be as good as money in the cash-box. The poor old man, resting his hands on his stick, gazed at the chickens and nodded approval. He actually grew so interested in all these plans that he said that if they bought back the house by the medlar tree they could rear the pig in the yard, because they could be sure of selling it to Peppi Naso at a profit. The house by the medlar tree also had a stall for the calf and a loft for fodder, and everything. He sought about with his dead eyes, resting his chin on his stick, and gradually remembered everything. Then he whispered to his granddaughter: "What did Don Ciccio say about the poor-house?" Mena scolded him like a child, and said: "Why do you worry your head about such things?" He listened in silence to all that she said. Then he repeated: "Don't send me to the poor-house, it's not what I'm used to!"

Eventually he couldn't get out of bed at all, and Don Ciccio said there was no more he could do, and that this settled the matter, because the old man might drag on for years in that state, and Alessi or Mena or Nunziata would have to lose a whole day's work looking after him all day long; otherwise the pigs would come in and eat him, if they found the door open.

Master 'Ntoni understood perfectly what the doctor said, because he looked at them one after another, with a heartbreaking expression on his face; and when the doctor left the room, while he was still at the door talking to Mena, who was weeping, and to Alessi, who kept stamping his feet and saying no, he beckoned to Nunziata to come near him, and said to her softly:

"It'll be better if you do send me to the poor-house. Here I eat up your whole week's earnings. Send me away when Mena and Alessi are out of the house. They'd never let me go, because they have the kind Malavoglia heart. But I'm eating up the money for the house, and the doctor said I might drag on like this for years. And here there's no more I can do. Only I shouldn't like to drag on for years in the poor-house!"

Nunziata started crying too, and refused to do what he asked, with the result that the Malavoglia became the talk of the village for wanting to be proud, though they didn't have enough to eat. With the whole family scattered—and just think where some of them were!—fancy being ashamed of sending their grandfather to the poor-house!

The chemist no longer talked politics in his shop, and when Don Silvestro came in he would always be busy with his pestle and mortar, to avoid compromising himself, for it was necessary to beware of everyone who was associated with the Government and ate the King's bread. The only people to whom he unburdened himself were Don Giammaria and the doctor, Don Ciccio, when he left his donkey at the chemist's shop and went to feel Master 'Ntoni's pulse. Don Ciccio no longer wrote out prescriptions for the Malavoglia, because he said they had no money to waste.

"Then why don't they send the old man to the poorhouse?" everybody said. "Why do they keep him in the house to be eaten alive by the fleas?"

The doctor kept on repeating that he was wasting his time and coming to the house for nothing, and when he found neighbours at the bedside—Grazia Piedipapera or Cousin Anna or Nunziata—he always repeated his refrain about the futility of letting the old man lie there to be eaten alive by the fleas. Master 'Ntoni, with his white, distraught face, hardly dared even to breathe, and, as the neighbours went on talking, in the end Nunziata gave in one day when Alessi wasn't there and the old man said: "Fetch Alfio Mosca for me, for he'll do me the kindness of taking me to the poor-house in his cart!"

So Master 'Ntoni was taken to the poor-house in Alfio Mosca's cart. Alfio put a mattress and pillows in it for him, and the poor old man, though he said nothing, looked all round him as they helped him out of the house, supporting him under the arm-pits, on a day when Alessi had gone to Riposto and an excuse had been found for getting Mena out of the way, because they would never have let him go. All the way down the Strada del Nero, and when they passed the house by the medlar tree, and when they crossed the square, Master 'Ntoni kept looking about him, to stamp everything on his mind. Alfio walked on one side of the mule, holding the reins, and Nunziata, carrying a bundle of Master 'Ntoni's things, on the other. She had left Turi in charge of the calf, the turkeys and the chickens. When the cart passed, everyone came to the door to see. Don Silvestro said the Malavoglia had done well to make up their minds at last—this was the purpose for which the commune paid its contribution to the upkeep of the poor-house; and, if Don Silvestro hadn't been there, Don Franco would have made the speech he had all ready in his head.

"At least the poor devil will have a little peace!" Uncle Crocifisso remarked.

"Pride goes before a fall," Master Cipolla answered, and Santuzza told her beads for the poor man. Only Cousin Anna and Grazia Piedipapera wiped their eyes with their aprons when the cart slowly moved away, bouncing over the stones. "Why are you snivelling like that?" Tino Piedipapera snapped at his wife. "Am I dead by any chance? Why should you care?"

Alfio Mosca, leading the mule, was telling Nunziata how and where he had seen Lia, who had looked exactly like St. Agatha; he still couldn't really believe that he had seen her with his own eyes, and his voice faltered as he talked about it, to relieve the tedium as they made their way slowly along the dusty road. "Oh! Nunziata," he said, "when we used to stand and talk from one door to the next, and the moon was shining, and you could hear all the neighbours' voices, and St. Agatha's loom clattered all day long, and the chickens recognised her by the way she opened the gate, and you heard La Longa calling out in the yard, because one could hear everything as distinctly as though it were happening in one's own house—who would have believed it? Poor La Longa! You see, now that I've got my mule, and everything that I desired then, though I shouldn't have believed it at the time, even if an angel from heaven had come to me and foretold it, I'm always thinking of those evenings when I used to hear all your voices while I was grooming my donkey, and used to see the light in the house by the medlar tree, which is all shut up now; and when I came back I found that nothing was as it had been, and even Mena no longer seemed the same. If one leaves one's village one should never return. You see, now I even think of that poor donkey that worked with me for so long, in fair weather and foul, with its long ears and drooping head. Who knows where it's being driven now, and what loads it's pulling along what sort of roads, with its ears lower still, so that now it must be actually nosing the earth that must soon receive it, because it's getting old, poor beast?"

Master 'Ntoni, stretched on his mattress, could hear nothing of all this. They had put a canopy over the cart, so that it looked as if they were taking away a corpse. "It's better that he shouldn't hear any more," Alfio went on. "He knows what happened to 'Ntoni, and one day or another he would have found out what became of Lia."

"He often used to ask me about her when we were alone," Nunziata answered. "He often wanted to know where she was."

"She went the same way as her brother. We poor people follow each other blindly, like sheep. You mustn't tell him, or anyone else in the village, where I saw her, because it would be like stabbing St. Agatha with a knife. She certainly recognised me when I passed the door, because she went white and red in the face, and I whipped the mule, to pass as quickly as I could, and I'm certain that the poor girl would rather have been trampled on by the mule, or stretched out on the cart as her grandfather is now! Now the Malavoglia family is destroyed, and you and Alessi must start rebuilding it."

"The money for the things is already there. And on St. John's Day we shall sell the calf."

"That's excellent! When you've got the money laid aside, there'll be no danger of its all disappearing one fine day if the calf should die, which heaven forbid! Now we've reached the first houses of the town, and if you don't want to come all the way to the poor-house you can wait for me here, if you like."

"No, I'll come with you. Then at least I'll see where they put him, and he'll see me right till the last moment."

Master 'Ntoni was able to see her until the last moment, and when she and Alfio left, walking softly through the long ward, as though they were walking down the aisle in a church, he followed them with his eyes. Alfio Mosca and Nunziata climbed on to the cart, rolled up the mattress and the canopy and came back along the long, dusty road without speaking. When Alessi found that his grandfather had gone, and saw them coming back with his mattress rolled up, he struck his head with his fists and tore his hair, and he started scolding Mena, as though it had been she who had sent the old man away. But Alfio Mosca said to him: "What's the use? The house of the Malavoglia is destroyed, and now you must start rebuilding it."

He wanted to start all over again going through the calculations about the price that they would get for the calf, and the other things which he had discussed with Nunziata along the road. But Alessi and Mena,

with their heads between their hands and their eyes
bright with tears, sat at the door of the house, in which
they were now really alone, and paid no attention to
him. Alfio tried to comfort them by reminding them of
what the house by the medlar tree had been like when
they had stood at their doorways and chatted in the
moonlight, and you had heard the clatter of St. Agatha's loom all day long, and the chickens had scratched
about, and La Longa, who had always been busy all
day long, had kept calling out. But everything had
changed now, and if you left your village it was better
never to return, because even the street no longer
seemed the same, with no one walking down it now
for the sake of the Mangiacarrubbe girl. Even Don
Silvestro, waiting for Barbara Zuppidda to fall at his
feet, was no longer to be seen, and Uncle Crocifisso
had barricaded himself in his house, to look after his
property and quarrel with La Vespa, and no more arguing went on in the chemist's shop, now that Don
Franco had seen justice face to face, and always re-
tired into a corner to read his newspaper, and relieved
his feelings by using his pestle and mortar all day long.
Even Master Fortunato Cipolla, having lost his peace
of mind, no longer sat and gossiped on the church steps.

One fine day the news went round that Master Fortunato was getting married, to prevent his wealth from
falling into the hands of the Mangiacarrubbe girl. That
was why he no longer sat and gossiped on the church
steps; and his bride was to be Barbara Zuppidda. "And
he used to warn me that marriage was like a rat-trap!"
Uncle Crocifisso grumbled. "Now you can see how far
men are to be trusted!"

All the girls were mad with jealousy, and said that
Barbara was marrying her grandfather. But sensible
people, like Peppi Naso and Piedipapera, and even

Don Franco, said that Venera Zuppidda had scored a tremendous victory over Don Silvestro, and that it was such a terrible blow to him that he would be well-advised to leave the village. "Out with the strangers!" they said. In their village strangers had never taken root. Don Silvestro would never be able to talk to Master Cipolla on equal terms.

"Did you expect my daughter to throw herself away on somebody who hasn't got a penny?" Venera Zuppidda declared with her arms akimbo. "This time I made my husband understand that I was in charge! A good dog feeds in its own kennel. We don't want any strangers in our house! Before all these strangers came to the village to write down on paper how many spoonfuls of food you ate, like Don Silvestro, or to pound marshmallow with a pestle and to fatten themselves on the villagers' blood, we were all far better off! In those days everybody knew everybody else, and knew what he was doing, and what his father and grandfather had done before him, and you even knew what everybody ate; and when you saw somebody passing, you knew where he was going, and the farms belonged to those who had been born on them, and every Tom, Dick and Harry couldn't set himself up as a fisherman, and families didn't scatter all over the place, and people didn't go away to die in the poor-house!"

With all these marriages taking place, Alfio Mosca would have liked to marry Mena, whom nobody else wanted, now that the Malavoglia house had been broken up; Alfio, with his mule, could be said to be a good match for her. So on Sunday, while sitting next to her outside the house, leaning against the wall and snapping twigs from the hedge between his fingers to pass the time, he thought over all the reasons why he should pluck up courage and ask her. They both looked at the people passing by, and that was how they enjoyed their Sundays. In the end Alfio said:

"If you still want me, Mena, I'm still willing."

Poor Mena didn't even blush at being told in so many words that Alfio had known all along that she would have liked to marry him at the time of her engagement to Brasi Cipolla; all that seemed so distant now, and she no longer felt herself to be the same person.

"I'm old now, Alfio," she said, "and I shan't get married any more."

"If you're old, well, so am I, because I was years older than you when we stood at the window and talked. It's still so fresh in my mind that to me it seems to have been only yesterday. But more than eight years must have passed. And now, when your brother gets married, you'll be left high and dry."

Mena shrugged her shoulders, because, like Cousin Anna, she was used to accepting the will of God; and Alfio, seeing this, said:

"Then it must mean that you don't like me, Mena, and forgive me for implying that I might have married you. I know that you're better born than I am, and your family has always been its own master. But now you have nothing left, and when your brother Alessi gets married you'll be left stranded. I have my mule and cart, and you'd never be short of bread, Mena. But forgive me for the liberty."

"You haven't offended me, Alfio; and when we had the Provvidenza and the house by the medlar tree I should have said yes to you, if my parents had been willing, because God knows how I suffered when you went away to La Bicocca with your donkey cart; and I can still see in my mind the light in the stable, and you, loading all your things on to the cart in the yard. Do you remember?"

"Of course I remember! Then why won't you say yes to me now, when you have nothing left in the world, and I have a mule instead of a donkey to pull my cart, and your parents are no longer alive to say no?"

"Now I can't get married any more," Mena repeated, with lowered head. She was snapping twigs from the hedge between her fingers too. "I'm twenty-six, and it's too late for me to get married now!"

"No, that's not the reason," Alfio insisted, with his head lowered like hers. "You won't tell me the real reason!"

They remained silent, twisting and snapping twigs between their fingers without looking at each other. After a time Alfio rose and went away, with heavy shoulders and his chin on his breast. Mena followed him with her eyes as long as she could see him, and then looked at the wall opposite and sighed.

As Alfio Mosca had foreseen, Alessi married Nunziata and bought back the house by the medlar tree.

"I can't get married any more," Mena said to Alfio again. "You get married, because you still can!" And she went to live like an old maid in the upstairs room in the house by the medlar tree, and set her heart at rest, and waited for Nunziata's children to be born, so that she could look after them. There were chickens in the fowl-house, and a calf in the stall, and wood and fodder in the attic, and nets and all kinds of gear hanging in the yard, just as Master 'Ntoni had said; and Nunziata, with those delicate arms of hers, which didn't look as though she had done so much washing and brought into the world those fine, pink, plump babies which Mena carried about as though they were her own, replanted the garden with cabbages and broccoli.

Alfio Mosca shook his head whenever he saw Mena pass, and turned away with heavy shoulders. "You didn't think me worthy of the honour," he said to her at last, with a heart heavier than his shoulders, when he could bear it no longer. "I wasn't worthy of you!"

"No, Alfio, it's not that," said Mena, with tears springing to her eyes. "By the pure soul of this innocent child that I carry in my arms, I swear to you that it's not that! But I can't get married any more!"

"Why can't you get married any more, Mena?"

"Please don't ask me, Alfio, please don't force me to speak! If I got married, people would start talking again about my sister Lia, because after what happened nobody would dare to marry a Malavoglia girl. You would be the first to regret it. Leave me alone, because I can't get married any more, and set your heart at rest."

"You're right, Mena," Alfio Mosca replied. "I never thought of that. Cursed be the fate that led to so many misfortunes!"

So Alfio set his heart at rest, and Mena went on carrying her little nephews and nieces about in her arms, as though her heart were at rest too, and she kept the upstairs room clean and tidy in case the others should return—as though they had gone on a journey from which they would return, as Piedipapera remarked.

Meanwhile Master 'Ntoni had set out on that long voyage—longer even than the voyage to Trieste or Alexandria in Egypt—from which there is no return; and if his name cropped up in conversation while they were resting, or counting up the week's money, or making plans for the future in the shade of the medlar tree, or sitting with their plates between their knees, a silence would suddenly fall, and they would all remember how they had seen him for the last time, in that long room with rows of beds in it, so many beds that you had to search before you could find him. He had been waiting for them like a soul in purgatory, with his eyes glued to the door, although he could hardly see, and he had to touch them to make sure it was really they; and then he hadn't spoken, although he had obviously been bursting with things to say, and the grief in his face that he couldn't express had been heartbreaking. When they told him they had bought back the house by the medlar tree, and were going to take him back to Trezza again, his eyes answered yes! yes! and a light came into them again, and he nearly smiled; it was the smile of those who smile no longer, or smile for the last time—a smile which transfixed their hearts. On the Monday they had gone back with Alfio Mosca's cart to bring their grandfather home again, but he was no longer there.

Remembering all these things, they dropped their spoons in their plates and pondered and pondered on all that had happened, for it all seemed dark, as though obscured by the shadow of the medlar tree. Now, when Cousin Anna came to spin for a time with the women-folk, she had white hair, and she said she had lost her smile, because she had no time to be cheerful, what with the family she had on her hands, and Rocco, whom she had to go and look for somewhere or other every day, in the streets or outside the tavern, and drive home like a vagabond calf. Two of the Malavoglia had turned out to be vagabonds too; and Alessi racked his brains to think where they might be, on the roads parched by the sun and white with dust; because after all this time they would never come back to the village again.

Late one night the dog started barking behind the yard door. Alessi himself went and opened it, and did not recognise 'Ntoni standing there with his bundle under his arm, so much had he changed. He was covered with dust, and had a long beard. He came in and sat down in a corner, and they hardly dared welcome and make a fuss of him. He no longer seemed the same, and looked round the room as though he had never seen it before. The dog, which had never known him, actually barked at him. They gave him a bowl of soup, because he was hungry and thirsty, and he put it between his knees, buried his nose in it, and wolfed it in silence, as though he had not seen God's blessing for a week. The others were too overcome to be able to eat with him. As soon as he had satisfied his appetite and rested a little he picked up his bundle and rose to go.

He had changed so much that Alessi had hardly dared speak to him. But when he saw him pick up his bundle his heart nearly leapt from his breast, and Mena in dismay said:

"Are you going?"

"Yes."

"Where?" asked Alessi.

"I don't know! I came to see you. But since I've been here the soup has turned to poison inside me. I can't stay here anyway, because everyone knows me. That's why I came at night. I shall go a long way away, where I shall be able to earn a living, and nobody will know who I am."

The others hardly dared breathe, because their heart was caught in a vice, and they realised that what 'Ntoni said was right. 'Ntoni went on gazing all round him, and he stood at the door and could not make up his mind to go.

"I'll let you know where I am," he said eventually, and when he was in the yard, under the medlar tree, which was all in darkness, he added:

"And grandfather?"

Alessi did not answer. 'Ntoni remained silent too. After a pause he said:

"And Lia? Because I didn't see her."

And, as he waited in vain for a reply, he added in a trembling voice, as though he were cold:

"Is she dead too?"

Alessi did not answer. Then 'Ntoni, who was standing under the medlar tree, with his bundle under his arm, made as if to sit down, because his legs were trembling, but he quickly pulled himself together and muttered:

"Good-bye! Good-bye! Don't you see that I must go?"

Before going 'Ntoni wanted to look round the house, to see that everything was in its place; but though he had been brave enough to leave home and stab Don Michele and face imprisonment, he was afraid to walk from one room to another without being asked. Alessi saw the desire in his eyes, and took him and showed him the stall, on the pretext of wanting to show him the calf which Nunziata had bought; and it was plump and sleek; and the broody hen and the chickens were in the corner. Then Alessi took him into the kitchen, where they had installed a new oven, and into the room next to it, where Mena slept with Nunziata's children. 'Ntoni looked at everything, and nodded his head in approval, and said: "Grandfather would have wanted the calf to be put there; this is where the broody hens used to be, and that's where the girls slept when her sister was here . . ." Then he stopped and said no more, and stood quietly looking round, with shining eyes. At that moment the Mangiacarrubbe girl went by, scolding Brasi Cipolla all the way down the street, and 'Ntoni said:

"So she's found herself a husband! When they've finished squabbling they'll go home, and go to sleep."

The others said nothing, and there was a great silence over the village, and there was nothing to be heard but the occasional slamming of a door, and, at these words of 'Ntoni's, Alessi plucked up courage and said:

"There's a home for you here if you want it. There's a bed for you in there."

"No," 'Ntoni answered. "I must go away. Mother's bed, which she wetted with her tears when I wanted to go away, was in there. Do you remember the conversations we used to have in the evening while the anchovies were being salted? And how Nunziata asked us riddles? And Lia and mother were both there, and you could hear voices all over the village, as though we were one big family. I didn't understand then, and I wanted to go away, but now I understand, and I've got to go away."

He stared at the ground as he spoke, with his head buried in his shoulders. Alessi flung his arms round him.

"Good-bye!" said 'Ntoni. "You see that I'm right to go, because I can't stay here. Good-bye, and forgive me, all of you!"

And he went away, with his bundle under his arm. He walked some distance, and stopped in the middle of the dark and deserted square, in which all the doors were shut. He waited and listened for the door to be shut at the house by the medlar tree, while the dog barked after him, telling him by its barking that he was the only person in the village out of doors. The only sound was the murmur of the sea, murmuring its old refrain among the Fariglioni, because the sea is homeless too, and can be listened to by anyone anywhere in the world, wherever the sun rises and sets, though at Aci Trezza it has a special refrain, which you can recognise at once, because of the way it gurgles and breaks among the rocks, and seems like the voice of a friend.

'Ntoni walked on, but stopped again in the middle of the road to look at the village lying in darkness, as though, now that he understood, he hadn't the heart to tear himself away; and he sat down on the low wall which runs along Massaro Filippo's vineyard.

And he stayed there for a long time, thinking of many things, looking at the village lying in darkness and listening to the murmur of the sea beneath his feet. He stayed there until he heard certain sounds that he knew well, and voices calling each other, and doors opening and shutting, and footsteps passing along the dark streets. Lights appeared in little groups at the end of the square. He raised his head and looked at the Three Kings shining, and the Pleiads which announce the dawn, as he had seen them so many times before. Then he dropped his head on his chest again, and thought again about his whole story. Gradually the sea started to grow white and the Three Kings grew pale, and one by one the houses, all of which he knew, became distinguishable along the dark streets, and all the doors were shut. The only light was outside Pizzuto's shop, and there was Rocco Spatu, with his hands in his pockets, coughing and spitting. Soon Uncle Santoro will open the door and sit down beside it and start his day's work too, 'Ntoni said to himself. He looked again at the sea, which had grown purple, and was covered with boats, which had also started their day's work. He picked up his bundle and said to himself that it was time to go, because soon people would be passing. But the first of them all to start their day's work was Rocco Spatu.

GIOVANNI VERGA (1840–1922) was born and educated in Sicily. From 1865 to 1880 he lived in Florence, then the center of the Italian literary world, where he became a writer of popular sentimental novels. But Verga did not reveal his true greatness until he returned to his native Sicily and began to write amid the scenes of his early life. His present reputation rests on the works of this period, which include two collections of short stories: *Vita dei Campi,* translated into English as *Under the Shadow of Etna* (1880); and *Novelle Rusticane* (1882); and the novels *Cavalleria Rusticana* (1884), *Mastro-Don Gesualdo* (1889), and *I Malavoglia* (The House by the Medlar Tree), first published in 1881.